The Carpenter and the Lady

But then the professor walked around the truck, and Jake's curiosity glued him in place. She was tall, too, taller than her sister. She had the same messy top-knot in her hair, but the professor's hair was darker, nearly brown. And she didn't have thick ankles, not that he would have minded. She was wearing cut-off denim shorts, and they were short enough to see that her legs were tanned and muscled—not the legs of a woman who spent all day reading.

Jake shook his head. He didn't do professors, not in any sense of the word. The Pembroke people had nothing to do with people like him, people who barely finished high school, who worked with their hands.

Besides, this professor was wearing a baggy, purple sweatshirt with a cat on it. The cat was wearing glittery sunglasses and striking a weird, sexy pose next to the words "Check Meowt." Also sparkly.

Still, she was the hottest crazy cat lady he had ever seen.

Also by Sarah Title

Kentucky Home
Kentucky Christmas

HOME SWEET HOME

SARAH TITLE

KENSINGTON BOOKS
KENSINGTON PUBLISHING CORP.
www.kensingtonbooks.com

KENSINGTON BOOKS are published by

Kensington Publishing Corp.
119 West 40th Street
New York, NY 10018

All Kensington titles, imprints, and distributed lines are available at special quantity discounts for bulk purchases for sales promotion, premiums, fund-raising, educational, or institutional use.

Special book excerpts or customized printings can also be created to fit specific needs. For details, write or phone the office of the Kensington Special Sales Manager: Kensington Publishing Corp., 119 West 40th Street, New York, NY 10018. Attn. Special Sales Department. Phone: 1-800-221-2647.

Kensington and the K logo Reg. U.S. Pat. & TM Off.

First Electronic Edition: April 2014
eISBN-13: 978-1-60183-115-6
eISBN-10: 1-60183-115-3

First Print Edition: April 2014
ISBN-13: 978-1-60183-136-1
ISBN-10: 1-60183-136-6

Printed in the United States of America

To Toni B., the only person I know who loves books more than I do.

Acknowledgements

First I have to thank Anne McConnell, Dr. McConnell if you're nasty, for all of her help in clarifying the particulars of academic life. I thought, as a former English major, that I knew enough to write a convincing professor, but her information about the hiring process and conferences, and just general life in an academic environment was invaluable. If there are any inaccuracies, it's because I wasn't listening well enough. I also want to thank her in advance for naming her baby after me.

I also have to thank the Kanawha County Public Library, where I was able to access both *What Matters in Jane Austen?* by John Mullan, and *Be Jane's Guide to Home Empowerment* by Heidi Baker and Eden Jarrin, which ended up being equally useful. Public libraries, people.

Thank you to Alicia Condon for giving me permission to explore the story I was feeling, and to Louise Fury for saying "a magic house, yes." That is a paraphrase.

Finally, I want to thank this huge list of people who deserve much more: Marsha Alford, convention partner and cheerleader; Tricia Stringer, for enforcing the joy of kittens; Matt Wolfe, for just the right amount of academic satire; Shirley Audetat, Midwest sales rep; Mary Ellen Maguire, who made sure every woman in New Jersey got a postcard; and my family, for being more excited than weirded out by this venture.

"My dearest sister, now be serious. I want to talk very seriously. Let me know every thing that I am to know without delay. Will you tell me how long you have loved him?"

"It has been coming on so gradually, that I hardly know when it began; but I believe I must date it from my first seeing his beautiful grounds at Pemberley."

—Jane Austen, *Pride and Prejudice*

Prologue

Barbara remembered those lonely first nights when she bought the house in Willow Springs. She would stay out on her porch, forcing friends to sit with her until they nearly keeled over from exhaustion. She hated that stereotype, the lonely old spinster. She wasn't that old—she refused to believe her late forties were old. And she wasn't lonely, usually. It was just being in that house all by herself.

The one person who came to see her every day was Bert. True, it was his job, but he was always so friendly. He would knock on her door and actually hand her the mail. Such manners! She thought he was just being polite, but then he started knocking on her door on Sundays. There was no mail delivery on Sundays. It was nice to have someone to bake for. Years of ballet training included years of watching her figure, and she had trouble indulging in the decadence of the brownies and cookies she suddenly felt inspired to make. But Bert loved them. And so what if sometimes she felt bad letting him eat alone. She had never been much of a baker before, but there was something about Bert, and she couldn't resist feeding him.

Barbara locked the door behind her for the last time. Bert had accepted a supervisor position in Columbus, which meant no more bad weather and overly friendly dogs. Barbara would open a dance studio in the basement of their new house. She turned the lock with her left hand just to watch the light glint off the simple diamond. He was a wonderful man. She'd thought she was done with romance, that she was too old (not *that* old) to be swept off her feet. And here she was, ready to start a new life with a new, wonderful, wonderful man. Even though it hadn't been for very long, she was so grateful that she had moved to Willow Springs.

As the moving truck pulled away from the curb, Barbara's eye caught a sudden movement under the house. Probably one of the cats that roamed the neighborhood. Bert honked and waved from the road. She ran down the steps and got into the passenger seat, not sparing a second glance at her old house.

The house felt her pull away, and felt that old empty feeling again. It would pass. The house knew that. Someone new was coming. The weeds would sprout overnight and the house would let go of its tight hold on the shutters. Someone new was coming, and the house would start all over again.

Chapter 1

"What the June Cleaver do you think that means?"

Grace Williams rubbed her still-sore neck and smiled at her sister's creative cursing. Immediately after being shocked awake, she'd recounted her strange dream to Jane. In her dream, she was baking. With an apron. She might have been wearing heels while doing it. She was in a bright, sunny kitchen and birds were chirping outside. Jane asked if Cinderella came down the stairs looking for mice to help her put her shoes on. Grace ignored her and went on to describe the sound of the front door opening and Dream Grace turning with her apron and a plate of cupcakes (the cupcakes actually looked really good—go Dream Grace) and Real Grace was overwhelmed with this feeling of joy and happy expectation as she waited for whoever was walking through the front door. Then there were footsteps, and the kitchen door swung open and the whole space was filled with even more light, and Grace felt warm and happy, and then . . .

"Maybe it's something all women go through when they buy their first house," she shrugged, then winced when her sore neck protested. She didn't regret agreeing to let her sister drive the U-Haul from northern California to Willow Springs, Kentucky, but regretted the awkward sleeping positions she kept falling into.

"You didn't have creepy Stepford dreams when you bought your condo," Jane said.

"True. But this wasn't creepy, exactly. It felt kind of nice."

Jane looked at her. "That's the creepy part."

"Don't worry. I'll always be your spinster older sister."

Jane snorted. "Hardly."

Grace sighed and watched the Midwest go past in a flat, corny blur. Domesticity had never been her idea of bliss. She wasn't quite as violently disgusted by heteronormativity as her sister was, but sometimes she felt that Jane just used that as an excuse to get out of folding laundry. In fact, Grace had folded Jane's laundry many times growing up. And now Jane's husband, Dev, had taken over laundry duties. Jane was a lucky woman.

The dream shook Grace up. Their mother had been a housewife. Not a normal housewife, but one of those super housewives with twelve arms, and eyes in the back of her head. She cooked, ironed, and managed play dates and crafty birthday parties. She was warm and creative, and a light, soft presence that her two daughters couldn't resist hovering around. Unless there were chores to do.

All that changed when their father was killed in a car accident on a twisty Ohio back road. The girls had been in college, but they'd rushed home to be with their mother. It didn't do much good, though, because she died of a heart attack just days after her husband did. People said it was so romantic, that she'd died of a broken heart. Grace thought it sucked.

So Grace never held much stock in dreams. Or in love, for that matter. But in this dream, it wasn't so much what she was doing that was appealing. And it was obviously a dream, because she'd never baked anything that looked remotely as appetizing as those cupcakes. It was the feeling she had—light, almost floating, and safe and happy down to her bones.

Grace had worked too hard to throw it all away for a batch of cupcakes and a dream guy. She had a mildly well-selling book under her belt, and was on her way to her first tenure-track position as an assistant professor of English at Pembroke College, a small but respected liberal arts school nestled in the hills of Kentucky. After years of grad school in California, she was finally back within driving distance of Jane, if she ever got a car. She'd be able to pop up to Columbus for the weekend to see her niece, Priya, and have dinner with Dev's family, who had embraced Grace as fully as they had Jane.

And she had her dream house. That was one dream she accepted without question. Grace pulled out her phone and started scrolling through the photo gallery. She'd found herself doing that a lot over the past several months, whenever she became overwhelmed by the stress of moving, of grading the last of her English 101 papers, of finding out that Lou was actually, in fact, still married.

Pictures of her dream house never failed to slow her heart rate to a normal, functioning level. It was, honestly, the cutest house she'd ever seen. The architecture was decidedly Victorian, but it was small and compact. A dollhouse was how the realtor described it, although the circular turret in the front reminded Grace more of a castle. A very groovy castle with stained-glass panels above the normal windows. The house itself was painted an odd shade of blue, somewhere between royal blue and turquoise. The trim was a soft white and needed touching up in places. Grace scrolled through the window shots—and there were plenty, because there were a lot of windows.

The interior photos showed small-ish, empty rooms—there hadn't been time to stage it, because Grace had snatched it up almost as soon as it went on the market. She swept her finger over the fireplace in the living room, the antique wall sconces, the built-in cabinets that she was imagining filled with books. She kept swiping. The realtor had told her the kitchen could use an upgrade—which was part of the reason it was such a bargain—but Grace loved the old gas range, the slightly wonky-with-age glass cabinets. She didn't plan on changing a thing. Maybe put up some fresh paint, find some interesting window treatments. But she loved the house as it was.

"Quit drooling over house pictures, Grace. You're going to wear out your battery."

"Keep your eyes on the road, Mario." Jane's legendary lead foot had gotten them halfway across the country in record time. The whole process of packing her small condo had been infinitely faster with Jane there, even if Jane insisted that it didn't matter what order the books went into the boxes, and did she really have to take *all* of them with her?

Jane was a pain and a joy, as only a little sister could be. But she was also a speed demon, and easily distracted. So Grace obeyed her and started to put her phone away as they entered Kentucky, where the roads got windier as the speed limit went up.

Grace checked the GPS, then put her phone on the dashboard. Jane followed the curve of the road, and Grace moved the phone to the center console. But her racing heart had nothing to do with Jane's driving. Just a few more hours and her new life would start. She had almost two months to get settled in before classes began. That was practically a whole summer to turn that cute little Victorian dollhouse into her dream home.

Jake Burdette looked over at his sister. Mary Beth was standing on the sidewalk, hands on her hips, the expression on her face making Jake feel as if he'd done something wrong.

"How did this even happen?" she asked the house.

For once in his life, Jake could say, unequivocally, that this was not his fault.

Mary Beth had called him in a panic about an hour ago. She'd interrupted a perfectly good pizza and *Die Hard* marathon to have him stand with her in front of that old house on Grant Street that looked like it was falling apart. He remembered her telling him that she'd sold it to a professor or something. Someone who'd never owned a house before, and so would probably need a little guidance in the fix-it department. Even though Jake didn't have much use for the professors at Pembroke College, Mary Beth was his sister and he couldn't say no to her. She'd probably break his thumb if he did.

"Listen, Mary Beth, I'm no landscaper. And I'm definitely not a miracle worker."

"What, so you couldn't mow the lawn? To welcome a new person into the town?"

"I did mow the lawn," he argued. "Three days ago, like you asked."

"Then why does it look like a jungle?"

Jake didn't know about a jungle. More like an idyllic meadow, complete with patches of wildflowers and mushrooms. Which hadn't been there when he'd left the freshly mown yard three days ago.

"She's going to be here soon." Mary Beth started pacing the sidewalk, pushing the gate to the short picket fence closed. "And the house is looking like this? Oh, she's going to regret moving here and then she'll leave and then . . ."

"What do you care? You already sold her the house." The fence swung limply open. Jake was sure that latch had worked three days ago.

"Jake Hanson Burdette, that is not the point. It's important to make new people feel welcome in Willow Springs. Make her feel like this is a place she'll want to settle. There's enough separating Pembroke people from the town already. We don't want her to think we're trying to take advantage of her."

"Right. Because Pembroke People always have such a high opinion of townies."

"Jake—"

"It doesn't matter what you do, MB. Give her a few days at Pembroke and she'll be looking down on us like the rest of them."

"Grace isn't like that," Mary Beth said. "She's sweet. Besides, she's young and I'm pretty sure she's single."

"I don't do professors."

"Don't be crude."

"You just like her because she wrote that book about what's-her-name."

"Jane Austen is her name, and don't you dare say a bad word about her or her books."

Jake raised his hands in surrender. He'd read Jane Austen in high school, and all he remembered about the novel was the girls in class mooning over Mr. What's-His-Name. And the long sentences. He remembered she wrote really long sentences.

"Professor Williams is a Jane Austen expert and we need her."

"You just want her to join your book group. Which she won't be-cause it's at the public library and Pembroke People don't go to the public library." Jake pulled up a purple wildflower and twirled it be-tween his fingers.

"Don't worry about what I want." She grabbed the flower out of his hand and threw it onto the sidewalk. "Just make this yard look nice. She said she wasn't far." When Mary Beth had earned her re-altor's license, she'd made a point of taking a picture with every client in front of their new house. Her office was wallpapered with smiling families: longtime residents, people new to the town, a lot of guys with their dogs. All giving a goofball thumbs up, holding a "Sold" sign. It made Mary Beth happy to make her clients happy.

Even if that involved torturing her younger brother.

It wasn't his fault the housing market had tanked. Mary Beth was all right—the presence of the college ensured there were always people coming and going in Willow Springs. But Jake's business was flipping houses, updating them with the pseudo-authentic fixtures that yuppies wanted, and then making a lot of money off them. He'd started right out of high school and had his own successful business before his classmates were out of college. Even without college, though, Jake was smart about the market. He saw how the rest of the country was going, and knew Kentucky would eventually catch up. So he saved, did a few commercial projects, worked in his dad's garage for a bit, and saved some more so he had enough to live on until more opportunities presented themselves. And, slowly, they were. In the meantime, he lived in an apartment above his sister's garage, helped her and her husband, Todd, pay the mortgage and, apparently, answered her beck and call.

He supposed he could pull a few of the big weeds from around the "Sold" sign, clear more of a path to the front door. He was just about to start complaining about his lack of a living wage when one of those rented moving trucks came barreling down the street.

"Crap," said Mary Beth. Too late for him to do any work. Okay, he'd just stick around and see what this new professor was all about. She was probably frumpy and wore cat sweaters and big glasses, and had thick ankles. Not that he minded thick ankles. He had an appreciation for many different shapes of women's legs, so long as they weren't attached to someone who looked at him like he was dirt on her shoe. But his distaste for Pembroke faculty manifested itself in a sort of sick curiosity, and he found he didn't want to leave.

Mary Beth was waving at the truck, her business smile plastered on her face. She was business-smiling within an inch of her life. He saw a woman in the passenger seat—couldn't see much, except that she was a woman. The woman waved at Mary Beth, then he saw her face drop as she got a good look at the house.

He didn't think it was that bad. It wasn't as nice as it had looked last week, but it wasn't that bad.

But he'd seen enough. "See you, sis," he said, heading over to his truck.

"No," she said, grabbing his arm in the death grip he recognized from many childhood torture sessions. "Stay and take the picture."

"You sure she's going to want a picture?"

The U-Haul pulled into the driveway and lurched to a stop. He saw the Professor say something to the woman who was driving, who said something back with her hands, then one more thing with her finger, and the driver opened the door and spilled out.

The driver was tall and slender, with a mop of bleached-blonde hair piled on top of her head in a messy knot, and thick glasses perched on her nose. She stretched, leaned forward to touch her toes, then stood up to wait for the professor, who was climbing out of the passenger side.

"You are the worst driver ever," he heard from the other side of the truck.

"Love ya, sis!" the driver said.

Mary Beth started toward the two women, but Jake hung back, hoping to make his escape. The sister could take the picture. If there was going to be a picture.

But then the professor walked around the truck, and Jake's curiosity glued him in place. She was tall, too, taller than her sister. She had the same messy top-knot in her hair, but the professor's hair was darker, nearly brown. And she didn't have thick ankles, not that he would have minded. She was wearing cut-off denim shorts, and they were short enough to see that her legs were tanned and muscled—not the legs of a woman who spent all day reading.

Jake shook his head. He didn't do professors, not in any sense of the word. The Pembroke People had nothing to do with people like him, people who barely finished high school, who worked with their hands.

Besides, this professor was wearing a baggy, purple sweatshirt with a cat on it. The cat was wearing glittery sunglasses and striking a weird, sexy pose next to the words "Check Meowt." Also sparkly.

Still, she was the hottest crazy cat lady he had ever seen.

Chapter 2

"I don't remember it looking this bad," said Jane in the loudest whisper known to man.

Grace didn't remember either. When she'd come for the job interview at Pembroke in early spring, her sister had driven down from Columbus to meet her and they'd gone house hunting together. Grace fell in love, signed the contract, and went back to California with a phone full of pictures.

Grace was glad she'd had a witness. Jane had fallen in love with the house almost as much as Grace had, although Jane had reservations about its age. Mary Beth had seemed reluctant to show them the place, said it might not be Grace's taste. It probably wasn't a lot of people's tastes. It was gaudy and weird and old. But there was a turret, complete with funky stained glass, and Grace could see herself creating a reading nook in there. And there were windows everywhere! She could just imagine how wonderful it would feel to sit in the sun, or to light a fire in the fireplace when it was overcast and cold. It was never overcast and cold in California. She would never find a house like this in California. This was a New Life house.

And the porch! The porch had made her sad to go back to her second floor balcony-free condo. She loved sitting outside, and this house not only had a front porch, but a gorgeous, winding garden in the back. Grace had always suspected she had a green thumb, but apartment living was never very conducive to keeping plants alive. If she bought the house, she would have flowers and tomatoes and cucumbers and more flowers and a gorgeous dreamy yard that required hardly any mowing but would be the perfect spot to have garden parties and to concoct brilliant ideas about literature.

Now she wasn't so sure that she hadn't bitten off more than she could chew. Mary Beth had sent her pictures a week ago, showing her the work her brother had done on the house. Everything was neatly trimmed and pruned and there was a potted plant on the front step. Now the plant seemed in danger of sliding off the crooked step, and it looked as if the yard was not as familiar with a weed whacker as she'd been led to believe.

She turned to Mary Beth, who had seemed so sweet and nice and genuine. She'd made Grace feel like it was her life's mission to get her into the perfect house. Mary Beth had gotten her a good deal and everything. At least Grace thought she had. Was she being hoodwinked? By this nice, snappily dressed realtor and her too-hot-for-his-own-good brother?

Because the brother introduced as Jake was ridiculous in his handsomeness. Even Jane, who was very happily married and who didn't put a lot of stock in people's looks, was gobsmacked. "Is this a joke?" she whispered to Grace when Mary Beth made the introductions. "This has to be a joke."

"What?" asked Mary Beth, because Jane was the loudest whisperer ever.

"Nothing. I was just saying that your brother is so handsome that he can't be real. Are you real?" Jane poked him on the forehead.

Mary Beth laughed, and way-too-handsome Jake smiled (which, damn him, made him even handsomer). The tension melted around them but Grace remained firm. She crossed her arms over her weird ironic cat sweater, and watched everybody laugh at her sister's charming goofiness while the house she'd just spent all of her money on crumbled around her.

She was a little cranky from the drive. Then she caught Jake looking at her. He rolled his eyes and she got even crankier. Because it was one thing to be completely not attracted to a handsome man, but it was another thing entirely to be dismissed by him. She shouldn't be cranky about that, she told herself, which made her even crankier. Plus she was tired, she was dirty, and she wished she hadn't worn the ironic spinster cat lady sweatshirt Jane had given her for her birthday last year. To top it all off, the realtor Grace had thought might be her first friend in this town was sheepishly handing her the keys to a quirky, Victorian dump.

"I mean, it's not that bad," Jane said, as Mary Beth and Jake climbed the wonky steps behind them. "It's pretty nice, really."

Grace rolled her eyes at her sister. Jane's true feelings about the house were written all over her face. Thankfully, once she rattled the door open, the inside wasn't as bad as the outside. It wasn't great, but it wasn't turn-the-truck-around terrible. The sun shining through the old lace curtains revealed some swirling dust, and as Grace ran her finger over the mantelpiece, it came away with more dust. It seemed to swirl and dance in the sunlight and if it hadn't been *dust*, for crying out loud, it would have looked magical. But just dust, she could handle. Just dust assuaged her impending panic attack when she thought about how much work she'd have to do to make the house livable before the semester started. If it was just dust on the inside, the outside could wait.

"It's just dust." Jake was inside the living room, running his finger over the windowsills. He looked up at the curtains as if to confirm, yup, those were dirty too.

"I know," said Grace.

"I'm just saying, because you looked like you were about to storm out of here and turn that truck around."

"Jake . . ." Mary Beth warned.

"I'm sure you can get someone to clean it for you," he added with a shrug.

"I can clean it all by myself, don't you worry about that." Grace flounced away from the fireplace and headed toward the swinging door to the kitchen. In the time it took her to cross the floor, her cranky brain had conjured a dramatic exit, a perfect cut expertly delivered to the too-handsome Jake, then a flourishing turn through to the kitchen.

"I can handle—" she started, before being cut off by the swinging door crashing off of its hinges. The momentum she'd put into dramatically pushing the door open brought her down on top of it. Smooth, she thought. She'd really showed him. Half of a cut direct and now she was on her butt in the kitchen, on top of the door, a cloud of magical pixie dust settling around her.

Grace sneezed. What had she gotten herself into?

Jake was not sure which instinct came first—the one to laugh as Grace Buster Keaton-ed through the kitchen door, or the one to run to her and pick her up because the fall kind of looked like it hurt. He decided to pretend he was the better man and rushed forward to check on her. She was fine. Red as a beet and scowling, but no injuries. Grace reached for her sister's outstretched hand, but Jake didn't like the way she ignored his. So he stuck his hands under her arms and hauled her up.

The look on her face as she got her feet underneath her was pretty much what he expected: angry, horrified, embarrassed.

"Jake," Mary Beth said behind him. Fine, yes, he shouldn't manhandle her clients. But he was just trying to help.

"Are you okay?" Jane asked, putting a protective arm around her waist.

"Yes, fine," Grace said, pulling her sparkle-cat sweatshirt back into place. Jake tried not to observe that the sweatshirt was doing her no favors, and that underneath she felt soft and solid.

"What's the deal, Mary Beth?" Grace whirled that soft and solid body on his sister. "I thought this house passed inspection?"

"It did! I don't know what—"

"Is this some kind of joke?" said Grace. "Get the new girl to buy a piece-of-crap house and laugh because you got your swindle on?"

"I swear to you, Grace, I have no idea why this is happening. You're right, the house passed inspection, and nobody has been in here since the old owners moved out."

"You're sure there wasn't a bunch of, I don't know, dismantling elves in here?"

Jane snorted. Jake tried not to.

"Because if this is how you do business—"

Mary Beth took a step back and Jake stepped in. He was willing to make allowances for Grace's anger because she was in a pretty tough position and she had just made a fool of herself, but stepping up to his sister like that was not going to fly.

"Watch it," he warned.

"Watch it? Watch it? What is that supposed to mean? You gonna manhandle me some more if I get in her face about the fact that I just got ripped off?"

Mary Beth looked close to tears. "I promise you, I have no idea—"

"Skip it, lady."

"Don't you talk to my sister—"

"Hey!" Everybody froze, fingers pointed at each other, as Jane shouted from on top of the kitchen door.

"Thank you," she said when everyone was quiet. "Let's talk about this like adults."

"I am—" Grace started.

"Don't make me use my teacher voice again," Jane warned.

Grace scowled at her sister, but she stopped talking. She crossed her hands angrily over her chest, but she stopped talking.

"Grace, did you do your due diligence when you bought this house? Inspections, certifications, all that stuff we talked about?" Jane asked, hands on her hips.

"You know I did."

"Mary Beth, did you talk to my sister about the possibility of things needing repair in an older house, even though there were perfectly fine new houses available in the neighborhood?"

"I did. But she fell in love with this one," Mary Beth said, choking back a note of desperation. "I can't blame her, it's a beautiful house. But, Grace, I did warn you that it would need some work."

" 'Some work!' " Grace shouted. " 'Some work' is different from doors falling off!"

"It's not a big deal," Jake said. "Look." He nudged Jane aside and hoisted the door up. He lined up the hinges, and the door clicked back into place.

Which was much easier than he expected it to be.

He thought he would have to prop it up, then go out to his truck to get some tools, or maybe run downtown to get some new hinges. But he stood it up, then *click*, and the door was working again. He gave it a tentative swing. It swung.

"No problem," he said, turning to the three amazed sets of eyes staring at him.

"It shouldn't have fallen in the first place," mumbled Grace.

"No, but Handsome Jake here was nice enough to fix it for you, so no problem," said Jane.

"No problem now, but what am I going to do when the next thing falls apart? What if this chandelier falls on our heads?"

Everybody took a little step back from the center of the room, where an antique iron lighting fixture was hanging.

"Grace, I know this is upsetting, and I really can't explain why that door just fell off," Mary Beth said, leading them toward the living room windows.

"Which was easy to fix," said Jake.

His sister shot him a look. "But," she continued, "everything should be fine. We did the inspection, the last owner replaced the water heater, the things that needed to be updated have been updated. That was part of the contract we signed. But it is an old house. I told you, it is livable, but it will require some TLC."

Jane looked at her sister even as she addressed the realtor. "Are you suggesting, Mary Beth, that my sister heard your well-informed advice, but ignored it and did what she wanted to anyway? How unlike my sister to do something like that. How very, very unlike her."

Jake guessed by the sarcasm dripping from Jane's tone that this was par for the course for Grace. Of course. People like Grace, they got what they wanted no matter what.

And based on the scowl covering Grace's face, she didn't like hearing it.

"I tell you what," said Mary Beth, ushering Grace into the sunny foyer. "What if we work something out? What if I got someone to come over here and help you fix things when they break? That way, you can enjoy the charm of this gorgeous old house, and you won't have to feel like I did you wrong in any way."

The back of Jake's neck prickled.

"Let me guess," said Grace. "You have the perfect guy lined up and his rates are completely reasonable."

"No charge," said Mary Beth calmly as she opened the front door. "The guy I'm thinking of doesn't need the money, and he owes me a favor."

Now Jake's neck was on fire. There was no way . . .

"He owes me a lifetime of favors," Mary Beth said, and looked right at Jake.

"Mary Beth—" he started to protest.

"She'll take it!" Jane said, and slammed the front door in their faces.

The house shuddered at the slam of the door. Things were not working out yet, but they rarely did at first. The heavy footfall on the front steps definitely belonged to the one, but now he was going away angry, muttering to the woman who had taken such good care of the house. The man had mowed the lawn and painted the porch rails. But if the house hadn't been careful, the man would have finished everything before the new owner moved in, and that would never do. The house had a job to do, and no matter how much it hurt, the job would get done.

Chapter 3

"What did you just do?" Grace stared at her sister, who was smirking in a way that looked as if she was pretty pleased with herself.

"What?" Jane blinked, and Grace didn't buy her innocent act for a second. "You don't want that hot guy helping you with stuff around your house?"

"No! He's a jerk."

"You don't have to talk to him. You just have to call him when something breaks and then ogle him from the corner while he works."

"Jane, that is beyond creepy."

"I wonder if he'll take his shirt off if it gets too hot? Your air conditioner isn't broken, is it?"

There was a quick knock at the door, and then Mary Beth's head appeared through the opening. "I just wanted to give you this," she said, thrusting a business card through the open door. "Jake's cell is on the back."

"Thank you!" said Jane, far too cheerily. "We'll be sure to give him a call!"

Grace rolled her eyes at her sister. On one hand, Jane was right. Grace was not handy, and owning a condo with a twenty-four hour handyman had not filled any holes in her education. She had stubbornly pushed ahead with buying the house because she'd wanted it so badly. She'd figured she could get a few library books, learn along the way.

But things take on a different urgency when a girl is sitting on her own kitchen door.

On the other hand, Jane was totally, one hundred percent wrong. Jake was not the right man to help her out. He hated her, or at least he looked down on her. Even if he hadn't acted like a jerk, she'd felt his disdain the second she got out of the truck. And she didn't need a man who thought she was an idiot hanging around her house, proving himself right about her own idiocy by doing manual tasks that she was incapable of doing.

Plus, he was hot. He was tall and broad, and his jeans were just snug enough to make her want to see if it was possible to bounce quarters off a guy's butt. His hands were big and rough, and he'd picked her up off her kitchen door like she weighed nothing. Grace knew she didn't weigh nothing.

The worst part, though, was when he'd stood her up and she faced him. She was mad, and then she'd got a good look at his eyes. They were a rich, dark brown, and in them she saw some mockery, yes, but also concern and intelligence. Those were deep eyes. She didn't do deep.

She couldn't afford to like him. She couldn't afford to like any man. She was done with that. She had taken the job at Pembroke to begin the spinster life she wanted to be destined for. No more men, no more distractions, no more lies. The last guy she'd let in, and she had only let him in a little, turned out to be a lying jerk with a superiority complex and a wife.

Plus, living for another person was not how she wanted to live her life.

"Hey," said Jane, fingering Mary Beth's business card. "Tell me again why we sent the guy with muscles away when we have a truck to unload?"

Grace looked out the window at the rented moving truck. "I thought Dev was coming."

"Ha. You underestimate the number of distractions a four-year-old can provide when you're trying to do . . . anything."

"Priya is good, she won't get in the way."

"Again, I say 'ha.' I know you. You'll get distracted by her cuteness and then Dev and I will have to do all the heavy lifting."

"You shouldn't have had such a cute daughter."

"I still think we should chase Handsome Jake down and ask for his help."

"No!" Grace knew Jane was joking—sort of—but she couldn't help the panic that seeped into her voice.

Jane put her arms around Grace, rested her head on her shoulder. "Not all men are egomaniacal jerks."

Grace snorted. "So far, Jake seems to fit the bill."

"And not all love stories have to end badly."

Grace shut her eyes even though she knew Jane couldn't see her face. Jane was less than two years younger than she was; how had she been able to do it? How did she have a normal, happy marriage while Grace still ran screaming from any sign of commitment?

"Okay." Jane swatted Grace on her butt. "No more pity party. You're a successful writer, a brilliant professor, and the proud owner of the cutest money pit in town. Shake it off."

Grace shook, hokey-pokey style, like they used to do when they were little.

"Good," said Jane. "Now stop shaking and get those boxes moved, you crazy spinster."

Jake followed Mary Beth to her office, hoping to get out of the deal with the new professor. It was either that or change his cell phone number, and he didn't want to do that. All of his friends and all of his business contacts knew his cell number. And a lot of women.

On second thought, maybe he should change it.

Not that he minded a lot of women calling him. He liked women. He liked talking to them and hanging out with them. He had a different relationship with his female friends than he did with his male friends, and he liked that. Even though his female friends tended to try to set him up with their friends. The women around here usually knew Jake from high school, or knew someone who did, and they were just out for a good time.

He wasn't complaining; he liked a good time. But sometimes he felt . . . cheap, maybe. Like they were just using him for his body. His head stepped in to remind him that he worked hard for his body; why shouldn't he want people to use it? But there was another part of him, a deep, secret part he usually only let out when he was drinking alone, that wanted more. That wanted someone to want him for every part of him.

Jesus, he was hanging out with his girl friends too much.

All he knew was that Grace was a double-whammy—a woman who would just want him for his body, *and* a professor. His experience with professors was that they had a lot of smarts and no idea how to use them, at least not in any practical way. What was the point of speaking Latin?

"I can't believe you did that," he accused, sinking heavily into one of the chairs facing Mary Beth's desk.

"You owe me, remember?" she said as she started up her laptop. He didn't say anything back, just glared at her. She ignored him and started typing.

"I don't owe you that much."

"Sorry, are you still here? Darling brother, I have many appointments this afternoon, so while I'd love to sit and argue with you about how right I am, I'm afraid I just don't have the time."

"You're such a snot."

"You're an ungrateful little brother. How many times did I bail you out? How many times did I say the beer cans under the couch were mine? How many times did I run out in the middle of the night because you got stranded somewhere by one of your meathead friends?"

"Fine. Yes, you did all of that. You were a wonderful sister. But that stuff was in high school. How long am I going to have to pay for stuff that happened over ten years ago?"

"Probably forever."

Dammit. Jake regrouped. Their mother always told him, when his temper got too hot, that he could catch more flies with honey than with vinegar.

"You know," Jake said, leaning back and folding his hands in front of him. Just real casual-like. "If it wasn't for my bad behavior, you never would have met Todd."

Mary Beth just sighed. Jake hoped it was a wistful sigh full of love for her husband.

"If you didn't have to bail me out so many times, you would be a lonely old spinster, just like Professor Grace. You'd probably have a whole collection of cat sweatshirts."

"Jake," Mary Beth warned, "don't make fun of my clients. And don't make fun of new people in town! I think she seems nice." Jake snorted. "Well, she seemed nice the other times I met her. She's very smart, and she's actually pretty funny. I think I'm going to ask her to join my book club after all."

"MB, no English professor is going to want to join your dinky book club."

"Well, thank you, Jake, for your confidence in my intelligence. Don't let your phone die—you're going to have a lot of calls to answer."

"Is this guy bothering you?"

Jake didn't even look up. He knew that voice, and he knew that joke. Todd Brakefield, Chief of the Willow Springs Police Department and Husband to His Sister, made the same joke every time he saw Jake and Mary Beth together. Todd insisted that it was so not-funny that it was starting to get funny again. After more than a decade of it, Jake wasn't so sure.

Not that he'd argue with the man wearing a gun.

"Hey, sweetheart," said Mary Beth, getting up from behind her desk.

"No, don't get up," said Todd, as he always did. Then, as always, he walked around her desk and gave her a peck on her cheek, and stood there a second, hovering over her, until she turned her head and he kissed her gently on the lips.

Since Jake had seen this every time he was with Mary Beth at work and Todd stopped by, Jake had to imagine it happened every time Todd came in. His sister was six years older than he was, and Todd was only four. And yet the two of them had turned into old farts.

"Well, if you two are going to start making out," Jake said, standing up.

"No, don't go," said Todd. "I just stopped in for a little sugar."

Jake threw up.

Metaphorically.

But still.

"Todd, you're making Jake sick."

"I'm not going to lie, that was part of my goal," Todd said. "That, and some sugar." He leaned down and kissed Mary Beth again.

"Okay, seriously. I'm leaving now." Jake really stood up this time.

"Wait, what're you going to do?" asked Mary Beth.

"I'm just going to go home, change my phone number, and move to Arizona where my sister won't pimp out my immensely impressive home repair skills to every person with a bad attitude who moves to town."

"What's this about?" asked Todd, and Mary Beth filled him in on Grace and the state of the house, with Jake interjecting rolled eyes and sarcastic snorts.

"Wait, the Spinster House?" asked Todd. "You sold the Spinster House?"

"No," said Mary Beth. "The Spinster House is over on Walnut."

"That house? Baby, you know I hate to interfere in your business, but that pile of crap is a meth lab waiting to happen. That's not the Spinster House."

"Yes, it is! The logging heiress built it on the outskirts of town and then left with her new husband before she could move into it. And it was scandalous because she built it on one of the out-of-the-way streets so people assumed she was up to no good."

"No, that's the house built by her no-good brother. It was a brothel. That's why it has all those porches and those tiny rooms."

"Todd, I hate to disagree with you, seeing as you're carrying a gun and all," said Jake, "but I'm pretty sure my sister's right. Look how big that place is. And, yeah, it's falling apart now, but it has big money written all over it. The house that Mary Beth sold Grace is just . . . weird."

"You ever heard of an eccentric millionaire?" Todd asked.

"Todd, I'm sure you're wrong." Mary Beth started clicking through on her computer. "See? It has a Wikipedia entry and everything."

Jake joined Todd behind Mary Beth's desk and they scanned the article together. Sure enough, the Spinster House in Willow Springs, Kentucky, was a dilapidated brothel-looking house on the outskirts of town. Not a cute but strange mini-Victorian in the center of town.

"You believe everything you read on the Internet?" asked Todd.

"That's one thing I love about you," said Mary Beth, wrapping her arms around her husband. "You're always willing to admit when you're wrong."

They started whispering in each other's ears and Jake knew it was time to get gone.

"I knew my sister was right," he said, heading toward the door. "Otherwise, I would've bought that house and fixed it up. But I'm not touching anything called the 'Spinster House.' Not for a million bucks and a life free from professors."

"Ah, yes—my brother, the confirmed bachelor."

"I think that's a euphemism for being gay," said Todd.

"You wish," said Jake.

"Boys," said Mary Beth. "Jake, go away. And close the door behind you. I want to make out with my husband."

Jake got whiplash on his way out the door.

"Oh!" Mary Beth called after him. "Mom wants to know if you're coming to dinner on Sunday. Will is making lasagna."

Jake scowled. His mom knew he couldn't resist her husband's lasagna. "Fine."

"And Jake, be nice to the new girl."

Jake growled.

Mary Beth laughed and put her arms around her husband. "She's probably not going to call anyway," she told her brother's retreating back.

Good, thought Jake. He didn't want her to call.

Chapter 4

Grace held out for almost two weeks before she called Jake. Jane and Dev helped get her moved in, despite Priya's best efforts to distract them with cuteness. There was a freezer full of homemade food from Dev's mother, who had absolutely no confidence in Grace's ability to feed herself, which was fine with Grace. Her books were still in boxes until she painted, her clothes were mostly in the closet, and she finally found her favorite moisturizer after a week of going without. She met with the head of the English Department, got a university-issued laptop, and set up her office in the creaky old brick building in the middle of Pembroke's campus. She rode her bike into town for coffee, for lunch, for library books.

She was especially impressed with the Willow Springs Public Library. It was small and dark, but it had an amazing stained glass window that took up almost the entire south wall of the building. It was an abstract design, a jumble of colors and shapes that shouldn't make sense, but did. It kind of reminded Grace of a Jackson Pollock painting—it looked haphazard and easy, but there was an unconscious order to the madness that drew her in. The Library Window, as it was cleverly called, was impressive, and so was the library's collection of DIY books. Grace had a pretty good selection checked out: *How to Maximize Small Spaces*, *The Modern Chick's Guide to Home Improvement*, *You Don't Need a Man, You Need a Hammer*, and, just for fun, *The Greek Tycoon's Virgin Secretary*.

She had used the books to guide her through fixing a wonky kitchen cabinet. She found instructions on how to replace her broken toilet seat, which made her very proud, even if she almost snapped her cheap-o wrench trying to get the rusted old bolts off. The process for replacing a loose top piece for the newel post on her banister seemed too complicated, so she just glued it, which seemed to work.

But none of the books, not even her new home-repair confidence, was helping. She sat at her kitchen table, her panicked gaze switching between the pages of *The Home Plumber's Guide to Home Plumbing* and her misbehaving kitchen sink. She was working up the courage to identify the source of the leak, which would entail turning the water back on. If she turned the water back on, her kitchen would flood again. She wasn't sure if the checkerboard linoleum could handle another rush of misbehaving kitchen water.

But the plumbing book made no sense to her. There were diagrams and pictures and words, and those three things had gotten her through other projects. But anxiety made the augers and pivot balls and bibs swim before her eyes. Plus, she needed a pipe wrench. All she had were pliers.

They didn't work. She'd tried.

And when she called Jane to freak out and maybe get her much-more-practical-and-handy sister to come down and fix her sink, Jane told her that the two things she never messed with were plumbing and wiring. Because only idiots messed with plumbing and wiring when they didn't know what they were doing.

"But you know who does know what he's doing?"

Grace hung up before Jane could tell her to call Handsome Jake.

So, instead of calling someone who would help her out, Grace sat at her kitchen table with her legs crossed (no water meant no toilet, she soon realized) and risked a glance at her refrigerator, where Jane had tacked Mary Beth's card with Jake's number on the back.

She shouldn't ask him for help. She should just call a regular plumber. She could just get a recommendation. But the only person in town she knew well enough to call so early in the morning was Mary Beth, and if she did that, Mary Beth would just send her brother over. That would save Grace the trouble of calling Jake herself, which would limit her exposure to his patronizing tone. But then Jake would know she was, too—what was she, annoyed? Intimidated? Chicken?

Yes.

But she was going to have to be able to use her kitchen and bathroom eventually.

Letting out the kind of heavy, self-pitying sigh that she only indulged in when she was alone, Grace got up from the table and plodded miserably to the refrigerator. She pulled the horse magnet, which apparently came with the house, off the clean, white surface. She held the card to the fridge with one finger.

"Grace Williams, you are being ridiculous," she told herself. Out loud. Because she'd rather start talking to herself out loud than call a perfectly competent person who was sort-of-willing to help. She bopped her head on the refrigerator door once, then once more, then she peeled off Jake's number and started to dial.

Jake's head was buzzing.

He shook himself awake, but it still took him a second to recognize where he was. Brown plaid couch, neon beer signs on the wall. Kyle's house.

Kyle had been on call all weekend, and, in solidarity, Jake had behaved himself. He was gone so much with work that he couldn't join the Willow Springs volunteer firefighters, but he could do his part by commiserating with his best friend who was, frankly, a drama queen. Of course, no fireman wants a house to catch on fire on account of lives endangered and property damaged. But Kyle was an adrenaline junkie and a rowdy, and being on call meant he had to stay close to home and sober. He used to spend his weekends on call with the other guys and gals at the fire station, but the captain had begged Jake to have mercy on all of them and babysit.

So Jake was doing his part for the citizens of Willow Springs.

Kyle was particularly grumpy because while he was on call, sitting around and not drinking like a normal red-blooded American man, Missy was out at the bars with her girlfriends. Kyle and Missy had only been dating for a few weeks this time, but they had dated for a couple of weeks on and off since high school. Jake wasn't sure why, if they drove each other so crazy, they couldn't just quit it. He liked Missy well enough, but he really couldn't see going out with someone who drove him as crazy as she drove Kyle. He asked Kyle about it once, and Kyle had slugged him. So they didn't talk about feelings anymore.

Missy was out and Kyle was home, and he'd been a beast all weekend, torturing himself with the kinds of trouble Missy was getting into without him. She wasn't helping, sending pictures of herself doing shots, hugging the bartender. If Jake didn't know Missy so well, he would've said she was being cruel. Well, she was being cruel, but Jake knew she was just giving Kyle hell. And Kyle had moped and whined, and Jake finally had to hide his car keys so Kyle didn't go out and chase Missy down.

So on Monday, no longer on call, Kyle staked out the hospital where Missy worked, finagled her into the car when she was done with her shift, and Jake didn't hear from either of them until Tuesday afternoon. By then, Kyle was feeling tied down and claustrophobic, and Missy was sick of his crap, so Jake invited himself over to Kyle's house where they basically did what they'd done all weekend, but this time with beer.

Jake had spent more nights than was probably healthy on Kyle's couch. He had even gone out and bought his own pillow to keep in Kyle's linen closet. It was the only remotely linen thing in there. But last night Jake had had too much whiskey on top of his beer, and he'd made do with the scratchy throw pillows and his sweatshirt.

Which was now buzzing on his cheek.

He dug around the mess until he found the pocket, then pulled out his cell phone. He didn't recognize the number, which usually meant he shouldn't pick up. But he was tired and hungover and wanted to take it out on someone, so he picked up.

"H'lo?"

"Hi, is this Jake?"

A woman. He squinted across the room at the neon Schlitz clock. It was awfully early for him to be staring at neon, let alone for a strange woman to be calling.

"Hello?" the woman asked.

Jake grunted in response.

"Hi, this is Grace Williams. Um, your sister sold me that house?"

Right. The professor who lived in that money pit. He thought he was off the hook with that obligation. If she needed him to hang her cat pictures, he was going to be pissed.

"Yeah, hi. What's up?" he said in the most uninterested way possible.

"Sorry, did I wake you?"

Years of maintaining relationships with difficult clients had taught Jake to politely deny when he was being inconvenienced, no matter how big a lie it was.

"Yeah," he replied. He wanted her to know that she was inconvenient.

"Oh. Sorry. Like I said."

"What do you want, Professor?"

"Um. You know what? Never mind. I'm fine."

He heard her hesitation, and he knew she wasn't fine.

"What do you need, Grace?" It did not, in fact, kill him to be a little bit nice.

"I told you, I'm—"

"I promised my sister I'd help you out, and if she finds out you need help and I wasn't there for you, I'll have to pay big time. So do me a favor and tell me what's wrong."

He heard her dramatic sigh loud and clear.

"What do you know about plumbing?"

Jake thought briefly about all of the bathrooms he'd upgraded or built from scratch, but he didn't like the way that Grace asked. It sounded as if she assumed he didn't know anything.

"Enough," he told her.

"Okay. Mary Beth said you were handy, but I didn't know if that would apply to plumbing."

Mary Beth had said he was *handy*? That's the last time he fixes her garbage disposal.

"Or do you know a plumber I can call? Someone with a good reputation who won't charge me too much."

"What's wrong?"

"It's my sink," she said.

He waited for her to give him a little more information.

She didn't.

"What's wrong with your sink?"

"It sort of exploded all over my kitchen floor."

Great. Of course that house would have leaky pipes.

He heaved himself off the couch and gave his own dramatic sigh. "Do you know how to turn the water off?"

"I'm not an idiot, Jake."

Whoa. Sassy. "I didn't say you were."

"No, but your tone implied it. Mary Beth showed me the water shut-off and the breakers before I bought the house. So I do know enough not to kill myself, thanks. But I'd really like someone to come take a look at this so I can go to the bathroom sometime before the end of the week."

Well, this should be fun, he thought, sliding his feet into his shoes. "I'll be over in a minute. Just let me stop at home and get some tools."

"Oh, you're not at home?"

He thought she sounded surprised, which offended him. He was a single, red-blooded man. Why should he sleep at home every night? Then he thought there was some judgment in her surprise, which offended him even more. He was going over there to fix her plumbing for free and now she was judging him?

He also blamed her for causing his intense overreaction. Normal women didn't push his buttons the way the professor did.

Jake put his hand over his phone, just enough so the sound was muffled, but she could still hear. "I'll call you later," he said in the loudest whisper he could muster.

"Okay, Professor, see you in a minute," he said into the phone.

She didn't say anything. Well, she might have, but Jake hung up before he could hear it.

"Who are you talking to?"

Jake looked up to see Missy, in one of Kyle's oversized T-shirts, coming down the stairs. When had Missy gotten here?

"I gotta go fix a sink," he told her, trying not to notice that the shirt was the only thing she was wearing.

"Oh, for that new girl?"

Jake stared. At her face. Only at her face.

"Mary Beth told me. She said she was nice. Really funny."

"That's not my impression of her."

"Yeah, MB told me she was kind of a b when she first moved in."

"Kind of?"

"Please, Jake, like you're never a jerk when you're cranky."

Jake just grunted. He wasn't cranky, dammit.

"Okay, well, have fun. I'm going to make pancakes if you want to come back when you're done."

Missy made the best pancakes. If it wasn't for the professor, he could hang out, not look at Missy's legs, and enjoy pancakes. There would probably be bacon and everything.

"Of course, Kyle will probably eat them all. And I'm trying not to fight with him, so I don't want to make him save any for you. So I guess there's no point in your coming back."

"Thanks, Miss. You know how to make a guy feel wanted."

"Hey, you know who wants you? That cute professor with the broke-down house. Go on. Go on and be her knight in shining armor."

Jake snorted.

"You know you love it. 'Bye, Jake," she said, shoving him out the door.

This professor better really need him.

Chapter 5

Grace saw Jake sitting on her porch swing as she pedaled up to the house. His hair was shoved under a baseball cap and his face looked as scruffy and disheveled as the rest of him. He did not look happy.

But he still looked handsome.

"Sorry," she said, jumping off her bike and hauling it up to the porch. "I had to pee."

Now he looked unhappy and confused.

"No water," she reminded him. "So I rode to the Daily Drip, which is a terrible name for a coffee shop, by the way."

He didn't laugh. "Let's look at this so-called plumbing problem."

She unlocked the front door and led him into the kitchen. "It's not a so-called problem. When I turn on the tap, the water comes out everywhere but the tap."

"Did you turn the water back on?"

"No. Because of the 'water comes out everywhere but the tap' problem."

"Let me turn it on and then we'll see what's really going on."

He was talking like he didn't believe she really had a plumbing situation. But she could not imagine why he thought she would call his grumpy butt, not to mention bike into town to use the bathroom, if she didn't really have a problem. She started to lead him to the water main in the basement, but he held a hand up to stop her.

"I know where it is. I'm the one who showed Mary Beth," he said as he stomped down the stairs.

"Okay, Smarty," she said under her breath to his retreating back. She pretended she didn't see his shoulders shake in a laugh. She also pretended not to notice how nicely those scruffy jeans fit.

In no time at all, Jake was back and sliding under the kitchen sink while Grace propped the swinging door open with her hip, ready to make a run for it.

She told herself she was standing in the doorway so she could revel in her victory when he discovered she was right about the plumbing. She told herself she was not standing in the doorway because of the way his long legs stretched out across her kitchen floor, or the way his shirt rode up a little, revealing a taught, tanned stomach. Or the way the muscles in his legs played against his jeans when he moved.

It was just so she could prove herself right.

Although she should probably not drool.

"Okay, turn the faucet on," he called from under the sink.

"Are you sure?" Grace asked. "Because last time . . ."

Jake edged out from under the sink and gave her a look she was becoming familiar with: the Why-do-you-think-I-don't-know-what-I'm-doing? look. She should give him the benefit of the doubt, even though all her recent experience with the kitchen sink told her that what he was asking her to do was also asking for disaster.

Fine, she told herself. If he fancies himself the expert, I'll follow his instructions. The worst that can happen is that he'll be right and I'll get my sink fixed. So she scurried over to the sink (all the while reminding herself never to scurry again), and pulled the faucet handle up.

And jumped back as water shot out of the pipes under the sink.

Right onto Jake.

And his shirt.

Which was now sticking to his chest.

She was so distracted by the wet shirt and the chest that she didn't hear Jake yelling at her to turn the water off, but she did register him scrambling to his feet and lunging over the sink. She also registered him whirling on her, his eyes on fire, his shirt dripping. She tried not to swoon.

Because she hated this guy. And he had just proved her right, that she needed a professional to do this job, not some guy who was trying to prove how manly he was by throwing his tools around. She was right. Therefore, he did not deserve the swoon.

Although, standing in front of her, dripping and seething, he looked pretty damn manly.

Jake continued to stare, and she continued to will her knees not to buckle. Then he reached down and tore his shirt over his head and she was pretty sure she was going to die.

I hate this guy, she reminded herself as she counted . . . yup, that's a six-pack.

She peeled her eyes away from those abs and, holy crap, that chest, to meet Jake's eyes. They were still dark, and he still looked peeved. She'd never appreciated how expressive brown eyes could be, but these were really quite fine. She would hate to have to re-think . . .

"Can I have a towel?" he growled.

She shook off the fine eyes and scurried (no more scurrying, she reminded herself) toward the linen closet. He was arrogant and rude and he had seriously just growled at her. No amount of physical beauty could overcome that personality. She ventured one glance behind her. Well, probably not.

Jake caught the towel Grace tossed at him. He noticed that she was no longer meeting his eyes. Good, he thought. He knew he was being childish, but he was glad that she was embarrassed. He was embarrassed, dammit. That was a rookie mistake, blasting the water through the pipes to see where the leak was. Still, he had just turned the water on. It shouldn't have had time to build up that much pressure. He shouldn't be standing in Grace's kitchen, sopping wet and pissed off.

He'd been fixing up houses since he was in high school. Heck, before that, even. His earliest memories involved following his dad around their old farmhouse, handing him tools whether he needed them or not.

That was before his dad screwed everything up and moved into the apartment above his mechanic shop. It didn't matter that his mom was deliriously happy with Will, or that it really was all his dad's fault. Or that Jake was now living in an apartment above Mary Beth and Todd's garage. There was no parallel; that was Jake's choice. Jake knew the housing market hadn't recovered enough for him to start flipping houses again, so he didn't. There was no sense in losing money on a mortgage for a house he couldn't sell, not when he could live off his plentiful savings and pick up odd jobs now and then just to stay out of trouble.

He'd flipped his first house the summer after he graduated from high school. He'd used the money he got for graduation and a loan from his dad to buy one of the falling-down houses right off Main Street. Then he fixed it up, Mary Beth sold it, and Jake was able to pay his dad back with enough left over to put a big down payment on his next flip. Sometimes he took his business further out of town—the closer he got to the big cities, the more lucrative the sale. He did most of the work himself, or he got Kyle and some other buddies involved. He was banking on his good reputation to keep him going while the market recovered. His reputation was every-thing, and he made sure he earned it. He never did shoddy work, and he had the clientele and the experience to back that claim up.

Which was why he was so pissed off at being sopping wet in Grace's kitchen. He had made a fool of himself. This damn sink should have been an easy fix. But Grace had been standing there, watching him work, and that made him just want to get out of the house as quickly as possible.

He couldn't leave a job half-done. And this job wasn't even close to half-done. He picked up his shirt and wrung it out in the sink. Then he tossed it on the counter and got himself back under the sink.

"Can you hand me the pipe wrench?" he asked, sitting up just enough to see whether Grace was still in the room. Of course she was. She was probably going to make sure he didn't break anything else with his cloddish workingman's hands.

"This claw-looking one?" She held up the pipe wrench, which looked nothing like a claw.

He rolled his eyes and held out his hand for it. Maybe it was a little claw-like, but he refused to be charmed.

After some tightening and re-tightening, he asked Grace to run the water again, slowly. He braced himself to jump out from under the sink, even though he didn't see how, at this point, getting wetter would make a difference. But it didn't matter. There was no leak.

Jake wasn't really sure what had been broken, but it looked like he'd fixed it.

He heard Grace kneel down next to him. "Is it leaking?"

He scooted over so she could see for herself. She hesitated—surely he didn't smell bad after that impromptu shower—but then her head joined his under the sink. The water was running into the drain above them, and through the pipes so smoothly it was like music. Grace was close enough that some of the hair that had come loose from her ponytail tickled his chin. Close enough that he could see that her hair wasn't just brown, but had hints of red in it, too. Close enough that he could tell she smelled like citrus.

Jake was having a moment with the professor.

"It's staying in the pipes!"

And the moment was gone.

Her lack of faith in him was really getting on his nerves.

"That's what pipes are for," he said, disentangling himself from her citrus-smelling hair and sitting up.

"Well, it wasn't doing that before. What did you do?"

He shrugged. "No big deal. You just have to know what you're looking for."

"Can you show me? That way I can fix it if it happens again."

He appreciated her initiative, and he would've liked to make her more independent—that way she wouldn't have to call him again. But he really had no idea what he'd done. He'd just tightened a joint that wasn't loose to begin with, and it was fixed.

And he'd taken his shirt off. He'd taken his shirt off and tightened something.

Well, it could be interesting to show Grace his new method of home repair. She was wearing another one of those horrible cat sweatshirts again, this one featuring an orange cat with rhinestone earrings. It was truly appalling. It was, Jake thought, a shirt made for tearing off.

"Like I said, you have to know what you're looking for. It shouldn't happen again." He hoped.

She rolled her eyes. "Okay. Well, thanks. I really appreciate it. Can I pay you something? I know Mary Beth said—"

"You don't have to pay me. Mary Beth is making me do you a favor."

"I know, but that doesn't seem right."

"Well, I gave her my word, so it's as right as it's going to get."

"But still, if you need the money—"

Whoa. Whoa whoa whoa. She thought he needed her money? That he was some charity case? That *she* was doing *him* a favor by being incapable of finding a plumber on her own?

"Forget it, Professor. On the house." He stalked toward the door, then turned back to grab his shirt off the counter. It was still soaking, but he wrestled himself into it anyway. It clung to his armpits and his shoulder blades, but, dammit, he was working on a dramatic exit.

She started to say something, but he didn't want to hear it. Shirt half-on and all wet, he stalked out the front door, got in his truck, and prepared to drive away from Grace and her arrogance forever. As he pulled out of the driveway, he caught a glimpse of her in the doorway, her arms crossed over her cat sweatshirt. She caught him looking, and she slammed the door.

Good, he thought. Good riddance.

Chapter 6

Grace signed for the package and as soon as the UPS man's back was turned, she did a little happy dance. Of course, trying to carry it upstairs was another story. Was it packed with stones?

She had seen the Regency reproduction wallpaper online, and she simply had to have it for her office. The aesthetic of the rest of the house was basically transported from her condo—modern and comfortable—but she was going crazy on the walls. The home-owner's association at her old condo had rules about painting only neutral colors—pretty lame considering she owned the unit, but she had complied. This house was her first chance to paint with actual colors.

The logistics of getting gallons of paint home from Harry's Hardware on her bicycle were easily managed by the friendliness of the eponymous Harry, who sent his nephew Dylan (and Dylan's car) over with her order. She had barely opened the first can of paint before she realized the handle of the roller she bought was way too short to reach the tops of the tall walls. So she biked back, and rode home one-handed with a four-foot retractable pole tucked under her arm. Fortunately, the drivers of Willow Springs were pretty bike-friendly and gave her a wide berth, or stopped to offer her a ride. Well, all of them except for Jake, whom she ran into at an intersection. He didn't offer her a ride, which was fine because she wouldn't have accepted anyway.

Her back was still killing her from her marathon painting week, but a nightly soak in her gigantic claw-foot tub gave her plenty of time to fantasize about living in a house without cardboard boxes everywhere. And the wallpaper was the last step of her aesthetic stamp before she started unpacking in earnest. This wallpaper was the icing on the cake.

Grace wanted her office to look like what she imagined Jane Austen's writing room would. Regency reproduction furniture was a little out of her budget, though. So she settled for a garage sale chaise longue, the deceptively sturdy writing desk she'd used as a child, and lots and lots of bookcases. The Regency touch would be the wallpaper. The more she looked at Regency patterns, though, the more she thought they were probably a little much for her modern sensibility (and her budget—even on sale, that wallpaper was expensive), so she settled on one accent wall.

They must have packed the wallpaper in bricks, though, because the long, narrow box was heavy.

She dragged the package inelegantly up the stairs and into her office. She'd pushed all the furniture in front of the bookcases, then piled all the boxes of books on top of the furniture. When she tore the package open and unraveled the first roll, she held it up to the wall and imagined her desk there. And then she dropped the wallpaper and clapped and giggled. It was going to look amazing once the whole wall was done.

There was still the problem of the high walls, though. Even upstairs, the small rooms had high ceilings, giving the illusion of space without actually being spacious. She thought about using her trusty retractable roller, but Harry told her that, to wallpaper properly, you need a brush. And her brush was short. So she needed a ladder.

Fortunately, she had friends in town now, and those friends had ladders. Mary Beth, who had forgiven her for her moving-day snootiness after Grace apologized profusely, was going to drop her ladder off after work and would stay to help her put up the wallpaper. Grace thought of the bottle of Pinot Grigio chilling in the fridge, and imagined sitting on the porch with Mary Beth, tired and satisfied after a job well done, watching the sunset. So she practically ran down the stairs when the doorbell rang, ready to start.

"The paper just came in! Just wait until you—" She stopped, mid-door swing, when she saw Jake standing on her porch with a ladder leaning against his shoulder.

"Oh," she said.

"Mary Beth couldn't make it," he said, picking up the ladder and barging past her into the house. "She had a showing. Where do you want this?"

"Upstairs. Hi, Jake."

"Hi, Professor. Where upstairs?"

"The office. First door on the right. Please."

She followed him and the ladder and pointed him in the right direction. He set up the ladder, then stood there, looking around.

"So this is where you write your famous books?"

She was surprised that he'd heard about her book; it didn't seem like his style. But then, most people in Willow Springs seemed to know that she'd written a mildly popular book about Jane Austen. The librarian had practically jumped on her. "Mostly it will be where I grade my students' papers."

"Ah. So this is where you do the dirty work."

"I see you've been reading undergraduate English papers."

"What's that supposed to mean?" Grace was shocked by the aggression in his tone.

"It was a joke."

"You think just because I didn't go to college, I won't get what some kid says about some old book?"

"No, Jake. I meant that when you say something snippy to me, I'll say something snippy back. Gosh, I'm not sure how you managed to carry that ladder up here with that gigantic chip on your shoulder."

He narrowed his eyes at her. But, whatever, it had been a joke. What did she care that he hadn't gone to college? He'd already proven himself more qualified than she was for the job.

"What's this wallpaper you're putting up?" he asked. "Mary Beth was all excited about it."

Fine. If he wanted a truce, she could give him a truce. "It's right here," she said, picking up the partially unraveled roll. "It's a design from the Regency era. Jane Austen's time. That's what I write about."

"I know."

"Okay. Well, here it is."

She watched him take in the soft rose color, the flocked, damask pattern.

"It's kind of a lot, isn't it?" he asked.

"You mean you think it's ugly."

He shrugged. "It's your house."

She sighed. "I'm just doing the one wall. I thought an accent would be nice."

"And a lot more palatable." He held the sheet up to the wall. "This will be nice, actually."

"Well, I appreciate your good opinion. And the ladder."

He stood there a moment longer, looking between her and the wall. "Are you going to do this by yourself?"

"Well, I had hoped for Mary Beth's help. But it looks like, yes, I'm going to do it by myself."

"She'll probably be able to help you over the weekend."

"I want to do it today. I need to get this room set up so I can start getting ready for my classes. And, anyway, I'm too excited to let it sit in a box until the weekend."

"Grace, it's Thursday."

"Patience is not one of my virtues."

He shook his head. "Fine. Where do you want to start? On this end? Do you have extra so we can match the pattern?" He started moving the ladder toward the end of the wall.

"You're going to help?"

"Yeah, if you can't wait. I have nothing better to do today."

"Of course not."

"What's that supposed to mean?"

"Nothing."

"Wait—" She stopped him again. "What do you mean match the pattern?"

"You have to line up the panels so the pattern matches."

"I know. But how did you know?"

"This ain't my first rodeo, Professor. I've hung wallpaper before."

"Oh."

"Yeah, oh. Do you want my help or not?"

"Sure." Why not? It would be fun spending the afternoon with such a chipper guy. Afterward, she could break the bottle of wine over his head.

Rich people and their accent walls, thought Jake as he started to cut the wallpaper at the top of the crown molding. This pattern was a special pain in his butt—it was so broad that he would think it was lined up in one spot, only to find one intricate swirl that didn't match a few inches down.

"Mother of—"

He stopped, mid-cut, at Grace's curse.

"Stop, stop," she said, putting a hand on his calf. He froze on the ladder, utility knife in the air, and tried not to shiver at the warmth of the contact.

"Dammit, it's not matching down here. Slide it up." She moved her hand to the wallpaper and started to move the panel up. "Whose idea was this stupid wallpaper anyway?"

"It's authentic," he reminded her.

"I wanted Jane Austen, not Charlotte Perkins Gilman."

He had no idea what she was talking about, but he didn't want another lecture. Not while he was holding a knife.

"Is it straight up there?" she asked him. He focused on the wall, not on the fact that when he looked down, he could see something pink and lacy through the neckline of her shirt.

"Yes. Ready to glue?"

She didn't respond, so he picked the brush up off the ladder's shelf and started the top coat of glue.

"How are we only on the second panel?" she whined. "How many more do we have to do?"

Jake did a quick visual measurement of the wall. It seemed to be getting bigger every time he did it. "Two and a half." Hopefully.

She leaned heavily onto her hands on the wall. Even though she was spiraling into a sulk, he appreciated that she held the wallpaper in place for him.

And he appreciated the pink bra.

"Trust me, this would feel a lot longer with Mary Beth," he said between brush swipes. "She's even more impatient with home improvement projects than you are."

He heard her sigh.

"Just keep your eyes on the prize, Professor. Every time you look at this accent wall, you can remember how hard you worked on it."

"That's nice of you, but you're doing all the work. I'm just holding the paper up."

"Don't forget how nicely you're bossing me around."

She laughed. "Sorry. I thought I knew what I was doing."

"Even though you've never wallpapered before?"

"I watched a video on YouTube."

He snorted. She was cute when she wasn't biting his head off.

"So you do a lot of this stuff?" she asked.

"Wallpapering?"

"Yeah, and other home improvement stuff."

He shrugged. "Sure. I like working with my hands."

"Better you than me," she mumbled, wiping one of her glue-y hands on her shorts.

A few hours ago, Jake would have taken that comment to mean that it was better for him to do the dirty work since he, as a dirty, working man, was much more suited to it. But now he knew that she was making a self-deprecating joke. Which he appreciated, because she really was not very handy.

He was beginning to see maybe she wasn't a total judgmental diva.

Not judgmental. He still wasn't sure about the diva part.

"Where do you park your car?" he asked. He hadn't seen it in the driveway, and he wasn't sure of the state of the garage. She probably had one of those tiny little hybrid things.

Although Missy had a hybrid and she seemed to be able to make it go pretty fast. Every cop in the county would probably agree with him.

"I don't have a car," she said.

"What?" Maybe she was one of those crazy earth-mother chicks who thought even a hybrid was too much carbon footprint. "Why not?"

She and her pink bra shrugged. "I don't really like driving, and Willow Springs is small. I'm hoping I can get away with not having one."

"So you just expect other people to chauffeur you around?"

She looked up at him, sharply. "That's a pretty big assumption. Have I ever asked you for a ride anywhere?"

"No."

"Or your sister? Or anyone you know? Have I ever, in the weeks that you've known me and decided I'm worthless, asked anyone for a ride anywhere?"

"Not that I know of." He didn't like how that made him feel, that she was aware of his disgust for her. No, it wasn't disgust, it was just . . . he just didn't like professors. But he didn't like that she knew.

"Well, I haven't, because I purposely bought a house close to town with a nice, flat bike ride to campus so I won't have to offend people like you with my grubby neediness."

"People like me?"

"Yes, people like you. People who don't know anything about me, but decide I'm useless."

"Please, you professors are all the same." He stopped wallpapering to glare down at her. "You think you're so smart and so great just because you have a fancy degree."

"I have several fancy degrees, Jake, but that's not what makes me smart and great."

"Not so smart that you can hang wallpaper on your own." He watched a drop of wallpaper glue land in the knot of hair piled on her head. She must not have felt it, because she didn't react.

"No, Jake, I'm not an octopus. I only have two hands." She stepped away from the wall. "You know what? You can go. I'll get someone else to help me."

The panel that he had half-glued unstuck itself from the wall and peeled slowly down. Onto Grace's head. She floundered and flailed and finally came unstuck.

"Very funny, Jake."

"You're the one who let go!"

"Just go."

A few seconds ago, he wanted to go. He wanted to just say, screw it. He had so many better things to do with his time.

But then the wallpaper had come down on her and she looked flustered and he felt bad about the blob of glue he'd dropped in her hair. Not, like, let's be friends forever bad, but bad enough that he remembered he was not a jerk, that he was the kind of guy who finishes what he starts. No excuses.

He still didn't like her. "I said I'd help you, so I'll help."

"That's not necessary, Jake. Especially since I don't really want to be in the same room as you are."

"Fine. Go. I can finish."

"It's not a one-person job." She threw his words back in his face.

"I'll call a friend to help me." Kyle owed him a favor—probably. And Kyle didn't hate him.

"I don't think this house is big enough for two self-righteous butt faces."

He had to hold on to the ladder rail to keep from falling off. She was funny. He thought he might put "self-righteous butt face" on his business card.

"Let's just finish," she said, picking up the fallen wallpaper. "Can we still use this?"

He nodded, then took it from her. "You just want to make sure I line it up right," he teased. But she didn't say anything back. They wallpapered in silence, and he had no choice but to think about Grace and what a strange person she was. When he was a teenager, he couldn't wait to get his license; to him, driving meant freedom. He could go wherever he wanted, see whomever he wanted—until his parents gave him a curfew and took away the car when he broke it.

But Grace didn't drive at all. He'd seen one of those Schwinns from the seventies on the porch, basket and all. He thought it was just a decoration. That, apparently, was her car. No wonder she had such great legs.

Great legs and a pink bra. The glue fumes must be getting to him.

The wallpaper finally stuck. And the wall wasn't letting go—the house made sure of that. The house liked this one. She had good taste in wallpaper, and she took care to clean the house's nooks and crannies. Grace *liked* the nooks and crannies. She didn't drag furniture across the floor without putting something underneath the legs first, she didn't put four thousand little nails in the walls, and every time she came home, she let out this happy sigh and the house would take it into its walls and ceilings and nooks and crannies.

The house knew that Grace just needed time to see that Jake was as right for her as the house was. But time wouldn't do anyone any good if they were never together. And Grace needed to be periodically reminded of how handsome Jake was, and how useful. A woman liked a man to make her feel special and taken care of. The house knew Jake could be that man.

If only they didn't kill each other first.

Chapter 7

"Hi, Jake. I'm sorry to bother you again, but I wasn't sure who to call." Grace peeked nervously around the doorway as she left a message for Jake. "I think something is living in my oven. Or behind it. It sounds big. Can you, I don't know, come take out the oven?"

She hung up, then took one step into the kitchen. The furious scratching paused. Don't be such a baby, she told herself. Then another scratch, and she ran out of the kitchen as if her bunny slippers had wings.

She stopped at the top of the stairs, feeling like an idiot. It was probably a mouse. Or a rat. Ugh, a rat would be so much worse. Or a raccoon. With rabies. Oh, God. She was going to have to just move. She didn't want to move. She loved this house.

Her cell phone rang, and since she was still clutching it within an inch of its life, she jumped out of her skin. Thank God, she thought. Jake to the rescue.

"Happy Fourth of July!"

That sure didn't sound like the voice of the man who was going to save her from the hell-beast trapped behind her stove.

"Mary Beth?"

"Yes, hi. What are you doing today?"

Grace knew she should spend the day working on the syllabi for her upcoming classes, or maybe unpack a few more boxes. But another round of furious scratching from the kitchen reminded her: Hell-beast.

"Nothing. I'd love to get out of the house."

"Great! Come to a barbecue. I'll pick you up at one. Super-casual, just bring something to drink if you don't like beer."

Grace didn't like beer. She wished she liked beer. It would be much cheaper to drink beer than those fruity umbrella drinks she usually ordered. She had perfected her mean margarita recipe. That could be fun for a barbecue. But that would mean digging out her blender, which was definitely in a box, and that box was probably in her kitchen.

She'd figure something else out.

Her groceries were still in the foyer, a bottle of red wine perched on top. She liked wine, and this wine was not in the kitchen. She ran up the stairs to shower and change. She couldn't hear the scritch-scratching from upstairs, and when she listened at the top of the stairs, it seemed to have stopped. Which either meant the mouse had gone back to its family in a different part of Willow Springs, or it was loose in the house. She shivered, threw on the first set of clean clothes she could find, grabbed the bottle of wine, and went outside to wait for Mary Beth.

Jake needed another beer, but he wasn't sure how to make that happen. He was sitting in the sun, which was making him hot, but his feet were in the kiddie pool, which was making him cool. It was all balancing out to perfect comfort—well, almost perfect. He was out of beer.

He threw a pleading look at Missy, but she just rolled her eyes and went back to talking to her girlfriends. Kyle was over at his massive grill with every other male in the county, so that wasn't going to work. This was it. Jake was just going to have to die of thirst. With his feet in a kiddie pool.

He jumped when he felt something cold and wet on his neck. "Here you go, lazy." Mary Beth was standing in his sun, but she'd brought him a beer so he forgave her.

"Hey, sis. What'd you bring?" He hoped potato salad. She made a mean potato salad.

"Nothing but Grace," she said, stepping aside to reveal the professor, wearing a short pink sundress and clutching a bottle of wine. Jake wished she was potato salad.

"Hi." Grace waved, and when she lifted her arm, her dress rode up a little. That was a pretty short dress for his professor. She must have caught him looking, though, because she blushed and looked away.

"Todd is coming later with the potato salad when he gets off work. He said he didn't trust you to leave any for him," Mary Beth told him with a scowl.

"I'm deeply offended. My own brother-in-law."

Mary Beth snorted at him, then flipped his baseball hat off his head. "Come on, Grace. I'll introduce you to people."

"Nice to see you, Jake," Grace said. She was polite now. She must have her company manners on. Jake rolled his eyes, and tried to recapture that perfect comfort equilibrium. But the sun was too hot and the kiddie pool water was starting to boil. He got up to stand with the other men, supervising the meat.

Grace had never had an easy time talking to strangers, and if her house wasn't being overrun by gigantic hell-beasts, she would have stayed away from the barbecue. Everyone else was wearing red, white, and blue, drinking beer, and being normal, barbecue-going Americans. Grace was holding a completely inappropriate bottle of wine and wearing the first thing she'd grabbed on her way out of the house.

So she was now at a Fourth of July barbecue with strangers, carrying around a bottle of wine (and no corkscrew), and wearing her pajamas.

Her pajamas were clean, and in a pinch they could pass as a cute, if short, sundress. But they were neither red, white, nor blue, and she felt sure they weren't fooling most of the women at the party. Mary Beth hadn't said anything, but she did look at her funny when Grace climbed into her car.

Jane always said that when Grace found herself in situations like this—which she often did—she needed to raise her chin and brazen through it. Nobody ever need know that Grace was doing absolutely everything wrong. Of course, Jane's idea of brazening through it was admitting her mistakes and charming everyone into laughing with her.

But Grace had never found it easy to talk to strangers. She got so nervous that all of her polite small-talk skills, practiced with Jane over the phone, went flying out of her head like a woman with a mouse in her kitchen.

"Hey, Missy," said Mary Beth, hugging a woman in a red halter top and blue denim shorts. "Great party."

"Thanks," said Missy. "Just do me a favor, and let Kyle pretend he did all the work? He gets cold feet when he thinks we're throwing parties together."

That sounded like a terrible boyfriend to Grace. But what did she know? She didn't have one.

"Missy, this is Grace. She moved into the old house on Grant."

Grace took Missy's outstretched hand and tried to return her warm smile. "I brought wine," Grace said. "And I'm accidentally wearing pajamas."

Missy's eyes widened for a second, but she quickly recovered her polite smile. "Thanks," she said, taking the inappropriate wine. "I'm not sure if we have a corkscrew."

"There was a mouse," said Grace.

Missy just smiled and took the wine into the house.

Grace turned to explain to Mary Beth that she was not having a stroke, but, really, it was all the mouse's fault, but Mary Beth had turned to talk to some friends on the other end of the long picnic table. Grace looked around, hoping for some kind of lifeline to pull her from the whirlpool of her own stupidity. The only other person she knew, though, was Jake, and he was scowling at her from under his baseball cap.

Fine, thought Grace. Brazen through it. She channeled her inner Jane.

"Beer?"

Grace hated beer. She knew red wine was a terrible thing to drink on a hot summer afternoon, but beer gave her a headache and she thought it tasted like smelly feet. But the guy standing in front of her was cute, and if he brought her a beer, he'd probably want to flirt with her. She didn't much like flirting, but at least she wouldn't be standing alone like an idiot.

"Thanks," she said, taking it from him.

"I'm Kyle," he said, holding out his hand.

Uh oh. Missy's Kyle. "Grace," she responded in her most platonic tone.

"So, Mary Beth tells me you're new in town?"

"Yes."

"Bought that old house on Grant?" Kyle asked after a long pause.

"Yes."

"Jake helping you fix it up?"

What a strange thing to ask. Was Jake telling people that he was fixing up her house? "Sort of." But that didn't feel right, to throw him under the bus like that. He had helped her out of a few bad spots. And she was probably going to ask him to catch a mouse later. "Actually, yeah. He's doing great."

"I'll bet," snorted Kyle.

Grace wasn't sure what that meant, but it was probably some sort of sexist innuendo. In the interest of small talk, she ignored it. "So, Kyle, what do you do?" she asked, doing exactly the thing Jane had told her not to do.

Kyle didn't seem to mind. "I do landscaping." His hand swept over the expanse of newly cut grass. "And I'm a firefighter," he added.

"Wow. That's a lot of responsibility."

"Yeah, well, the firefighting is volunteer. I just, you know, do what I can."

"Great," said Grace, meaning it, but not sure it came out that way.

"So, you're a professor?"

"Yes. I focus on British literature from the eighteenth and nineteenth centuries. I'm starting at Pembroke in a few weeks."

"Cool. You must read a lot."

"I guess," Grace said with a laugh. People always said that. She didn't know that she read more than the average person. She certainly didn't read for fun as much as she wanted to.

"I think the last time I read a book was in high school. What was that one about the rich guy and the eye thing and then he gets shot in the pool?" Grace had no idea what he was talking about. "They just made a movie of it with that kid from Titanic," Kyle added.

"*The Great Gatsby?*"

"Yeah, that one. Have you read that?"

"Sure, yeah. But that's not really my focus. My area of study is Regency-era British literature. Jane Austen mostly."

"Hmm," said Kyle. Then, after a long pause, "What kind of music do you like?"

"Oh." Grace was a little surprised at his topic shift, but she tried to keep up. "Um, I like all kinds, I guess."

"There you are." Missy came toward the table carrying a gigantic plastic container full of what appeared to be potato salad. She put it on the table, then put an arm around Kyle's waist.

"Hey, babe," said Kyle, shifting his beer and throwing his arm around Missy's shoulder. "This here is, uh—"

"Grace," said Grace.

"Yeah, Grace. She's a professor. English or something. Missy here loves reading," said Kyle.

"Great," said Grace, in her most chipper, I-swear-I-wasn't-hitting-on-your-boyfriend tone.

Missy shrugged. "Just trashy stuff. Probably not the smart stuff you read."

"Oh, I like all kinds of books," said Grace, thinking of *The Greek Tycoon's Virgin Secretary* on her bedside table.

"She does that one author you always talk about. The one with the movies you make me watch."

"Jane Austen?" asked Missy. "You teach Jane Austen?"

"Yes," said Grace. "Wait a second . . . Jane Austen's not trashy."

"No, that's my smart trash. To be honest, when I'm reading it, I'm mostly just picturing Colin Firth."

"Hey, I thought you were picturing me."

"No, babe, I picture you when I'm reading the really trashy stuff."

Kyle murmured something Grace pretended not to understand and leaned in to give Missy a kiss that made Grace blush.

"Knock it off," Missy said fifteen seconds after Grace was sure she would die of embarrassment. "That's cool that you teach Jane Austen. It must be fun to read those love stories every day."

"Oh, well, I don't really read them as love stories. I mean, there is love in them," Grace added quickly when Missy raised her eyebrows. "It's just not what I focus on. I'm more concerned with her advances in the structure of the novel, and the ways she used the form to address social irony and the situation of women. Women of her class, of course, but what I'm most excited about—" Grace stopped when she noticed that Kyle's eyes had glazed over. That was fast. Maybe a boring-strangers-at-a-party record for her.

Missy still had her eyebrows raised. "I just can't believe you don't think those are love stories. The end of *Persuasion*? That letter? 'You pierce my soul'? Are you kidding me? That's, like, swoon city. If someone said that to me, I swear I would do anything for that man."

"Hey, babe, I gotta get back to the grill," said Kyle. "And I need another beer. Nice to meet you, Grace. Good luck with the lady books."

"Lady books?" said Missy. "Get your own beer."

Kyle was already halfway to the grill. He shouted over his shoulder, "Hey, Missy! You pierce my soul!"

Missy, soul pierced, rolled her eyes and headed to the cooler.

And Grace was standing by herself again. She edged over to one of the flowering bushes lining the garage and tilted her beer into it. Then, avoiding Jake's glare, she looked around for someone else to alienate with her awkwardness.

Chapter 8

Jake could not believe he'd been roped into driving Grace home. She barely talked to anyone at the barbecue, wasted a perfectly good beer, and now was sitting in his truck in a too-short dress and he didn't like it. Those cyclist's legs made him want to forget what a snob she was, and how she wasted beer. She'd only talked to Mary Beth and Todd, and Missy a little bit. Actually, she'd talked to most of the women at the party. And most of the single men. But she always had this weird look on her face like she couldn't wait to get out of the conversation. Like she was scared of talking to regular people.

That's what Mary Beth got for bringing a professor to a townie party.

And now he was stuck driving her home.

Which was also Mary Beth's fault. Grace had a mouse, apparently, although she repeatedly referred to it as a "hell-beast." So Big Manly Jake had to get involved. All the stores were closed for the Fourth of July, so they couldn't get any traps, and he was going to have to use all of his MacGyver skills to catch this sucker. He had to admit, he was a little excited about that. Poor mouse didn't know what was coming at him.

If the mouse was smart, it would get out of that house fast, and not just because of Jake's ingenuity. The house was falling apart. No, that wasn't it. It was a good house, solid bones, and, frankly, it was in excellent shape for its age. Jake probably would have passed on a house like that. There wouldn't have been enough work for him to do to justify flipping it. Maybe he could have updated the kitchen. But he liked that old gas range and the big checkerboard tiles. The built-in glass cabinet was in kind of a strange spot—across from the stove and the sink, totally inconvenient for fast dish-reaching—but it was a beautiful piece of carpentry.

Whenever he bought a house to flip, he would walk through each room and close his eyes until he got a vision for what it should look like. Then he had to think about neutral décor and neighborhood comparables and all the stuff that made his job work. Then he'd measure and calculate and make it happen.

He'd have to spend some time in Grace's house. He'd barely seen the living room when he came in to do the wallpaper, and was so annoyed with her when he left that he forgot all about his curiosity. But he was curious. He wanted to see how Grace envisioned the rooms, how she used the unusual spaces in the house. Probably a lot of throw pillows. She probably embroidered them. With pictures of cats.

By the time he pulled into her driveway, he realized he'd barely said two words to her the whole ride over. A taste of her own medicine, he thought, but that idea didn't turn out to be very appealing. He didn't have to sink to her level.

She climbed out of the car and yanked her sundress down. She'd seemed uncomfortable all afternoon in that thing. Why did she wear it, then? What was she trying to prove?

"Would you mind going in first?" she asked, holding out her keys. "I'm sorry. I know this is ridiculous, but it has been a very strange and stressful day, and I'm pretty sure if I see a mouse, I'll cry."

The only thing Jake disliked more than snotty professors was a crying woman. He took the keys from her and led the way up the stairs. But when he turned the key, nothing happened. He tried jamming it to the left, then to the right, but it was so stuck that he was afraid he was going to break the key off in the door.

"Is it stuck again? Here, let me," Grace said, reaching around him for the key. She reinserted it into the lock, jiggled it up and down twice, pulled it out a little, and turned. The door opened.

"Interesting," he said, stepping into the house in front of her.

"I like to think of it as a home security system."

"Grace, I don't think a burglar is going to try the lock."

He could see on her face that she was working on a pithy come-back, one of her self-deprecating little barbs that would have him laughing despite himself. But then her face turned ghost-white and he could actually see the scream working its way up her throat.

He turned just as she threw herself onto his back. The scream worked its way out, straight into his ear. He wrestled her off his back, but held her close behind him. She was annoying and deafening, but he was a gentleman.

And what kind of gentleman lets a terrified woman face down a cat sitting proudly in front of a dead mouse?

Not Jake.

"Do you have a cat?" he asked her as soon as her screams devolved into breathy whimpers.

"No," she whispered.

Jake looked at the cat. It was black and its long hair was surprisingly neat and clean. If this was a stray, it had been well-loved by the neighbors. Jake leaned down, and Grace came with him, crouching behind him crouching in front of the cat. He felt for a collar, and when the cat didn't attack him, ran a hand down its back. It seemed too skinny under all that fur. Its yellow eyes were a little too close together, making the cat look young and innocent and pleading. Jake stood up, and so did Grace. The cat followed their movements with its eyes, then stepped over the dead mouse to wind its way between their legs, purring so hard Jake felt it through his jeans.

"I think you have a cat now," said Jake.

"I can't have a cat." Grace leaned down and gave the cat a tentative rub. It stopped in its tracks and pushed its head against her hand. Grace scratched its ears and leaned in to touch noses.

She didn't look like a woman who couldn't have a cat.

"If I get a cat, then my spinsterhood will be complete. I'm already independent, bookish, and terrible at small talk. I can't have a cat on top of that."

"But you have all those cat shirts," he pointed out.

"They're supposed to be a joke," she said. "Jane and her daughter find them at thrift stores."

"But you wear them anyway?"

"They're comfortable," she said with a shrug. "Would you believe me if I said I was being ironic?"

"Nope," said Jake. He got a handful of paper towels from the kitchen and scooped up the mouse. Grace's back stiffened, but she stayed calm—relatively. He took the unfortunate creature out to the garbage can, then went inside to wash his hands and make sure there was nothing else Grace couldn't handle.

He came through the kitchen door—which happily stayed on its hinges—to find Grace on the floor in front of her sofa, dangling a shoelace in front of the cat. The cat swatted and climbed on her lap and swatted more.

"You definitely have a cat now," he said, sitting on the couch next to her shoulder. The cat looked up at him with those wide, too-close eyes, then curled up to lick its butt.

Grace sighed. "He's pretty cute. And he's too skinny. I'll have to get some cat food and some proper toys. Oh, God, I really have a cat now." She scooped the cat up and nuzzled its neck. "I'm going to call you Mr. Bingley."

The name rang a vague bell in Jake's head. "What if it's a girl?"

"Hmm. If you're a girl, I'll still call you Mr. Bingley," Grace said to Mr. Bingley. "Because Mr. Bingley is Mr. Darcy's best friend and I just know that you're going to be . . . oh God."

"Too late," said Jake. "I heard it. The cat is your best friend."

Grace turned to him long enough to glare at Jake, then returned to Mr. Bingley's ears.

Jake decided he would put Grace in touch with his cousin, Keith, who was a vet over in Hollow Bend. He was the only vet nearby, and Jake knew he would have enough sense to convince Grace not to call a girl cat "Mr." At least he hoped so. For the cat's sake.

Mr. Bingley seemed to have Grace's rodent problem under control, but Jake wasn't ready to leave yet. The room was comfortable, and he found himself appreciating the way she'd arranged the big sectional sofa, and the way the soft yellow of the walls set off the eclectic colors of the rest of the furniture. There were a few boxes around the room, and he peeked into the one closest to his elbow. Books. Of course.

He picked up the one on top. *What's Love Got To Do With It? Beyond Romance in Jane Austen* by Grace Williams.

"You wrote this?" he asked, even though, duh, there was her name.

She looked up, and he enjoyed watching the flush that spread from her cheeks down her neck.

"It's based on my dissertation. I tried to get it published by a university press, but it got picked up by a more mainstream publisher. So I didn't get a ton of academic cred out of it, but it made the outer reaches of the *New York Times* bestseller list."

Jake didn't understand the disappointment in her voice. She was upset that her book made money? Her peers didn't appreciate that it did?

He put the book on the couch next to him. When he read, he stuck to biographies and spy thrillers. Definitely not the kind of stuff the professor would be into. He went back to the box.

"Are you unpacking for me?" she asked, her attention back on the cat.

"Just curious what kind of books a smart lady like you likes to read." He pulled out a worn paperback. *Tempest of the Heart* it declared, in shiny, raised script. There was definitely a storm going on, and it was a windy one. The woman's dress was being torn off her shoulder, and the man's shirt was hanging on by a thread, his hair flowing dramatically behind them both.

He held it up to her, his eyebrows raised. He watched that blush creep lower down her neck onto her chest.

"That's an old one."

"Looks steamy," he said. It looked like the kind of book his mother read. She probably had this on one of the shelves in her basement.

"It was very educational the first time I read it. I was thirteen."

"My mom says these books aren't about sex, they're about love." He held up the book Grace had written. "I'm getting conflicting messages here, Grace."

She rolled her eyes at him and grabbed the romance novel. "This is fiction. An escape."

"So you don't want to get swept up on a windy moor by a guy in a blouse?"

She hit him on the knee with the book. Mr. Bingley jumped up on the couch and sniffed the other book, then lay down on top of it.

"Seriously, Grace. I thought all women wanted happily ever after."

Grace fingered Mr. Bingley's furry ears. "Not me."

"Then why do you read this stuff?"

"I read mysteries, too. Does that mean I want to murder someone?"

"You wanted me to get rid of that mouse for you."

She raised her eyebrow at him.

He took the paperback from her and slid down to the floor next to her. "Angelina drew her dressing gown tighter around her bosom," he read. "Rupert stalked forward and tore her hands away. He drew her roughly to him, his hard body crushing her lush curves as she struggled in his fierce, manly grasp. 'Oh, Rupert,' she cried. Rupert? What kind of hero is named Rupert?"

"Shut up," she said, grabbing the book away from him.

"Hey, I'm not done with that! I want to find out what Rupert does with his manly grasp!" He reached for the book again, but she held it behind her back. They went horizontal in a tangle of limbs and musty pages, and suddenly Jake found himself on top of the professor, her lush curves very decidedly pressing against his manly . . . grasp.

Grace stilled. Her breathing picked up. He felt every inhale in his own chest. He noticed her green eyes had flecks of yellow in them. He appreciated again the fine hints of red in her brown hair. Her lips were pink and soft and full.

Terrible idea, his brain said, as he leaned closer to those lips. But by then it was too late. He pressed closer into her, and he felt her hands go around his neck, tangle in his hair. He deepened the kiss, feeling her open beneath him. He wrapped his arms around her, trying to get her closer, and he felt her arch up in response.

He was so lost in the kiss, in that lush, soft mouth, that he barely registered Mr. Bingley jumping onto his back and then onto the floor. But Grace must have heard, because she pulled away. Her eyes were dark and her breath came even faster.

That kind of vivid response was not at all what he was expecting from the uptight professor. He brushed a lock of hair off her forehead. But the moment couldn't last. Mr. Bingley was trying to snuggle between them. Jake sat up, and Grace followed, pulling at her sundress even as Mr. Bingley insinuated himself onto her lap. Lucky cat.

"I wasn't expecting that," she said, not meeting his eye.

Jake felt a moment of panic. Had he crossed a line? He thought for sure he had seen sudden desire flash through her eyes.

"Jake." She turned to face him, finally. "That was . . ." She fingered her lower lip absentmindedly, and he had a hard time listening to what she was saying. "That was unexpected. And nice."

"Nice."

"You didn't think it was nice?"

"Not the word I would have chosen," he growled.

"Jake," she said, taking his hand. "I don't do this."

"What? Don't kiss men?"

"No, I mean—"

"Don't kiss the help?"

"What? No! Jake—"

"It's fine," he said, and started to get up. It was fine. He didn't even like her that much anyway.

"Jake, listen." She stood, too, and put a hand on his arm. Mr. Bingley tangled in his feet. "I don't do relationships. I don't do love. It's just . . . it's not something I do, okay?"

"Love? It was just a kiss, Grace. Don't flatter yourself."

Grace just stared at him, dumbstruck.

"I should go," he said. He practically ran to the front door, tripping over the cat. When he tried to turn the knob, it wouldn't turn. He jiggled it, then yanked it in desperation.

"Here," said Grace, and she came up behind him and gently pulled the door open. "Jake—"

"I gotta go," he repeated, then capped his graceful exit off by tripping on the bottom stair. He didn't turn around to see if Grace was laughing at him; he was sure she was. He just kept his head down, got in his truck, and pulled away.

So they still hated each other. But the house remained optimistic. The two of them had admitted their attraction, and even though Jake had angrily stomped off the porch, the living room practically sparked with the energy they had set off. Grace had made herself vulnerable, which the house counted as progress, too. And even though she was now sitting on the floor telling the cat how strange men were, the house was hopeful. Grace and Jake were well on their way.

No matter how much they fought it.

Chapter 9

Grace took one more look around her office in the Pembroke English Department building. Her own, real-life office. When she was teaching in California, she shared an office with two post-docs and an adjunct. She was the only full-time professor in there, but she was just an assistant professor, and it was her first year, and the department knew her because she'd just finished her PhD there, and Lou, as the head of the department, wanted to make sure it didn't look like she got preferential treatment. There were many reasons Grace was glad to be out of that office, not the least of which was the one post-doc who refused to wear deodorant. It got pretty hot in California.

And, of course, Lou. That turned out to be a great reason to leave.

Here at Pembroke, Grace had a nice office in a quaint brick building with stairs that creaked. Her office—her own office—was small, but there was enough space for a desk, a floor-to-ceiling book case, and enough chairs for her and two students. The window looked out over the academic quad, and Grace looked forward to watching the seasons change. She missed seasons.

Grace secured the tie on her wrap dress one more time, just to make sure. She was nervous. She shouldn't be nervous. Gatherings with strangers were not her forte, but she found that she could easily relate to other professors. But the last time she'd been to a faculty party, it was a holiday gathering in California. She wore a red dress and was looking forward to meeting Lou under the mistletoe. Everyone else was bringing their spouses or dates, but Grace didn't care because Lou would be coming alone, too. He was separated from his wife, and the divorce was just about final.

Except that his wife showed up at the party. With Lou. They had decided to work things out, he told her in the hallway outside the bathroom. For the kids. Grace got on her bike and pedaled home and immediately updated her CV.

But, surely, this faculty party would be nothing like that one. For one, the party was at the dean's house, which was just across campus. If she had to make a quick escape, it wouldn't need to be by bicycle. And Grace hadn't been here long enough to entangle herself with someone inappropriate. She was done entangling. She was going to be a lone wolf. She was going to be like Jane Austen, ward off suitors and focus on her work. That was probably a misrepresentation of Jane's love life, but it suited Grace's purpose. The comparison was just for a little pep talk. Besides, she didn't really want to model her life on Jane's. Nobody wanted to die of tuberculosis.

She coughed, then picked up her purse. This would be fine. She'd met a few of the other English professors on her tour of campus last spring, and they were great. The department secretary was friendly and helpful. Even the night janitor was nice. She and Grace had had a long chat when Grace had lost track of time working on a syllabus the other night, and Carrie had come in to empty her garbage can. Carrie had three kids, the oldest of whom was about to start her freshman year at Pembroke. Then, when Carrie found out Grace had ridden her bike to campus, she'd offered to drive her home. Grace declined, and Carrie only relented when Grace showed her the headlight she would attach to her handlebar and the reflective strips on her helmet.

She doubted she would see Carrie at the party. These faculty things tended to include only, well, faculty. It was too bad; she would have liked to see a familiar face.

"To new familiar faces," she told herself as she strode across campus. Her wrap dress flipped perilously in the light breeze and she nearly tripped over her sandals as she tried to maneuver herself into decency. She stopped in the middle of the sidewalk and took a deep breath. These were her people. She could relate to brainy academics. There was no reason to be concerned.

Jake dumped the last of the homemade potato chips into a bowl and handed them to the white-shirted undergrad who was probably being paid pennies to serve as a waiter at this thing. She smiled and thanked him in a breathy voice. He grunted in response.

"Charming the ladies, as always."

Jake turned to Will, who was arranging tomato pastry things on a tray. Another undergrad came and swept it up as soon as he was finished.

"Can't help it," Jake said, snatching one off the tray as it left the kitchen.

"Hey, those are for the guests," scolded Will.

"Mmm . . . what a waste. You got any more?"

"There's a container of them at home. You'll have to fight your mother for them."

"Is she here? I thought this was a faculty thing," Jake asked around a mouthful of tomato pastry thing.

"Yes, but you know how she likes to make sure everyone is getting along," Will said with a smile. For a big guy, he sure had a soft spot for Jake's mother. That was a good quality in a husband, Jake acknowledged, even though part of him wished his father would be that guy.

"She'll get roped into cleaning up," Jake said, crankily.

"No, she won't." Will leveled a gaze at Jake. "You seem to have this idea that just because your mother is nice, she has no backbone."

Jake shrugged. "I just don't want these people to push her around."

Will shook his head. "Jake, you're a snob."

"I'm a snob?" Jake waved a hand at his jeans and T-shirt. "Does a snob wear work boots?"

"Thanks for dressing up, by the way," said Will with a tilt of his eyebrow.

"I just didn't want to be mistaken for a poor, underpaid, Pembroke scholarship student."

Will rolled his eyes. "I appreciate your help all the same. I didn't want your mother helping me load all this food in here. I know she wanted to be out there." He waved his hands in the general direction of the party.

"Yeah, well, I'm doing everybody favors lately," said Jake.

"Why is that, Jake? Housing market still that bad?"

Jake shrugged. "It's getting better. I just haven't found anything that calls out to me, you know?"

"And you're enjoying being a bum?"

"Hey, if I could get away with being a bum, I would. But the women in this family have other ideas. Maybe I should take on a new project, even if I'm not inspired. It'd probably be less work."

Will just smiled and chopped a pile of sundried tomatoes. When Jake stood there, watching him, Will tossed him a peeler and pointed him toward a basket of apples.

"I saw your father today," Will said.

Jake gave Will a wary glance. Will and Jake's father didn't always see eye-to-eye. Maybe because they were both in love with his mother. And Will was the one married to her.

"He said he hasn't seen you in a while."

That was true. Jake loved his father, but he was hard to be around. If Grace thought *he* had a chip on his shoulder, she should meet Don.

Not that she'd be meeting Don. But in comparison, Jake was an angel.

Don had been an okay father, but he spent a lot of time in his shop. He would come home regaling them with stories of incompetent professors who didn't even know that a car had oil, let alone that it needed to be changed, and how Don was happy to take their money. His mother always chided him—she worked for those professors, after all. Which always led to a fight, that Marilyn didn't think Don was good enough for her, that she would rather be with one of those eggheads than a man who worked hard to provide for his family.

Of course, the fact that Don couldn't keep his hands to himself didn't help.

They finally split up when Mary Beth went off to college. It was amicable, as far as divorces go. Marilyn didn't ask for anything from Don, and he just slunk back to his shop, where he could be a miserable bastard in peace.

And aside from the fact that Don drank too much at family gatherings and tried to pick fights with Will, it was fine. Will never took the bait. Well, almost never. A few Christmases ago, Don got into the whiskey and started saying not-very-flattering things about Marilyn, and Will laid him out with one swift punch. Jake didn't blame him. If Will hadn't been there, Jake would have done it himself.

So, no, he didn't see his father much. "I'll stop by this weekend."

"Good. I think someone needs to check up on him every now and then, and I'd prefer if it wasn't Marilyn." Will wasn't jealous, Jake was pretty sure. But they both knew his mother had a soft spot for sorry cases, and Don was about as sorry as they come.

"Are you just going to stand there, or are you going to help me assemble canapés?"

"Ugh, no. I should go." Jake didn't really have any plans this evening, but beer and TV sounded a lot better than hanging around in the kitchen while a bunch of academics whipped out their degrees at each other.

The door swung open, and a third undergrad came in with an empty tray. As the door swung on its hinges, Jake got a look at the crowd. Standing in the middle of a group of stuffy cardigans, he caught sight of Grace, her hair swept up off her neck and wearing a dark red dress that clung in all the right places.

He could hang out for a minute.

Grace wanted to find the dean's caterer and marry him or else get him to somehow cater her life. She'd been to faculty do's before, although hers were mostly of the happy hour variety and involved paying for your own drinks. Here, there were actual waiters—students, she imagined—and a small bar with more than one choice of wine.

And the house was gorgeous. It was like her charming Victorian dollhouse on steroids. The details, such as sconces and window treatments, were impeccable. The furniture looked antique, and if the way the dean's wife was walking around putting coasters under everyone's drink was any indication, it was. The carpet was a gorgeous off-white, and Grace was torn between taking off her shoes to do a little comfy-feet dance or switching to white wine. The more she thought about spilling, the more she wished she had a coaster so she could put her drink down.

Grace was the only new English professor this year, but there were new faculty in other departments. She had a brief conversation with a fine arts professor, who talked about movement and story and string, and also how he had a student last year who crocheted an Andy Warhol-inspired Mona Lisa installation, which Grace thought sounded kind of cool. Then Grace got distracted by a cheese puff and she lost him.

She was quickly drawn into a conversation with Helen Lee, Pembroke reference librarian, who had read Grace's book and admired it. But, like every woman Grace had ever met, Helen wanted to argue the importance of love in Jane Austen.

"I'm not saying that love is not important to the novels," said Grace, almost by rote at this point. "It's just that we get all distracted by the in-love-with-a-rich-man part, and we overlook the elements of her writing that truly make her a master."

"I know you're right," Helen sighed. "I agree with everything you say in the book about form and character and plot. But the thing that keeps bringing me back to Jane is not her creative syntax."

"It's Mr. Darcy," Grace finished. She was familiar with this argument.

Helen laughed. "Fine, you be the soulless academic, I'll be the fawning devotee."

Grace smiled and they were interrupted by a young man in a bow tie who wanted to know if Helen had heard that Professor Johnson had broken up with her husband, who was apparently a prominent journalist.

"It was the Oxford comma," he said.

Helen smiled and rolled her eyes. "Hi, Henry. Grace, this is Henry Beckham, History Department."

"Nice to meet you," said Grace, shaking his outstretched hand.

"Grace Williams? I've actually been looking forward to meeting you," said Henry. "I'm interested in local history, and I understand you bought the Spinster House?"

Grace choked on her wine. "The what?" she croaked out.

"That's not the Spinster House," said Helen. "The Spinster House is that one up on Walnut. The one that's falling apart. Hey, Grace, if you need any work done on your house, you have to call this guy Jake. He's terrific. And he's gorgeous. Sorry, Henry."

"Jake's okay," said Henry. "Not really my type. But you're wrong, Helen. I believe the provenance has been purposely misdirected."

"Because why would anyone try to hide the fact that they live in a place called the 'Spinster House'?" Grace asked, sarcastic, but alarmed. She joked about being a spinster all the time, but first Mr. Bingley, whose opinion she was beginning to rely on, and now this? Was this town conspiring to keep her single forever?

And why wasn't she happy about that?

"The realtor didn't tell you the story? Who sold you the house?"

"Mary Beth Brakefield."

"I know her," Henry said. "I mean, I called her to tell her what a goldmine she had on her hands, but she was convinced, as you were, Helen, that the Spinster House is on Walnut Street. But it's not, I can prove it if—"

"Hold on." Grace reached for another glass of wine from a passing waitress. "What is this Spinster House anyway? Did I just buy an ancient home for decrepit single women? Please don't tell me they're buried in the back yard."

"No, no," Henry laughed. "Nothing so sinister. The house was built, as I'm sure you've guessed, in the very early years of the twentieth century. This area was in the middle of a logging boom. And with industrial booms come captains of industry and their families. Nelson Summers had a big family, and one particularly troublesome daughter, Ree."

"Ree Summers was awesome," Helen piped in. "She's an icon. She did all the usual charity stuff women of her station were expected to do, but she didn't quite follow the rules, you know? Instead of sitting on the board of the Foundling Hospital, she volunteered there. Instead of just giving money to workers' charities, she threw the mill workers and their families a huge Thanksgiving party every year. And she wore pants."

"Scandal!" Grace liked the sound of Ree Summers. She would like to have known her.

"She also had a reputation for being bull-headed," added Henry.

Helen dismissed him with a wave of her hand. "That's what they always say about women with opinions."

"So she built a house." Henry ignored Helen and continued. "She chose a less-savory part of town, although it was by no means dangerous. She had everything built to her exacting specifications, even though she was repeatedly told that they made no sense. I have several letters between her and the builder. They're quite fascinating."

Grace had wondered about the turret and the window seats and the oddly shaped rooms. She felt as if they'd been designed just for her. She wanted to know more about Ree Summers.

Fortunately, Henry seemed willing to tell her.

"But she never moved into the house," Henry said ominously.

"Oh, no! What happened?" asked Grace, imagining a mill collapse or a bicycle accident or consumption.

"Nothing as dire as what you're thinking," said Henry quickly.

"Worse," interrupted Helen. "It was a man."

"What?"

Henry shot Helen an annoyed glance, and continued. "Nelson Summers's success drew the attention of logging men around the country. He had developed efficiency measures that ensured his mill had one of the highest outputs in the region. Now he is regarded as an equal to Henry Ford in terms of business acumen and—"

"Here's the good stuff," said Helen. "So this guy Charles Beaumont comes to town, and he's a young up-and-comer in the industry and wants to learn from Nelson Summers. And he does. Works under him for a while, but soon he gets restless for his own mill. Meanwhile, he keeps hearing about Nelson's daughter, who's building a house and who's kind of a weirdo. But he's never met her."

"They ran in different circles," explained Henry. "Although Charles showed such promise that he was soon allowed into Nelson's inner circle."

"Which meant he got to go to all of the fancy dinner parties." Helen took over the story again. "Which was a big deal for a guy like Charles Beaumont, who came from nothing and was doing that whole American Dream, pull yourself up by your bootstraps thing.

So one night, he goes to a dinner party at Nelson Summers's house, and whom should he meet, but—"

"Canapé?"

"Jake!" exclaimed Helen. "Grace, this is the guy I was telling you about. Jake, we were just telling Grace the Spinster House story."

"Oh, you mean the one where the crazy lady builds her dream house but then runs off with some West Coast logging magnate before she can even move in?"

"Yes," grumbled Helen. "Thanks for spoiling the ending."

"I know Jake," Grace said to Helen, as if Jake weren't standing right behind her.

"Of course, if Mary Beth sold you the house. He probably took the picture when you moved in, right?"

"What are you doing here?" she asked Jake, ignoring Helen. "I thought you hated professors?"

"Hello, son." Marilyn, the English Department secretary, came over and gave Jake a kiss on the cheek. Grace's head was spinning. She was not used to small towns where everybody knew each other. And where the beloved English Department secretary was the mother of her realtor and her arch-nemesis.

"Grace, I was so pleased when Mary Beth told me Jake had been doing some work on your house for you."

"Yeah," said Grace, dumbly.

"He's a good boy," she said, patting Jake's cheek. Jake blushed and rolled his eyes.

"Be a good boy and give me one of those canapés," Henry said, reaching forward. Grace watched, fascinated, as Jake's face turned an entirely different shade of red.

"So, what I was saying about the Spinster House," said Henry, his mouth full of canapé, "is that, like all good, older houses, it has a legend attached."

"Oh, that old legend," said Marilyn, waving her hand dismissively.

"What legend?" asked Grace. Because if the legend was that she would get a cat and die alone, she was pretty sure she was going to move.

"The house is destined to be bought only by single women," said Helen with unnecessary glee.

"Because a single woman of good fortune must be in want of a house?" asked Grace. Only Helen laughed.

"It's just a legend," chided Marilyn.

"Anyway, that house on Walnut Street is a wreck. Nobody, single or not, would live there," said Jake.

"Ah, that's where you're wrong, as I was just telling these ladies here," said Henry. His chest puffed up and he went on in a conspiratorial whisper. "I uncovered documents in a musty back room of the library—the public library," he added when Helen, who knew the Pembroke Library like the back of her hand, started to protest. "It turns out that Ree owned both pieces of land, and she built on each of them. The one commonly—and erroneously—referred to as the Spinster House was actually a home designed for unwed mothers. It is much larger than the one Grace owns."

Helen and Henry started arguing about the authenticity of the documents, and legend and proof, and a lot of other complicated things that Grace was too distracted to follow.

"Hey, are you okay?" Jake gently grabbed her elbow. "You look like you're going to pass out."

Which is funny, Grace thought, because I feel like I'm going to pass out. Instead, she turned to Jake. "If your sister sold me a house for spinsters," she said, leveling her most menacing gaze on him, "I will kill her."

The house felt the vibrations of a truck in the driveway and felt the faint stirrings of the charge that sparked between Grace and Jake. But then only one set of footsteps came up the walkway, and the only voice in the foyer was Grace talking to the cat. Maybe the cat had been a mistake. Grace acted as if she preferred the cat to Jake.

Vulnerable and safe at the same time. Grace felt both ways around Jake, but she just wasn't getting how important it was. And, frankly, neither was Jake. If Grace could see that Jake could make her feel this way, maybe she would spend less time talking to the cat.

Chapter 10

Jake had absolutely no intention of seeking Grace out again. He saw the way she was at the barbecue, then the way she was at the Professor Party. It was as if there were two different Graces. One was awkward and could barely talk, one laughed and smiled and charmed. From afar, he liked the Grace at the Professor Party much better, but what kind of person could make small talk in one situation, and be completely unintelligent in another?

She annoyed him; that was the only reason he couldn't get her out of his head. Not her surprising sense of humor, or the fact that she needed him. Definitely not the way that red dress clung to her curves. He did not care at all about that. Just because he'd been reliving it for the past several days, that meant nothing. She meant nothing to him.

Nothing.

So what if he went out for a run on Tuesday morning, and he happened to run by her house? He'd been too lazy this summer and needed a good, long workout.

And if he happened to look over at her house as he was running by, it was just general neighborly curiosity. He had put a lot of work into that house. Of course he'd be interested in seeing how it was holding up.

He was not, however, expecting to see Grace waving frantically at him. From the roof above her porch.

* * *

It wasn't that far to jump. She probably could've made it. But Grace was not a huge fan of heights, and when she saw Jake running by, she knew she was saved.

She shouted, but that didn't have any effect. So she waved so hard that she nearly threw herself off the roof—which would have solved her problem, but was exactly the solution she was trying to avoid. He saw her, then meandered across the street, pulling at his ear buds. When he got to her yard, he just stood there, hands on his hips, eyebrow in the air.

She tried very, very hard not to notice that his shirt was tucked into the waist of his running shorts. And that sweat was running down his chest. And that as he stood there, no doubt judging her, he shone in the sun like a radiant god.

She nearly fell off the roof again.

Too bad he was such a pain.

"What are you doing up there?" he asked.

"I'm stuck."

"Why don't you just climb in the window?"

Grace turned around to look at the window, then back at Jake. "Gosh, why didn't I think of that?" Did he think she was some kind of idiot? She might have very limited practical abilities, but she wasn't an idiot. She had a PhD, dammit.

"The window is stuck."

"You're stuck because the window is stuck?"

"Yes, can you stop shouting and come get me out of here?"

He disappeared from view, but then he came back. "Locked."

"Crap," she muttered. Stupid Todd and his safety reminders. *"Lock your doors," he said. "It's not a good idea for a woman living alone to leave an invitation like that to intruders."* Like an intruder wouldn't just break her window. And now here she was, stuck on the roof where she would surely die. She couldn't die; she had classes to prepare for.

"I'll try the back," said Jake. But she knew the back door was locked because she'd gone out in the morning to start weeding the garden and when she tried to get back in, she found herself locked out. So she had to come in the front door. Which she'd promptly locked behind herself in the interest of safety.

Jake came jogging back. "Uh, I don't suppose you left any windows open downstairs?"

She shook her head. "Air conditioning."

"What about that ladder we used for wallpapering?"

She thrust her thumb toward the window behind her. "Still in the office. I can see it from here if that helps."

"Not at all. Okay, I'm coming up."

"Wait, how—" How is that going to help? she started to ask. But then she got distracted by shirtless Jake swinging a leg over her porch railing and pulling himself up and over the edge of the roof.

Muscles, she thought. I might die.

"Okay," he said, a little out of breath from his gymnastic routine. "What's going on up here?"

"Muscles," she said.

Muscles, she said out loud, to the man she didn't like and who didn't like her but whom she was hoping to convince to save her from certain death atop a ten-foot roof.

He looked at her with that confused look on his face that she was becoming really familiar with. Well, she was confused, too. And not just because of Muscles.

"I came out here to paint the trim," she said, indicating the paint and brush she had leaning against the house. "So I closed the window, and when I was done, I tried to open it, but it's stuck."

"Did you paint the window shut?" he asked, as if she were an idiot.

"No, smarty. I wasn't painting the windowsill. I was doing up there," she said, pointing to the trim that had, until about an hour ago, been peeling and shabby-looking.

"You did a nice job."

"Thanks. I sanded it first and everything."

Jake looked around, so she added, "The sandpaper blew away. Hey, are you going to try this window, or what?"

"Step back, little lady," he said, and sauntered up to the window. What a goof, she thought. What a saunter.

And those back muscles. Good grief, they danced as he tried to pull the window up. Then they strained and his neck started turning red.

"Must be locked." He shaded his eyes and peered into her office.

"Lock's broken." She shrugged when he looked back at her. "It's on my list of things to fix."

"I can take a look at it."

"I don't want to bother you."

"It's no bother. It's a lot less bother than being stuck on a roof."

"Sorry. In my defense, it wasn't my idea for you to climb up here with me."

Jake moved to the edge of the roof and peered down, hands on his hips. Grace took a tentative step toward him, and the edge.

"Well, we're going to have to climb down," said Jake with a decisive nod.

"But—" Grace tried to think of a good reason why she couldn't climb. She had weak wrists. She had vertigo. She didn't want to die falling from a ten-foot roof. "I can't."

"Sure you can." He gave her a confident smile. "You won't fall. I'll make sure."

Damn that smile. That smile made her believe that she could make it off the roof alive. That she could rappel down a mountain if she wanted to. That smile made her consider hang-gliding.

"Okay, I'm going to go first," Jake said, tucking his killer smile away and getting down on his haunches. "Watch what I do. You just have to put your hands and feet where I do, and then I'll be at the bottom to catch you."

Grace kneeled by the side of the roof as Jake slowly lowered himself down. "*Catch* implies that I will be falling."

"Grace," he grunted. "Don't argue semantics when I'm climbing off a roof."

She watched him climb down. She watched his hands as they gripped the cornice, then leaned further to see his feet touch the top rail of the porch. He shifted his hands for a more secure grip, then gently swung his legs out behind him. She held her breath as his hands disconnected, and then he was crouching on the grass, smiling up at her.

"See? No problem," he said, wiping sweat off his forehead.

"No problem!" she called out, hoping she sounded more enthusiastic than manic. But she was not confident of that.

"Lie down flat," he instructed, and she did. He'd gotten down alive; he was obviously an expert.

"Okay," she called from her flat position on the roof.

"Now swing your legs over, nice and slow."

Was he crazy? If she swung her legs over, she would be half off the roof and then she would die.

"Grace?"

"Legs over," she muttered to herself, and swung one leg down. She felt Jake's hand above her knee.

"Great, now one more," he said.

"One more," and she slowly inched her foot off the roof until there was no more roof, and then there was just air and her one leg flying toward her other one with far more momentum than she could control, and she started to slide.

"Whoa! Okay, slow down, I got you," said Jake, and he did. She was hanging on to the edge of the roof with her fingers with a grip she could not sustain, but she felt his arms strong around her legs, his face pressed into her stomach.

"Grace—" His voice was muffled by her shirt. "One hand at a time, let go."

"I can't," she said.

"Sweetheart, I can't hold you like this for much longer."

"Are you calling me fat?" Perfect time for jokes, Grace!

"No, Grace, I'm calling you gravity. Come on, one hand. Just move it from the roof to my shoulder."

So she did it. She let go with her right hand, but she couldn't reach his shoulder, not while still holding on to the roof. So she grabbed on to his hair. He yelped, she apologized, but she still held on to the roof with her left hand.

"Grace." His voice sounded both muffled and strained now. "Other hand."

Even though she knew if she let go of the roof she would bend backward and fall to her certain death, Grace did as Jake asked. When she let go with her left hand, her whole body felt heavy, but Jake had her in a tight grip and he let go enough for her to slide down his body, and then her feet were on the grass, and she was not dead.

Instead, she was out of breath and face-to-face and chest-to-chest with a very sweaty Jake. Some of the sweat might also have been hers. They were so close it almost didn't matter.

"You okay?" he said, pushing a strand of hair off her face.

She nodded. She wasn't capable of speech.

His eyes were brown, but they had flecks of yellow in them. She hadn't noticed that before.

"You sure? You look kind of pale."

"I don't like heights," she croaked. Where had her voice gone?

"You did really well, Grace."

"I did?"

"Yes. You were very brave." She knew he was just saying that to make her feel better. She had been an idiot and a chicken. He probably said that to all of the women he pulled off roofs.

But his words felt almost as good as his arms, so she just let all of Jake surround her and leaned her cheek on his chest. His heart was still beating fast. Well, he had just pulled her off a roof.

"Of course, we're still locked out."

"Crap," she said into his chest. She reluctantly pulled away and took the few steps to the front door. Just for kicks, she tried the handle.

The door swung open.

Grace swung toward Jake.

"I swear it was locked!" He took a step back and threw his hands up. "It wouldn't open!"

Grace didn't care. She was suddenly very, very tired. She was tired of her strange house doing weird things when Jake was around. She was tired of her heart doing strange things, too. When he'd been holding her out in the yard, it felt good. He felt strong and sure and safe. That was three seconds ago. Now the old Jake was back. Jerk Jake was unpleasant, but she was, somehow, more comfortable with him.

"Grace—"

"I'm glad this is funny to you, Jake. Let's see how many crappy situations we can get the Professor in before she blows a gasket! Well, that's it, Jake. You win. You're better than me at everything. I won't call you again."

She started to slam the door, but his foot was in the way. "Grace—" he started again, and there was real hurt in his eyes. But she had seen those hurt-looking eyes before. Those eyes were liars.

"You win, Jake," and she shoved him back and slammed the door in his face.

* * *

The house was beginning to think it had lost its knack. But after one hundred years of happy couples, that could not possibly be the case. They were so close. Standing in the yard in each other's arms, Grace and Jake gave off electricity in waves. So the house thought they had worked hard enough, that now was the time for them to really get together.

Wrong again.

The house let go of its tight hold on the upstairs window. What was the point?

Chapter 11

Grace hadn't been sleeping well. She wanted to chalk it up to first-week-of-school stress, but that wasn't it. She'd had three days of classes, and they'd gone fine. Her Intro to British Literature class was full of eager freshman, and Grace felt enthusiastic after her office hours with each of her seminar students. Pembroke was a tough school, and the kids were taking their studies seriously. She knew that wouldn't last, not for all of them, but she felt optimistic all the same.

Henry had stopped by her office twice already, talking to her about her house. She finally relented and invited him to stop over on Sunday. She hoped "stop over" meant just come in and hang out and drink whatever she had in the fridge, because she really didn't feel like cooking for him. And Henry had an eager look about him—she didn't want to lead him on. God, even in her own head that sounded egotistical. But she hoped he was only interested in her for her house.

She shouldn't mind Henry stopping over. He was nice, if a bit uptight, and apparently bow ties were a thing for him. Still, on paper, he was perfect for her. He had an interesting career in a field related to her own, and he was certainly handsome. He looked nice in a bow tie. That wasn't really a prerequisite for a relationship with her, but it was nice to know. He didn't make her act like an idiot and blurt out stupid things like "muscles," so that was good.

If she wanted a relationship—which she didn't—Henry would be a good candidate. He was solid, smart, and decent. A girl could do worse, if she wanted to do anything at all.

But Henry Beckham hardly inspired her to break her no-relationship rule.

The problem was, quite simply, Jake. She hadn't seen him since he'd pulled her from the roof, not even to apologize. But she couldn't seem to muster up any real anger toward him. Her house was finicky; she knew that. Her front door stuck all the time. She would think she had the trick mastered, then it would stick again in another strange way. So even though Jake was obviously stronger than she (*muscles*, she thought), it was possible that he was telling the truth, that he hadn't played a trick on her to get her to climb off the roof even though it was terrifying and embarrassing.

She couldn't get him out of her head. Right before she left for her first-ever class at Pembroke on Wednesday, her Jane Austen portrait fell in the foyer, shattering glass everywhere. The picture hook just fell right out of the wall—there was a hole in the plaster and everything. If random stuff like that hadn't been happening all week, she'd think it was a sign. But the floorboard was still sticking up and now the window in her office wouldn't close at all. Her kitchen curtains kept going wonky and she was pretty sure something was happening with the throw pillows on her couch, although that was probably Mr. Bingley.

And every time something fell or broke or detached, her first thought was of Jake. Jake would know how to fix this. She should call Jake, he'd come right over. And he might have, if she'd called him. But Jake was too much for her. He made her feel . . . uncertain. One minute he'd be friendly and kind, the next he'd be storming out the door because he thought she called him stupid. And even though he probably wasn't screwing with her up on the roof, just the fact that he could have made her want to keep her distance. She was relying far too much on Jake. And what was she getting out of it? One hot kiss and a bruised ego.

She would not think of Jake any more.

It didn't help that everyone seemed to think she and Jake were a thing now. She'd run into her neighbor, Mrs. Wallace, yesterday afternoon when she was walking her wiener beagle, Lucy.

"I hear you're seeing that Jake Burdette," Mrs. Wallace had said as Lucy sniffed the fence.

"Really?" Grace had been bemused—where would Mrs. Wallace have gotten that from?

"Gail Plimpton said she saw you two embracing in the yard."

"Oh, well . . ."

"Now, I know how you young people are. It's none of my business. But I will warn you . . ." She leaned over the fence to Grace. "I've known Jake for a long time and he's nothing but trouble. Oh, you should have seen what he got into when he was in high school! Quite a rascal. And quite a heartbreaker. You seem like a nice young lady, and you're smart, too. Take my advice and stay away from Jake Burdette."

Then Lucy turned and peed on Mrs. Wallace's shoes.

When Grace went out to lunch with Helen on Thursday (a work meeting, to discuss bibliographic instruction for Grace's freshmen), Helen grilled Grace on Jake. But Grace couldn't answer any of her questions, even if she wanted to. (Well, she could answer the question about his chest hair—yes, he had it and yes, it was perfect—but she didn't. A lady doesn't ogle and tell.) Unlike Mrs. Wallace, Helen encouraged Grace to go for it.

"Oh, I know he's trouble," Helen said, mid-cheesecake. "I'm just saying that's not necessarily a bad thing."

But now Grace was tired and grumpy. She was grumpy at herself for thinking so much about Jake, and she was grumpy at the entire population of Willow Springs, who had put her in a relationship with a man she didn't even like. But it was Saturday, and she had nothing pressing to do. She could continue to laze about, maybe work on her garden, read a little more, and not think about Jake.

Ugh, even *not* thinking about him was a form of thinking about him. She needed to get out of the house.

She was just swinging her legs out of bed when her phone rang. She checked the caller ID—just to make sure it wasn't Jake because she didn't want to talk to him unless he was willing to apologize. And now I am lying to myself, she thought. But it wasn't Jake, so she answered.

"Hey, Mary Beth."

"Hi, Grace!" She sounded very chipper. "What are you doing today? Nothing? Good! We're going to the swimming hole!"

Grace tried to catch up to Mary Beth's monologue, which was tough on half a cup of coffee. "I have no fixed plans, but I was going to—a swimming hole?" That sounded weird. Like a lake, but terrible.

"Oh, good, I was hoping you'd never been to one! They're so much fun. This one is next to a biker church, but they only use it for baptisms on Sunday, and they don't mind if we use it on Saturdays as long as we clean up after ourselves. And no drinking; they're Baptist. You have a swimsuit, right? Otherwise you can borrow one of mine. I'm so excited!"

"I can tell."

"We barely got to the swimming hole all summer. Either Todd was on duty or I had a showing or it was raining or, you know, a million excuses. This is our last chance. It gets cold early in the mountains and, trust me, a swimming hole is no fun when your lips are turning blue."

Grace thought about it. She loved swimming, and she would love the chance to redeem herself among Mary Beth's friends. She'd run into Missy a few times, and Grace felt comfortable with her now, but she knew she had a long way to go before the rest of them stopped seeing her as a stuck-up professor.

Including Jake. Then Grace thought about swimsuits and wet bodies and that just seemed like a terrible idea if she was trying to forget about Jake.

"I don't know—" she told Mary Beth, stalling until she could come up with a good excuse.

"Please? You have to come. Jake's already backed out, and I want as many people as possible there. The last swimming hole trip of the summer! Do you hear me?"

"Yes! Yes, I hear you. What do you mean, Jake backed out?"

"He says he has work."

"And it's about time, the bum!" Grace heard Todd shout in the background. He must have been sitting right next to her.

"But it's the last swimming-hole trip—" Mary Beth whined to Todd.

"Babe, I don't think Jake really cares. Do you care, Jake?"

"I don't care," Grace heard, even more muffled. She flushed suddenly, as if Jake being in the same room as Mary Beth on the other end of the line meant he could read all of the dirty things she was trying not to think about him.

Mary Beth sighed into the phone. "Fine. So it's just me and Todd. And probably Kyle and Missy and maybe my cousins and a bunch of other people. But no Jake. Will you come?"

Grace hesitated. She loved swimming. And no Jake. "Okay. Okay, I'll go."

"I take it from your happy squeal that Grace is coming with us?" Todd asked his wife across the breakfast table.

"Yes. Unlike some people—" she waved her fork at Jake, "she's not a party pooper."

"Babe, he's got a lead on a house. That's not party-pooping."

"But I wouldn't go anyway," said Jake. "I would still poop on that party."

"You're gross. Why? You love the swimming hole."

"I just don't want to go, okay?"

"Because of Grace?" asked Todd.

Jake rolled his eyes. "No, not because of Grace." Even though it was completely because of Grace. "I wouldn't let one snotty professor ruin my weekend."

"You really are determined not to like this girl," Mary Beth said, wrinkling her nose at him. "I don't get it. Do you have some kind of vendetta against her profession? Was your heart broken by an academic? Did a professor somehow wrong our family and I missed it?"

"No, don't be stupid," Jake said.

"Don't call my wife stupid," Todd said back to him.

"Well, she's being . . . less than smart. And naïve, if you think someone like Grace could really be interested in friendship with someone like you," Jake said to Mary Beth, who crossed her arms at him.

"Right," Mary Beth said. "Because successful women have nothing in common."

"That's not what I mean . . ."

"Grace is nice, Jake. I know, I know—" Mary Beth held up a hand to stop Jake's comments. "I know she was weird at the barbecue. But she gets nervous around new people."

"She wasn't nervous at the professor party."

"And you were watching her from the kitchen like a weirdo, which, I hope, is not typical behavior for you either."

"That's a convenient explanation, MB, but I'm not buying it. Pembroke people just don't belong with Willow Springs people."

"You make it sound like we're the Jets and the Sharks," said Mary Beth, throwing up her hands.

"If you were from Pembroke, you would have said the Montagues and Capulets," teased Todd. "Jake, you're wrong about 'Pembroke people.' Sure, there are some weirdos, and, yes, there are some snobs, but there's no reason to universally dismiss them."

"Like they don't universally dismiss us?"

"You like Helen well enough," said Todd, getting up to refill his coffee. He brought the pot over and filled Mary Beth's. Then the pot was empty, so he just shrugged at Jake.

"Helen is a librarian. She's not a professor."

"Ha," said Mary Beth. "Don't say that to her face. She is a professor, she has tenure and everything."

"Fine, then Helen is the exception."

"Why can't Grace be an exception, too?"

"Why are you so up my butt about Grace?" Jake stood up from the table and slammed his dishes into the sink. "What possible effect could it have on you whether I like her or not?"

"Because she's my friend, Jake, and I don't want you turning all scowly every time I mention her name. And because I don't want you missing out on things you love just so you can avoid her."

He turned to face his sister. "I'm not. I swear. It's a good time for me to start a new project, so I'm going to check out this house. But if that were not the case, I would go to the swimming hole, even if there were ten thousand Graces there."

Mary Beth eyed him skeptically for a minute, then nodded. "Fine. I believe you. And I'll remember that comment and bring it up many times in the future if I have to."

"You have my permission. Now, if you don't mind, I'm going to go see a man about a house."

"That boy's got it bad," he heard Todd say as he turned out of the kitchen. Then he heard Mary Beth shush him. Jake went out the door and didn't hear anything else about Grace.

Chapter 12

"Let's go, Professor!" Kyle stood on the beach, if one could call the stones and dirt that led into the swimming hole a beach, and yelled up at Grace.

She gave him a weak thumbs-up and peered over the side of the rock again. It wasn't so high. Maybe eight feet. Probably ten. Certainly it was no higher than her porch roof.

Which she was also afraid of.

How had she allowed herself to be convinced to climb to the top of the rock with the goal of hurling herself off into the deceptively deep waters of a swimming hole?

It was all Jake's fault.

When Todd had pulled off the road, Grace thought it must be some kind of joke. There was no lake; there wasn't even a river. But he and Mary Beth got out, each grabbed a handle of the cooler, and started walking. Grace had no choice but to swing her beach bag over her shoulder and follow.

As she climbed up a gravel road and down a grassy bank, Grace was glad she'd listened when MB told her to wear old shoes. Every step deeper into the woods lowered her expectations of what a swimming hole was. By the time they could hear the shouts of the other swimmers, Grace was expecting a knee-deep puddle. But when they finally got to the beach, Grace had to catch her breath— and not just because that grassy bank was a killer.

The swimming hole was lovely.

The swimming area itself was maybe thirty feet across, although most of the water butted right against the woods. There was a nominally flat, rocky area where everyone was gathered, and it looked like someone was just getting the fire pit started. Across from the beach was an imposing rock face, flat on one section, almost stepped on either side. A slow stream of water ran down one of the stepped sides and fed into the swimming hole. Right above the dry, stepped side sat a small, white, clapboard building—the biker church, she guessed. There was a path worn in the grass and brush that snaked down from the back of the church to the beach.

With the sunlight streaming through the trees, the water looked like a jewel, like a rough-cut black diamond surrounded by emeralds.

She helped Mary Beth lug the cooler down the rocky beach to where the rest of the coolers sat. Kyle, it turned out, had driven his four-wheeler in, and he was busy hanging beach towels between the trees.

"Kyle, if you think any of us are changing behind those things, you're crazy," Missy called out from the front seat of the four-wheeler. She seemed to be wrangling something underneath her shirt, and a few seconds later, her bra came flying out and hit Kyle in the face.

"Babe, I told you to change before we left," Kyle said, and put the bra around his neck. "Chief! You made it!"

"Kyle. I see you've assigned a designated driver," Todd said, nodding to the beer in Kyle's hand.

Kyle smiled sheepishly and took the cooler from Grace and Mary Beth. "And your lovely wife, and the Professor."

"Grace," Grace reminded him.

"I know who you are, darlin'," and he brushed past.

"Hey, Professor!" Missy called as she climbed out of the four-wheeler. She shimmied a little, then threw off her cover-up to reveal a cute bandana-print bikini.

Grace pulled at the fabric of her bathing suit that clung to her stomach. She suddenly felt Amish. "Grace," she reminded Missy.

"I know, but it annoys Kyle and Jake when I call you that." Then she looked genuinely concerned. "Is that okay?"

"Uh, sure. Why does it annoy them?"

"I don't know. They think it's their secret nickname for you. Real original, right?"

They had a secret nickname for her? Did that mean they were making fun of her? She looked over to where Kyle was piling kindling next to the fire pit. What had she ever done to him?

Missy put a hand on her arm. "Don't worry about it. They don't mean anything by it. They're just being stupid."

"Okay," said Grace, not at all okay.

"Kyle, come over here and apologize!" Missy shouted.

"No, it's fine, don't—" Grace tried to stop her.

"For what?" Kyle shouted back.

"For being a jerk!" Missy called.

"Sorry for being a jerk!" Kyle called back.

Missy shrugged. "That's about all you're going to get, I'm afraid. But, really, it's nothing personal. Seriously. If you were, like, an insurance salesman, they wouldn't care."

"But because I'm a professor, they hate me?"

"They don't hate you, they just think you think you're smarter than they are. And with Kyle, you probably are."

Grace looked up at the treetops. Why was she even here?

"But, look, who cares? We came here to swim. C'mon. Take off this burka and let's go."

First Missy introduced Grace around, amending her nickname to "Professor Grace." Katie, MB's cousin from Hollow Bend, already knew about her from Keith the vet, which reminded Grace that small town news traveled fast. Billie, Katie's best friend, offered Grace a beer, which she declined.

"The Professor doesn't drink beer!" Kyle shouted. Did that guy have superhuman hearing? Grace wondered.

"I thought there was no drinking here," Grace said. "Because of the Baptist bikers."

"Eh, as long as we clean up, they'll never know," Billie said with a shrug.

"Besides, I can take a few bikers," said Katie.

Chase, a tall, cowboy-looking friend of Katie, took the beer out of her hand.

"Hey!" Katie yelled, and grabbed for her drink. But Chase was fast, and set the beer down on the ground, leaned into Katie, and threw her over his shoulder. He carried her, fireman-style, down to the water.

"Don't you d—" she started, but didn't finish, because Chase threw her in.

"Oh, Chase! With her clothes on!" Billie shouted. "He's gonna pay for that later," she told Grace.

Grace just nodded. Although if she were Katie, she wouldn't wait too long to make him pay.

"Does that make you want to go swimming, or what?" Missy asked her.

"Well, it certainly reassures me that the water is deep." Katie was standing a few feet from the shore, and the water came up to her waist.

"It's deeper than it looks. And there's quite a steep drop-off. The best thing to do is just jump right in," Missy reassured her. "Ready?" she asked. Before Grace could respond, Missy was ripped away and thrown into the water. She and Kyle both came up screaming, Missy from anger, Kyle from cold.

"Come on in, Professor!" Kyle shouted at her. "The water's fine!"

"Then why are your teeth chattering?" she asked him.

"Because he's a wimp!" Katie shouted, and dunked Kyle's head under the water.

"Don't you dare," Grace heard MB say to Todd as she pulled her shirt off to reveal a bright blue two-piece.

"Wouldn't dream of it, darling," Todd said, taking her hand. "You coming, Grace?"

She nodded, then turned from the group to pull off her cover-up. Her retro-style navy blue halter top felt too fussy for this environment, but there was nothing she could do about that now. Before she could properly steel herself for whatever reaction her swimsuit might cause, her feet were in the air and she was over Kyle's shoulder, which was wet and cold and bony and just slightly less pleasant than the freezing cold water of the swimming hole.

"Kyle! What the hell?" Missy splashed his face as soon as he came up for air. "You okay, Grace?"

Grace coughed and pushed her hair out of her face. Freezing was maybe too strong a word for the water. It was cold, but it felt nice compared to the humidity of the air. She leaned her head back and took off floating away.

"Kyle!" she heard Missy whisper urgently. Then she heard someone swimming up next to her.

"Hey, I'm sorry, Professor. It was a joke."

Grace just waved her arms lightly, letting the water decide which direction she would head in.

"Come on, Professor. I really didn't mean to hurt you. Did I hurt you?"

Grace's feet made their way around to Kyle's face. She felt the top of her shoe bump his nose.

"Professor, if you don't speak to me, Missy is going to kill me. Do you want my death on your conscience?"

Grace floated.

"Grace, please."

She tucked in and straightened out upright in the water, and beamed a beatific smile at Kyle. He looked confused, and Grace swam a little closer. Then she bobbed up and pushed his head under.

He came up sputtering and she swam as far away as she could. "I forgive you!" she shouted, and it echoed off the rocks, along with Missy's laughter.

Somehow that led to Kyle daring her to jump off the rock. First he climbed up and demonstrated how easy it was. He just stood at the edge and then he was a tangle of flailing limbs that worked itself into a ball and a tremendous splash. He came up shaking the water out of his hair. "I knew Jake was wrong about you!" he shouted after her as she found footing on the rocks.

Jake. What did Jake have to do with it? If she could get rid of Jake, her life would be great. She could teach, and research, and spend time with these people who she thought would become good friends. But she kept needing Jake, to fix this, to lift that, to pull her down off a roof.

By the time she got to the top of the rock, she had convinced herself that if she could conquer her fear of heights, she wouldn't need Jake anymore. She stood, knees shaking, and tried not to look over the edge.

"Let's go, Professor!" shouted Katie. Grace couldn't help it— she looked. Damn, it was high. But not any higher than her porch roof, she reasoned, and she hadn't died on the roof, so she wouldn't die jumping off this rock. She gave a thumbs-up, took a deep breath, and prepared to launch herself into her new, independent, Jake-free life.

But just as she launched, she saw a disturbance in the woods, and there, coming down the trail from the church, was Jake.

Jake.

She lost her footing, but it was too late. There was gravity, and then there was the water.

As soon as Jake pulled up to the house, he knew it was no good. There was a huge crack in the cement foundation and the only way to fix that was to re-lay the foundation or tear the house down and start over. He went in anyway, saw the water damage on the walls of the basement and smelled the mold in the kitchen. That, coupled with the complete unwillingness of the realtor to budge on the way-too-high price, convinced Jake that he'd be better off with an after-noon of swimming. So he went home, changed into his board shorts, and hit the road. Mary Beth was right—he loved the swim-ming hole, and he wasn't going to let some imaginary beef with the Professor get in the way of enjoying the last warm days before fall set in.

Besides, he wasn't really mad at her. He just . . . didn't like her.

That wasn't true. And that was the problem. He was attracted to her; no seeing man wouldn't be. And as long as she kept acting like she was better than everyone else, he had no problem staying away. But then she had to go and laugh. And she laughed at herself. He had never known a professor to laugh at herself.

Of course, he didn't know many professors that well.

So, okay, as a person, she was fine. She was great. She had a good sense of humor and was smart and liked to laugh. And she was gorgeous.

But she was still a professor. His father always told him that those Pembroke people thought they were too good for the people of Willow Springs. Don Burdette wasn't right about a lot of things, but in Jake's experience, he was right about Pembroke.

When Jake finally got to the swimming hole, he could hear the party was in full swing. Kyle must have had his high school boom box set up, blaring country music. As he started to climb down the hill, he counted at least a dozen people, eating and drinking and lounging in inner tubes.

He didn't spot Grace until he heard his cousin, Katie, shout out. Jake looked in the direction she was pointing, and there Grace was, like a Venus on top of the rocks. Her dark blue bathing suit looked like one of those old-fashioned pin-up styles, one that didn't show a lot, but hugged her everywhere. His mind immediately went back to the other day when he'd helped her climb off the roof. His body went back to holding her trembling body, feeling those curves cuddle into him for comfort. His hands clenched reflexively as he watched her give Kyle the least convincing thumbs-up he'd ever seen. He could swear he saw her knees knocking from where he stood.

What the hell was she thinking, jumping off that rock? She was clearly terrified.

But then he saw her take a determined breath and he stopped walking. She was going to do it. He couldn't believe it, but she bent her knees and prepared to jump. He must have moved, must have made some sound, because just as she sprang out, her eyes locked with his and whatever momentum she had built up got all messed up and she lost control. Down she went.

Hard.

Jake heard her whole body hit the water with more of a *splat* than a splash. He vaguely registered a couple of sympathetic groans from his friends, but just barely as his stride ate the rest of the distance down the hill. He took a running dive into the water, thinking only that she was hurt, that he had to get to her.

He reached her just as she came up with a huge gasp. Then she opened her mouth and let out one of the foulest curses he'd ever heard. She turned to raise a triumphant fist at Kyle, her eyes still closed and covered with her hair. Finally, she ducked back under the water and came up with her head tilted back and wiped the water out of her eyes.

When she opened them, she saw him.

"Jake!" she shouted and sent a huge splash of water into his face.

"Hey!" he sputtered, but she closed the distance between them and smacked him on the shoulder.

"What are you doing here?"

"I'm trying to save you," he said, snaking his arms around her waist. She could be in shock, after all. She could drown at any minute.

She gripped his shirt as their legs tangled under the water. "Why are you wearing a shirt?"

He let go of her long enough to push his hair out of his face. She didn't let go, so he took that as a sign that she was still unsteady and she needed him to hold on to her a little longer.

"I thought you were drowning." He shrugged.

"I don't suppose you missed that?" Her eyes flicked back to the rock.

"It's kind of why I'm in the water with my shirt still on."

"Well, it's your fault. You distracted me."

"Are you okay? Really? That looked like it hurt."

She snorted. "I'm fine. I mean, my skin burns and I think I broke my ego, but I'll live."

Jake clucked in sympathy when he saw that the skin on her chest had turned a very patriotic shade of red. He ran his hand gently between the straps of her bathing suit, and she shivered and pressed in closer to him.

"You sure you're okay?" Her mouth was a breath away from his, and he was so close he could see her cheeks flush and her eyes darken. She nodded and bit her lip and Jake urged her even closer.

"Just kiss her already!" Katie and Billie called from the shore, accompanied by a few catcalls from his friends.

Grace snapped her head to the shore and just like that, the moment was gone.

"Come on," he said, gently swimming her toward the party. "Let's get you to dry land."

If Grace had known that all it would take to make friends in this town was to make a complete fool of herself, well, she wouldn't have hidden all the ways she'd made a complete fool of herself already. Like wearing pajamas to the Fourth of July barbecue, for example. That, at least, had been a much less painful way to make a good impression.

Her body was fine. It wasn't like she'd never belly-flopped before. Never quite so spectacularly, but physically she could handle it.

Her ego might never be the same.

It didn't help that every time she looked at Kyle, he turned his hands sideways and clapped them together while making a *sploosh* sound with his big, dumb mouth. That made everyone laugh, which didn't exactly make Grace feel good.

Well, Jake didn't laugh. Apparently all she had to do to get him to be civil was appear to fall to her death.

But then Chase patted her on the back in sympathy and Katie reminded Kyle that if he had belly-flopped off The Rock, he would've packed up his high school boom box and gone home. So, really, they were all laughing *with* her. Well, they were laughing with her as soon as she started laughing. They weren't making fun of her—they were teasing her. God, had she been away from normal people so long that she forgot the difference?

Jake was right. Most of the time she did associate with other professors. That had certainly been her life in California, especially after she'd started seeing Lou. She had always bonded easily with her classmates, then her fellow post-docs—well, the ones who weren't insanely competitive alien people. And Lou seemed to only know other professors, so when they went out, it was always something academic.

And she didn't mind. Sometimes she'd idly wonder what it was like to sell insurance or work at a bank or fix cars. Lou said it involved a lot of fast food and reality television. Which was interesting because she frequently saw McDonald's wrappers tucked under the back seat of his car. And she would never tell him, but she liked having reality television on in the background while she graded papers. She could tune it out while she graded, then get distracted by it for a few minutes until she had to grade the next one.

Sometimes she wondered what Jane Austen would make of reality TV. She tried to imagine her as The Bachelorette, having to pick from a roomful of Darcys and Knightleys and Wentworths, maybe with a few Wickhams and Willoughbys thrown in. Surely, she would pick Darcy. If she didn't pass out from all of her dreams coming true.

"What are you thinking about?" Jake nudged her shoulder and she hunkered down further into the blanket wrapped around her.

"Reality television." The Jane Austen idea would never work. Time-space continuum aside, that would just reinforce the notion that her books were *just* love stories, that there was no art and genius involved.

"Ugh, you watch that crap?"

She laughed at the look of shock on his face.

"Don't be a snob, Jake," she chided, and held her hands up to the fire.

"Are you cold?" he asked, grabbing her hands and holding them between his. "Jesus, Grace, you're freezing!" He pulled the blanket tighter around her until it was practically smothering her, then he pulled her closer to him so that she was practically sitting on his lap.

She looked across the fire at Mary Beth, who gave her a bemused smirk. Grace just shrugged. *Hey, he's warm.*

"So, Professor," asked Billie, "if you had to go out with one Jane Austen hero, who would it be?"

Kyle snorted, and Missy shoved him playfully in the leg. "You're just mad because I like Mr. Darcy better than I like you."

"Yeah, but he's not real, I am. Besides, would Mr. Darcy do this?"

The dance Kyle did for Missy was not exactly vulgar, but Grace wished she hadn't seen it all the same.

"I don't really think of them like that," said Grace.

"Because they're fictional?" Todd asked from next to Mary Beth.

"No. I mean, yes, of course. I would never romantically identify with a fictional character."

Missy snorted. Grace smiled.

"I just mean that when you reduce Jane Austen's book to the love story, you diminish the value of her work," she said.

"Like a well-told love story isn't worth it?" asked Billie.

"No, of course it is. It's just . . . that tends to call into question her relevance. It invites dismissal."

"From other snobs," Missy said, her eyebrow firmly raised. "Male snobs."

Grace smiled. "Mostly."

"Listen," said Missy, pulling Kyle down to sit with her. He immediately wrapped his arms around her. "You don't have to justify your life's work to us. But if you think those love stories aren't important, you've been doing it wrong."

Grace laughed. "Fine, I surrender."

"Hey, how come you're allowed to say that stuff to her and I'm not?" Kyle asked Missy petulantly.

"Because you're an idiot," Missy said, and pulled his chin down for a kiss.

Soon they were making out full-throttle. Grace glanced at Jake, who was studiously watching the fire. Then Kyle abruptly stood, Missy still wrapped around him, and they stalked off into the woods.

"You want to get out of here?" Jake asked.

"Yes," said Grace, because she was cold, and people were making out, and because she wanted to get out of there with Jake.

Chapter 13

Jake didn't say much on the way home, and Grace was too tired to prod him into conversation. It felt nice, somehow, riding with the windows down, quiet radio noise in the background. She occasionally snuck a glance over at Jake, who kept his eyes studiously on the road. She braved a longer look, admired his strong jaw and the way the ridge in his nose stood out more in profile.

"What?"

She jumped in her seat, startled and embarrassed to have been caught ogling.

"Nothing!" she insisted.

"Why do you keep looking at me?" Even with his head still facing forward, she could see that crooked smile stretch across his mouth.

She shrugged. "What happened to your nose?"

He ran a finger gingerly along the ridge and said, "Broke it."

"What's the story?"

He just shook his head.

"Come on, there's always a good story behind a broken nose. I'll tell you mine if you tell me yours."

"You broke your nose?" He turned his head to face her, squinted in the faint light.

"I fell off a horse. Jane was one of those horse-crazy kids, so my parents took us for riding lessons. And I fell off."

"Geez. You really should keep your feet on the ground, you know that?"

"It actually wasn't that bad a fall, but I got tangled in the stirrup and I hit my face against the horse's neck."

"So you broke your nose *on* a horse."

She laughed. "Yeah, I guess."

"Your nose looks fine. I mean, it doesn't look like it's been broken."

"Well, it healed. And . . . you know, plastic surgery."

"So you've had a nose job?"

"Yes, it's true," she admitted. "I've had some work done. Your turn. How'd you break yours?"

Jake rubbed the back of his neck. "It's not as whimsical as your story."

"I don't care, I want to hear it."

"I got into a fight in jail."

Grace sputtered out a laugh. That was not at all what she was expecting.

But Jake didn't laugh.

"Wait, you're serious?"

"I did a lot of stupid stuff when I was a kid. When I was a senior in high school, I got busted for underage drinking. Todd was just a cop then, but he was dating my sister. He saw what a pain I was to her, so he persuaded her to let him teach me a lesson, let me wait it out in jail overnight."

"Oh, my God. What did your mom say?" Grace really couldn't imagine Marilyn leaving her son in jail, even overnight.

"Mary Beth didn't tell her. Made up a story about me staying over at Kyle's or something."

"Did it scare you straight?"

Jake snorted. "Not hardly. I was a punk. I thought I was tougher than all those guys in there. I was younger, and I was faster. But faster only gets you so far when a guy outweighs you by about a hundred pounds and you're in a cage together."

"Jake," Grace said again, "you could have been killed."

"Nah, he just got in one good punch, and then some other guys pulled him off. Todd paid my bail and took me to the hospital. I think it hurt him more than it hurt me."

"I doubt that."

"I've never seen Todd scared before, or since. I think he thought Mary Beth would never speak to him again."

"He almost got you killed."

"Yeah, well. He's always been good to MB, and I was acting like a punk."

Grace just stared at that crooked profile. She wasn't sure she would be so forgiving.

Of course, she was confident she wouldn't last even the idea of a night in jail.

"Anyway," Jake said, "that's how I broke my nose."

"And now you're cursed to carry the scar of your misspent youth, huh?"

"Yup. No plastic surgery for me."

Grace stilled. Was he doing it again? Bringing up how different they were? She didn't want this nice night to end on a sour note, so she told him the truth.

"I like it. It's kind of . . . sexy."

His crooked smile broke out again, and he kept his eyes on the road.

When they got to Grace's house, she was almost sorry to say goodnight. Apparently so was Jake, because he got out of the truck with her. He walked around and opened the tailgate. She thought he might be getting his tool belt, but it was late and she didn't want him to fix anything. She wanted them to be friends. She was just starting to say as much when he came around the truck to meet her at the front door.

"You don't have to—" Then she saw a gigantic box of cat litter.

"Is that for me?" she asked.

"Will belongs to one of those warehouse club things. I got a deal."

"Jake, that's—"

"It's no big deal, okay? I just thought, since you ride your bike everywhere, that it would be hard to carry."

He was right. The smallest container of cat litter she could find had been fifteen pounds. She had to take her old lady wheeled cart into town to pick it up.

So, not only was she a single woman with a cat, she was seen around town wheeling a shopping cart full of cat litter.

And she lived in a house called the Spinster House.

At least Jake had saved her from any further cat litter humiliation. In time, she'd be able to function as a normal member of society. Tonight, she'd be satisfied with cat litter.

"Thank you," she said, and impulsively stretched up to kiss him on the cheek.

"No big deal," he mumbled, then reached around to open the door she'd unlocked.

She was momentarily distracted by his jeans. More specifically, the way his jeans stretched over his butt. Damn that perfect butt. And the way his triceps strained with the weight of the tub of cat litter. Good Lord, this man made cat litter look sexy.

"You coming in?" he asked with a smile.

She followed him in, leaned down to pet Mr. Bingley, then pointed Jake to the downstairs powder room, where the litter box was more or less hidden under the sink.

He came out, followed by the cat. "Thanks again," she told him. "You really didn't have to do that."

He just shrugged and she shook her head. Sometimes Jake could be so thoughtful. It almost made her forget that he was such a pain.

Jake didn't want to leave. He didn't want to stay—of course not, he didn't like Grace. As he continually reminded himself. Because he kept forgetting.

He still didn't like professors. They were smug and overbearing and looked down on people like Jake, people who didn't think it was fun to always have your nose in a book. Not that Jake didn't read. What was the point of having a library card if he didn't use it? And aside from having a knack for fixing things, the main thing he and his dad had in common was a love of suspense and thrillers. If Jake had read Jack Reacher when he was a kid, he would have dropped everything and gotten on a bus to save the world.

But professors managed to take the fun out of reading. He remembered when Henry was new at Pembroke and Marilyn had him over for dinner. Will liked to show off his cooking, and Marilyn liked talking to new people, even if she had to drag her adult children into it. When she told Henry about Jake's paperback reading habit, Henry feigned interest and started talking about the sociological implications of perpetuating a dangerous kind of masculinity, blah blah blah. Jake wanted to talk about the sociological implications of his fist in Henry's face.

And now Henry was sniffing around Grace, and they would sit around and talk about sociological implications and high art and Jake was getting bored even imagining it.

No, he wasn't getting bored. He was getting jealous. Grace wasn't like the other professors he knew. She knew how to laugh at herself, and at him. She was smart, sure, but she was also actually interesting, and she could talk about other things besides literature. And he hated to admit it, but she had kind of a hot-for-teacher thing going on. Her clothes were cute and fun and totally appropriate, but no matter how many cat sweatshirts she wore, she would never erase the mental picture he had of her in that bathing suit.

Doesn't matter, he told himself. Even if, by some miracle, she liked him despite his being a total jerk to her, it could never work. They had nothing in common, essentially. It wasn't so much that he thought Grace was too good for him. Just that they were, well, different.

Man, he really needed to fix something right now.

Instead, he just had Grace in front of him, toying with the string on her hoodie. She looked toward the powder room and let out the most pathetic sigh he'd heard since Kyle found out Missy had to work late.

"What's that forlorn sigh for?" he asked her.

"I'm not forlorn!" she protested. "I'm just . . . pensive."

"About cat litter?"

"A little," she said. "Not really specifically about cat litter, more about how excited I was that you brought me cat litter. And because I live in the Spinster House."

"Grace, this isn't the Spinster House."

"How can you be so sure?"

"I've lived in this town my entire life. They publicize the heck out of any little bit of local news. If the Spinster House was suddenly not where it was supposed to be, we'd all know."

Grace sighed. Again. "Well, even if it's not *the* Spinster House, it's certainly turning into a spinster house."

"What is your deal with spinsters?"

"I don't know! It started as a joke between me and Jane, and then the cat sweatshirts started, and it was funny for a while. It still is funny, with her. But now it feels like I'm fulfilling some sort of prophecy. Doomed to a life of spinsterhood. And the thing is, I don't really mind. I feel like I should mind, but I don't."

"You don't mind becoming a spinster?" Jake had a few spinster aunts, and he wanted to reassure Grace that she had a long way to go before she turned into Aunt May or Aunt Tess. She needed to wear her hair in a bun and work on growing a little hair on her upper lip. And she would have to get a roommate; spinsters always lived in pairs.

Then he remembered that Aunt May and Aunt Tess weren't sisters, and that they only had one bedroom.

Not exactly where he wanted the conversation to go.

"I admire the sensible shoes of the spinster," Grace said, as if she wasn't privy to Jake's internal monologue. Which was good. "And I like cats. And the being-single part, I like that. Oh, God, I am totally a spinster."

Jake raised an eyebrow. He had never met a woman who was happy being single. Well, except for Aunt May and Aunt Tess, and he wasn't getting that kind of vibe from Grace.

Not when she raised her eyes slowly. Not when they met his and he felt a jolt go through him.

Her eyes still on his, she just shrugged. Then she took a step forward.

He thought he should take a step forward too, but when he went to lift his foot, he realized he had already closed the distance between them.

"You like being single, huh?" He brushed an errant lock of hair out of her face.

"I like some parts about being single," she admitted.

He was curious about that. Really, he was. She was smart and warm and funny. It seemed a shame that she didn't want to share that with someone.

But he really didn't want to get into a conversation about her relationship status right now. He just wanted to put his arms around her, and to see where that would lead.

So he did.

As soon as his hands skimmed her waist, hers came up around his neck and she pulled him in for a kiss. He'd kissed her once before, right over there on the living room floor. Why had he waited so long to kiss her again?

"I thought I had sworn off men," she said, breathless, in between kisses. "But now I'm not so sure."

"I changed your mind, huh?" He nudged his hips against her, just so she could feel how much he appreciated her decision to swear back on to men.

She looked up at him and smiled like a cat. Then she wiggled out of his arms and he was about to protest, to reach for her because surely she was not done with him yet, when she grabbed his hand and led him up the creaking stairs to her room.

The stairs creaked and her bed squeaked and Grace couldn't hear any of it over the pounding beat of her heart. She wished she had picked up some of the clothes strewn about the room or maybe didn't have quite so many books piled within easy reach of her bed because the nightstand was too full. But then Jake walked in behind her, the hall light giving him a halo he didn't deserve, and he whipped his shirt over his head and tossed it aside.

She gulped. Not because she was afraid, but because . . . gaaah. He was perfect. Sculpted, but not too beefy. He had a fair amount of hair on his chest, which she loved, and that "v" on hips that she loved even more. She didn't think she had ever seen one of those in real life. He unbuttoned his jeans, but before he could get them over his hips, she hopped off the bed.

Jake let go of his pants and reached for Grace, just as she'd hoped he would. She stepped into him, but not so close that she couldn't explore the contours of his chest, run her fingers through the rough hair there, then follow the trail lower.

"Why are you still wearing this?" he asked, tugging at the hem of her T-shirt. But she wasn't done exploring him yet, so she ducked down out of his grasp and ran her tongue along that "v." She was becoming obsessed. She wanted to make sure it was real.

Jake cursed, but it was the good kind of curse, the kind that said he was surprised but not displeased with the sudden turn of events. She ran her hands up his sides, then back down, taking his jeans with her. She took a moment to appreciate the tone of his legs on the way down, then again on the way up when she hooked her fingers in the waist of his boxers. She looked up to give him a teasing grin, but Jake was looking at the ceiling. His fists were clenched and his neck was straining and—was he praying?

Grace let loose that teasing grin anyway and pulled his boxers gently down to join his jeans at his ankles, and then there he was, big and thick and bobbing in front of her. She licked her lips and reached out to take hold of him . . .

But found herself suddenly picked up by the armpits and thrown onto the bed.

"Sorry," Jake grunted at her. "I want this to be good for both of us."

That would have been good for me, too, she wanted to say, but the way he was stalking over her on his hands and knees left her a little tongue-tied. She opened her mouth as soon as he kissed her and when she felt his hands under her shirt she thought, well, that's it, I've melted. But Jake persisted and licked a trail up from her waist to her neck, pulling her shirt up and over her head as he went. She wiggled out of her shorts while she waited for him to take the initiative with her bra. When he didn't, she started to do it herself; she didn't mind. But then Jake stilled her with a hand on her arm and she looked up at him, surprised, but lay back down, hands at her sides.

"What is this?" he asked, running his hands gently over the whole front of her.

"Boobs?" She was teasing him, but also hopefully directing him.

"I never would have guessed . . ." He traced a finger around the edge of her bra. It was one of her more serviceable ones, gray cotton, designed for comfort. Jake's finger followed the bright pink lace sewn to the edges, then spread his fingers over the polka dots on the gray fabric. Grace tried her hardest not to arch into his touch, not to look too eager, but when he leaned down and kissed between her breasts, then ran his tongue along the outside of the lace, she didn't care how she looked.

She felt good. He felt good, the rough stubble of his cheeks brushing against her belly-flop sensitive skin, the calluses on his hands scraping gently as he ran his hands down over her hips, taking her underwear with him.

He spent more time—more time than she thought she could stand—trailing kisses all over her skin before he finally nudged her up and took her bra off. She really liked what he was doing, but she was ready for him to get on with it.

He must have felt that same mad impatience because he cursed and attacked her mouth and she held on, attacking back, as he worked his hips between her legs and settled in against her.

The feeling of him hard and bare against her brought her back to reality. Grace mentally ran through the contents of her bathroom cabinets, which was hard to do when Jake's hands and mouth were running through her contents. But she managed because she knew this would get even more dire soon. She was ninety-seven percent sure she didn't have any condoms, although there might still be that glow-in-the-dark one that Jane gave her as a joke last Halloween. Whatever, it would work. It was safe to put something glow-in-the-dark in her body, right?

But then Jake bit her neck and she squeaked.

"Get out of that head of yours," he said, gently licking over the spot, then trailing kisses along her chin and up to her mouth. "I'm trying to turn you on to men again."

"Jake," she said breathlessly just as he kissed her. He probably thought she was just sighing in pleasure. Which she was doing, but she also needed to apprise him of the condom situation. But as she tried to push his shoulders up she got distracted by how wide they were, and how the muscles played beneath her fingers as he shifted to pull her closer.

"Hey." Jake nipped her chin. "Stay with me, here."

"I know, I know. But I don't have any condoms," she said in a rush before he could distract her again.

He looked at her blankly, then rested his forehead on hers. Then, in a rush, he was out of bed. Oh, God, she thought. Is this the end? She didn't want to have unprotected sex, but couldn't they, like, do other stuff?

"Don't look so panicked, I ain't leavin'," he said, digging something out of his discarded jeans. He came up, muscled and victorious, a foil wrapped prize between his fingers. Before she could think of something clever to say to show her appreciation, he was back, his whole body covering hers, then inside of hers, and the only clever thing she could say was a loud, appreciative moan. He paused, brushed her hair back, so she wrapped her legs around his hips and he got the message and moved. She picked up his rhythm and they were moving together, his eyes locked on hers until she threw her head back and shouted, then he shouted, and they collapsed into each other.

"I should go," Jake murmured into her neck. Grace was glad he said it, because she was about to and she didn't want him to get offended. He felt good, if a bit heavy, lying half on top of her, their sweat-slicked limbs tangled in the sheets. She could get used to this kind of entanglement.

Which was exactly why he needed to leave.

"Okay," she said, and brushed the hair on the back of his neck. He had really good hair. It was thick and wavy and she liked that it was a little too long, because it gave her fingers something to play with as she worked up the energy to kick him out.

She looked over at the clock, but they had knocked it off the nightstand in their fervor. And what fervor. She stretched as best as she could underneath Jake, tilting her head back to look out of the open curtains. It was definitely late, and not quite early. He could probably get out unnoticed by Mrs. Wallace and her neighborhood watch.

"I should be able to avoid your neighbors if I go now. What time is it, anyway?"

She smiled up at him and he kissed her, hard and fast. He started to get up and she wanted to pull him back, to tangle the sheets up with him a little more, but she had to let him go. He was definitely trouble, and she was determined to avoid romantic entanglements.

Determined.

He climbed out of the bed, tripping over the sheets and pulling them to the floor. She sat up just enough to pull them back onto the bed. She was cold all of a sudden. She watched him step into his jeans, then look vaguely around the room for the rest of his clothes. His hair was sticking up in the places where she had toyed with it, and standing there, looking tired and a little confused in just his jeans, he was the most perfect combination of sexy and cute she had ever seen.

But she was determined.

She pointed to the back of the purple armchair in the corner. He smiled ruefully and retrieved his shirt, then quickly pulled it over his head. Hmph. Should have kept my pointing to myself, she thought. Then he bent down and found his boxers under the ottoman—how had they gotten *under* the ottoman?—and, shrugging, he stuffed them in his pocket. Oh, good Lord, she was never getting back to sleep now.

But she had to let the poor man out, so she rolled out of bed and grabbed her robe off the back of the door. He stuffed his feet into his shoes and followed her down the stairs. She started to open the door, but he pushed it closed, then pushed her up against it and kissed her so hard her insides rebelled and she wrapped her limbs around him.

"Good night," he said, that crooked grin teasing her.

She unwound herself but kept her head close. "Good night," she whispered, and kissed him on the nose.

As soon as she closed the door behind him, she died. She leaned against the door and squealed as quietly as she could, which was pretty difficult considering she was bursting inside. Holy crap. Jake, the pain in her butt, was a Love God.

No, not love. She didn't do love.

He was a Like God.

No, he was a Sex God.

Her toes curled just thinking about it. She thought about calling Jane, just so she would have someone to squeal with. But it was late, or early, and besides, Jane really didn't need to hear the details.

Just as Grace was deciding that she didn't want to share them anyway, there was a knock at the door. Since the knock was directly behind where her head was, she jumped, and, without thinking, threw the door open.

Jake was back.

"Uh, my truck won't start," he said, rubbing the back of his neck in that way that he did when he was feeling conflicted. "I must not have closed the door all the way."

"Oh," said Grace.

"I could call someone for a jump, or—"

Before he even finished whatever ridiculous solution he was about to propose, Grace grabbed him by the neck of his shirt and pulled him inside. Before she could even think about releasing him, his mouth was on hers and he hauled her up into his arms and carried her back upstairs.

The house finally, finally, settled down for the night.

Chapter 14

Jake woke up with a start. He'd been having this strange dream where everything smelled like cupcakes and he was coming home like Ward Cleaver, with briefcase and suit and tie. In the dream, he was happy—probably the cupcakes—but woke up with a strangled feeling—probably the tie. He didn't dream a lot, or at least he didn't remember his dreams, so he was already disoriented, and when he didn't immediately recognize his surroundings, he started to panic.

Then Grace moaned in her sleep and snuggled closer into his side and Jake figured it out pretty quickly. Grace was sleep-warm and smelled better than cupcakes. He remembered his car not starting, which was why he spent the night even though he never spent the night. He reached over to the nightstand, which was a mess, and fumbled with the alarm clock. It was late, but it was Sunday, so that didn't matter. He rolled out of bed and dug around for his cell phone, then sent Kyle a quick message to come help him start his car. That would take a while, he knew, so he shooed Mr. Bingley out of the spot he'd just vacated on the bed and curled himself around Grace. She probably had stuff to do today. He should wake her up, he thought. He should definitely not wrap his arms around her and go back to sleep.

Grace woke up to a pounding on her front door. She jerked out of bed, then remembered Henry. Crap. She looked at the clock, which had been righted on the nightstand, and frowned. He was early. And she was naked.

And so was Jake.

She debated waking him up and shooing him out the back door. Or letting him stay and hoping he slept through Henry's visit. She didn't regret having slept with him, but for some reason she didn't want Henry to know. She didn't really want anyone to know. That would make it real. And this wasn't real, this was just a sex thing. A really, really good sex thing, but not real. Not a relationship.

Although she would probably tell Jane.

Just not all the details.

The pounding on the door was getting more insistent and Jake was starting to stir, so Grace threw on her robe and ran down the stairs. Halfway down it occurred to her that greeting Henry in her bathrobe was probably not the most professional way to maintain their working relationship, but momentum propelled her forward and there was nothing she could do. As she was about to open the door, she heard the person on the other side yell, "Hey, lazy! I'm here to start your damn truck! Quit bonking the Professor and get out here!"

Kyle.

So much for nobody knowing about her and Jake.

Grace threw the door open and Kyle jumped back, his arm still raised to pound the door again.

"Uh, hi, Professor. Jake here?"

"Yeah, dumbass," said a bleary Jake, trudging down the stairs in his crumpled clothes, shoes in hand.

"I'm here to save *you*, buddy, so who's the dumbass now?" Kyle looked very confident when he started that rant, but sort of fizzled out in the end. "Never mind. I need coffee, bro, so let's do this."

"Go," Grace shooed when Jake gave her a sorry-for-my-friend look with a side of bedroom-eyes. Part of her wanted Jake to get rid of Kyle and just stay, but even if the other part of her didn't rebel and scream at that idea, Henry was due and she should probably put on clothes before he came over.

Jake kissed her on the nose and promised to call. She raised her eyebrows in a look that she hoped conveyed it-doesn't-matter-because-you're-not-my-boyfriend, but she was glad he said it all the same. And she did want him to call; they were friends. Now she supposed they were friends with benefits.

Was she turning into one of her undergrads? Was she going to start wearing sweatpants with inappropriate words on the butt? In public?

Or would she continue to become an old lady by complaining about what the kids were wearing these days?

Mr. Bingley did a figure eight around her legs, then Jake's, which tripped Jake up as he tried to get out the door. Kyle just shook his head and stalked down the front steps. Jake gave Grace one more kiss—she pushed him away before he could get too serious about it—and followed Kyle. Grace watched him go, laughing at the spring in his step and maybe also admiring the view a little, but shut the door as soon as the jumper cables came out. She leaned against it, listening to the sound of one motor, then two starting, then both fading away as the boys drove off in pursuit of coffee.

Grace leaned back against the door, sighing like an idiot. But she couldn't help it. Maybe it was just post-coital glee, but she felt really good about this. She had never had a purely physical relationship before. She had always felt like she shouldn't get intimate with someone unless she had feelings for him, and she followed that rule until the feelings became too strong—on either side—and backed off. Well, she usually ran screaming, but the end result was the same.

It hadn't been that way with Lou. Lou always maintained a certain distance with her, and that, in a strange way, made her feel safe. His heart was shielded, her heart was shielded, they could carry on and be close, maybe even forever.

Grace had discovered that he wasn't so much protecting his heart as keeping it aside for his not-actually-ex wife. She'd also discovered that she had become more emotionally invested than she realized. She couldn't understand why she couldn't stop crying, and it took Jane to point out to her that it was normal, that her heart was broken.

Jane rescinded her analysis when, a week later, Grace was back to normal, sleeping with a physics post-doc, and applying for jobs elsewhere.

Grace just didn't give her heart away. She never would, and was afraid of how close she'd come with Lou. She wouldn't fall into that same trap with Jake. She liked him, there was no denying that. He was clever and he was kind, when he wanted to be, and she didn't think she'd ever been so physically attracted to a man in her life. She shivered against the door frame, remembering the way he felt last night.

But there was a distance between them that could never be crossed. With Lou, there had been almost a hero-worship element to their relationship. He was a genius, and his literary brain was what had attracted him to her in the first place, and what fueled their passion. There were nights when they would start a debate at dinner that would become so heated they would just rip each other's clothes off, then continue the debate afterward, lying in bed. That would never happen with Jake. Not that they didn't have plenty to argue about, but it was different. They connected on a different level. It was physical more than intellectual, because their intellects worked so differently. Grace always joked that she had the ability to retain only the kind of knowledge that had absolutely no practical application. Jake's genius was entirely in the practical application. She liked that, not just because it meant he could fix stuff for her, but it was interesting to watch a brain so different from her own puzzle out a problem.

Interesting, but not clothes-ripping-off, heart-stealing exciting.

But, man, she was physically attracted to him.

She was just starting to get weak in the knees from remembering when there was a knock at her door. I really need to get a doorbell, she thought. Or just quit standing against the door frame. Then she smiled because she thought it might be Jake, and that he might have brought her coffee. She loosened her robe a little and flung the door open with an "I'm so glad you came back!"

Only it wasn't Jake.

It was Henry.

And he was staring at her boobs.

She shrieked and slammed the door. After a few deep breaths, she pulled her robe tighter and opened the door with a professional and welcoming smile.

"Good morning, Henry."

"Good morning. I'm early. I just didn't see how early. Sorry about that." His eyes twitched a little. She figured he was probably trying to avoid looking at her chest again, which she appreciated.

"That's okay, I lost track of time." And my mind, apparently. "Come on in. Do you mind waiting down here while I . . ."

"Oh, no, take your time. I brought a few things to show you." He held up a manila folder bursting with papers and clippings. "I'll just get organized?"

"Sure, and feel free to take a look around."

Henry's eyes lit up and she thought if he hadn't been holding that folder, he would have rubbed his hands together with glee. Well, at least he wasn't offended by her casual attire.

As she shut the door behind him, she saw Mrs. Wallace across the street, Lucy tugging at the leash while she stood staring, open-mouthed, at Grace.

So much for the Spinster House, Grace thought, and shut the door.

Two hours later, Grace was thoroughly sick of the Spinster House. She'd taken a quick shower and pulled on a cotton sundress (not pajamas—she made sure of that). Her hair was tied up in a messy bun on top of her head, and she hadn't bothered with makeup. After a few minutes with Henry, she thought she could have come down in her pajamas with a bag on her head and he wouldn't have noticed. Heck, she could have come down naked, and he still would have paid more attention to her sconces.

At first, it was great. She loved her house and she loved showing it off. She was proud of the work she'd put into it, although Henry seemed to disagree with some of her bolder paint choices. But a good way into the first hour of his visit, she realized that he was only half-listening to what she was saying. She knew this because at one point when he asked if the fireplace tile was original, she told him, no, she had artfully chipped the ceramic herself, and Henry just ran his hands over the tile, saying "remarkable, yes, of course it's original" and immediately asked her a question about the mantelpiece. It wasn't a very good joke, so she couldn't blame him for ignoring it, but why did he go to all the effort of asking her questions if he didn't care what the answers were?

She shouldn't blame him. She had gone on British Lit tangents that bored people to tears—Jane, in particular, was prone to crying when she brought up her work during holiday visits. It was an occupational hazard. Henry's thing was Kentucky history and he taught classes in the urban planning program, and every time he mentioned that he made a joke about most of Kentucky history hardly being "urban" planning.

When she invited Henry over, she'd been uneasy with the thought that she would have to spend an afternoon talking about spinsters. But Henry spoke more about architectural details—the features on the mantel that were unique to the period, the turret that Grace hadn't quite managed to turn into the reading nook she hoped for.

"I guess bookshelves won't work," Henry said, running his hands along the circular wall of the small turret space. "This window is gorgeous."

The turret had regular rectangular windows cut into the curved walls, but above them was a row of cut-out stained glass. The designs were abstract and quite progressive for the time, Henry assured her. Grace was surprised to hear that they were original. To her, they had more of a mid-century feel. She had taken to calling them "Mad Men Windows" in her head, and she was kind of annoyed that she'd have to stop. Although, she supposed, she could call them whatever she wanted. It was her head.

The windows, apparently were a gift from a secret admirer, and the key to the house's identity. "It's not a well-known story," said Henry. "Because it was a bit of a scandal. It would have been a much more destructive scandal if it had ever gotten out."

"The art is that controversial?"

"No, it's not the art. It's the artist. Do you see this signature?"

Grace squinted at the corner of one of the panes. There, in a section of dark red, was a faintly visible symbol Grace knew she'd seen before.

"David Tulley," said Henry proudly. "I'd know that symbol anywhere."

"Wow." Grace had heard the name when she first came to visit the Pembroke campus. David Tulley was a regional glass artist of some renown who had created the beautiful, stained glass mural in the Willow Springs Public Library. Alumni and townspeople alike were crazy about that window, and about the artist.

"I think I must be the first person to recognize the windows' creator here. You didn't notice it, did you?" Henry asked. When Grace shook her head, he continued. "I didn't think so. And I can't imagine how it happened, but somehow the realtor and the appraiser must have missed it as well. Otherwise the house would have been way out of your price range. No offense."

Grace shrugged. It was no secret, especially to a fellow professor, that they weren't exactly rolling in dough.

"This is indicative of his early work. I reckon this was done well before he refined his style enough to take on a huge project like the library window." Grace smiled. She hadn't noticed it before, but when he got excited, his language was a combination of highbrow and Appalachian.

"But why is it a scandal?" she asked. "Why would he keep it secret that he did work on a house for one of the prominent citizens of Willow Springs?"

"That, I had to dig for," he said, putting his folder on the floor to delve through it more thoroughly. "Ah, here it is." He held up a photocopy of what looked like a diary entry. "I noticed this when I was looking at some of Ree Summers's diaries. Look at this." He pointed to a spot on the page, then read it out loud to Grace. "Met DT today; acted, as always, as perfectly indifferent friends. Approved his drawings for the windows; how could I not? They are gorgeous. Upon leaving, he handed me a note, and I blush to even recall its contents: 'The windows are designed to perfectly reflect light on the most gorgeous features of your naked skin.' Of course, I burned it immediately. Probably shouldn't have transcribed it here, but I can't resist. There is little about DT that I can."

Henry was a little flushed after reading the note, and Grace didn't blame him. She thought the windows were pretty but had no idea they had such a steamy past. She also felt bad for Ree Summers. How terrible to try to gain one's eternal rest, only to have people like Henry—and Grace—always digging into one's private papers. She didn't blame Cassandra Austen one bit for burning her sister Jane's letters. Grace would give her right arm to read them, but she didn't blame Cassandra for honoring her sister's wishes.

And now here she was, prying into another woman's private past. So what if Ree Summers had a fling before she was married? She realized she had the benefit of benevolent hindsight, but did the affair really matter anymore?

"That's pretty steamy," Grace said, trying to figure out how best to address Henry's prudishness when it came to unmarried women having affairs.

"Yes, especially since David was married."

"Oh," said Grace. That put a slightly different spin on things.

"To Ree Summers's sister."

"Oh!" Love was nothing but trouble. Grace found more evidence every day.

"It was an unhappy marriage, by all accounts. Virginia Summers Tulley was considered to have married beneath her station when she took up with David, who was promising, but poor. What must have started as a love match was soured by the disapproval of her family and financial struggles."

"So he took up with the little sister?"

"Who knows how it happened?" Henry said, gazing up at the stained glass. "The three of them often spent time together, and as Virginia had children, David and Ree were left on their own. It seems as if it just happened."

Grace was all too familiar with that feeling. That, in fact, was how Lou had described falling in love with her. While he was still married.

"Poor Ree."

"Well, the story does have a happy ending for her. She fell in love with a man who took her away from Willow Springs before any scandal could come out. And it seems her marriage was a happy one. She raised three boys and a girl in the Pacific Northwest. She was active in women's suffrage, and was a great patron of the arts."

Grace snorted. Then regretted it. That wasn't fair. She didn't know this woman. People did stupid things for love.

"She never came back here, though. And she seems to have lost contact with her sister."

"What happened to Virginia?"

Henry shrugged. "Nothing. David's career skyrocketed, and she was known for managing his affairs. He often cited her as being his muse. Of course, given this information"—he brandished the diary page—"I might call that into question."

"Huh. Do you think you'll pursue that?" She didn't like the idea. On the one hand, even this little bit of information made her curious. But on the other, she wanted Henry to let the dead rest.

So she was relieved when he said, "I think David Tulley's art speaks for itself. I'm not sure if it matters who the muse was. Well, not to me, anyway. I'm more interested in the house. Thank you for showing me around."

She tightened her ponytail, which was threatening to spill, damply, all over her shoulders. "No problem. But . . . just to be clear. This *is* the Spinster House?" She wanted him to say no. She loved old houses, and the stories that came with them, but this was a little much.

"The windows confirm it, I'm afraid. Sorry." He gave her a comforting pat on her shoulder. "But if it's any consolation, I think the legend is wrong."

"So it's not the Spinster House?" She hoped she didn't sound as desperate as she was certain she did.

He laughed. "The legend is partly true. This house has been sold exclusively to single women since the first woman bought it from Ree Summers. A quick dig through the public records proves that."

"Great."

"But I've been working on a different theory." He leaned forward conspiratorially. Grace could smell the breath mint on him. "If you pair up the property records with marriage records—"

"Just another quick dig?"

"Right. It seems that this house inevitably goes on the market when the woman who owns it gets married. And the owner of the house *always* gets married."

If Henry hadn't still been standing in front of her, Grace would have sworn the floor fell out from underneath her. Married? She didn't want to get married. Suddenly she wished there was a chair in this turret.

Henry gave her a teasing smile. "I can see by your nauseous look that that idea does not appeal to you?"

Grace did her best to laugh back. "I just don't want to lose this house, that's all." And that was true, too. There had to be a finite number of things that would fall apart on her. Surely soon she would be on top of the repairs, and could do as she planned—to live in this house forever, to host dinner parties for her seminar students, to write books and rock on the porch and get fabulous silver hair and wrinkles, and soak her aching, arthritic bones in the claw-foot tub.

"And you won't, as long as you don't get married." He took a step forward. "Unless, of course, you marry someone interested in old houses."

Mr. Bingley slunk into the turret and hissed at Henry.

"Mr. Bingley!" she chided, and scooped him up. "Sorry, he's never done that before."

Henry took a step out of the turret into her office. "That's okay, I'm not a big cat guy. Allergic. Cute name, though."

She rubbed behind Mr. Bingley's ears. "Thanks. He really is a wonderful cat, but if you're allergic . . ." Henry was eyeing the cat nervously, and Mr. Bingley was growling softly, so Grace put him down. He scampered down the hall.

Henry sneezed.

"Wow," she said, her eyes wide with alarm at Henry's red eyes. "You really are allergic. Come on, let's get you downstairs."

But downstairs didn't help. Despite her regular vacuuming— Mr. Bingley had a lot of black hair, and he liked to leave it on every available surface—the house was, apparently, not dander-free enough for Henry.

"I'm so sorry," Grace said, plying him with tissues.

"It's never come on this fast before," he said with a wheeze. "I was fine until we went upstairs. I think—" he coughed, "I think I should go."

"Okay, yes. Here—" She handed him the box of tissues. "Sorry again. And thank you for bringing that information by. It was really interesting."

Henry took a deep breath as soon as she opened the door. "I'm glad. This house has an amazing history. I'm glad someone is finally living here who appreciates it."

He was gone before she could ask what he meant.

Chapter 15

Will was right; Jake hadn't seen his dad in a while. And he was riding high from his night with Grace, so he figured now was as good a time as any. Of course, Don Burdette had the unique ability to bring Jake down. But then, until last night, so did Grace. Maybe this was his weekend to shake up all of his relationships.

Not that he had a relationship with Grace. She had made that clear, and he was fine with it. He liked sex, especially the kind that came with no strings. If she meant what she said, and he was pretty sure she did, they could have a great time together. If last night was any indication, they definitely would. He'd thought she was uptight, that she would insist on under-the-covers, lights-off sex.

Boy, was he wrong. She'd pounced on him, and it was all he could do to keep up. And that underwear. Just thinking that she'd been in the woods, changing out of her wet bathing suit into that cute bra and panty set made his jeans suddenly feel a little uncomfortable. She had said something about it being casual underwear. Once he got beyond the fact that there was such a thing as casual underwear, he started to think about what would constitute un-casual underwear. What would that look like? On Grace?

If he kept Grace on his mind, he was going to have to start wearing bigger jeans.

He wondered if he should call her later. She probably had school stuff to do. Did she even have classes on Mondays? Did she have to go to work even if she didn't have class? He realized he had no idea what a professor's workload was like. Maybe it was like his, relatively flexible, but when it had to get done, it had to get done. That might be nice, if she had some afternoons off. He could stop by, see if she had anything that needed fixing, maybe hang out and see what kind of underwear she was wearing.

Should he call first? Or just swing by on his way back from his dad's? Or should he stop being such a girl about it and just see what happens? Maybe she would call him. He usually didn't like it when a woman pursued him—he was, as Mary Beth said, kind of a caveman like that. But he wouldn't mind if Grace called. She seemed to know what she wanted out of a relationship, which was not a relationship at all, so it would be kind of nice to know that she was thinking about him. That she wanted him.

He checked his phone. No messages. Well, it had only been a few hours. She'd call him. And if she didn't, he would call her.

And then he'd go home and try to find where he'd left his balls.

Jake tried his best to put Grace out of his mind as he pulled into his dad's shop. As usual, the Burdette Auto Body yard was clear of debris and parts and the usual crap lying around a mechanic shop. He went in through the bays, but no one was there—no surprise, it was a Sunday. He stuck his head into the spotless office and found his dad sitting at the desk, giving a mean look to the computer screen.

Don Burdette looked the same as ever—too-long gray hair slicked back, his tanned face a little rough and wrinkled from never wearing sunscreen. And perched on his nose was a pair of dark-framed glasses.

They suited him, in a strange way. Jake had never seen his dad with glasses before, and he was glad that after years of squinting over paperbacks, Don finally admitted that his eyesight might not be exactly perfect.

"Hey, Pop."

Don jumped and yanked the glasses off his face and down onto his lap.

"Hey, son. How are you?"

"Great. Are those your glasses?"

Don pulled them sheepishly from under the desk. "Yeah. Just got 'em. For the computer, mostly. And for reading."

"Good."

"I thought it would make using this damn thing a little easier."
He waved at the computer.

"Is it working?"

"Nah. Now I *see* all the ways it's screwing up."

Don was definitely a slow adopter when it came to technology.
He did okay with the computers in cars—there wasn't much about a
car Don couldn't fix, even without technological training. He had a
knack for understanding how a machine worked, and had been able
to incorporate computers into his thinking pretty easily. He still preferred old cars, which was good since most of his customers had
old cars—the ones with new cars tended to go to their dealership.
But Don was much slower to adopt a computerized billing system.
Jake remembered coming here as a kid and being fascinated by the
pads of carbon receipt paper. He loved that he could draw a rocket
once, and he would come out with two more underneath. Don
wouldn't have updated at all if Marilyn hadn't insisted. She thought
he was going to lose business if he didn't step it up.

Don sighed and tossed his glasses on top of the keyboard.
"How's your mom?" They'd been divorced for ten years and Jake
knew they saw each other at least once a week, but Don always
asked about her.

"She's fine."

"And Will? He still treating her good?" Marilyn and Will had
been married for five years, and Don saw him as often as he saw
Marilyn. But he always asked Jake if he was treating Marilyn well.
Mary Beth said he asked her the same thing.

"Will is fine, and he's still treating her like she walks on water."

"Good," Don said gruffly. "Good."

Jake shook his head. He had no idea what went through that
man's head.

"So what brings you here on a fine Sunday afternoon? Checking
up on your old man?"

"Maybe," Jake said with a shrug.

"Your mother put you up to it?"

"Will did. But I'm sure Mom put the bug in his ear," he added
quickly.

Don just grunted.

Jake rocked back on his heels. This was productive. As always.

"What's that grin for?"

Jake was not aware that he was grinning. "Nothing."

"I hear you're seeing that professor."

Jesus, word spread fast in this town. It had been less than twenty-four hours. And he wasn't exactly seeing her. Just having a non-relationship with her. Which was probably a type of relationship anyway . . .

"Fran Wallace was in yesterday to get her oil changed, finally. She was chomping at the bit to tell me you've been hanging around. That might have been the only reason she came in."

Great. If Mrs. Wallace knew, everyone in town knew. If she wasn't a little old lady with a cute little dog, Jake thought he might wring her neck.

"It's good, though. She was overdue," said Don.

"Huh?"

"For an oil change. You got it bad, huh?"

Jake shook his head. "No, we're just friends. And her name is Grace."

"Then why did Fran tell me you were all over each other in her front yard?"

The front yard? Oh, the front yard. "That wasn't what it looked like. It's kind of funny, actually. She got stuck on her roof and she's afraid of heights, so I had to talk her down—"

"Just watch out for her," Don interrupted.

"What do you mean?" Was Mrs. Wallace threatening him? Through his dad?

"Watch out for that professor, that's all. She's not your type."

"Dad, you've never even met her."

"Don't have to. Smart women like that don't go for guys like us."

"Guys like us?"

"Guys who work with their hands. Guys with dirt under their fingernails."

"Dad—"

"You're a good-looking guy, Jake, but trust me, she's not in it for the long haul. You'll have some fun, and then she'll think she's too good for you, and you'll be out." Don brushed past his son and practically stomped into the shop.

Jake was momentarily distracted by the Ford Taurus Don stopped in front of. "Is that Mrs. Flanagan's car?"

When Don nodded, Jake said, "I can't believe that thing is still running." Jake remembered Mrs. Flanagan carting him and Missy and Kyle and usually a bunch of other kids around in that station wagon. Missy gave Jake his first kiss in the way-back. They were about seven years old.

"Bertie doesn't want to buy another car. Can't blame her. It doesn't have that many miles on it, considering."

"It's got to cost more to fix it at this point," Jake said, admiring the familiarly shoddy touch-up paint job on the hood.

Don shrugged and pulled a wrench out of his back pocket. He opened the station wagon door and started the engine, cocking his head toward the steering wheel as if listening for something. Then he shook his head—must have heard something he didn't like—and turned off the engine. Don stepped around Jake and opened the hood.

It was strange. Don had earned his reputation as a fair and reasonably priced mechanic. If he thought it wasn't worth your money to fix a car, he'd tell you. Unless. "Unless you're not charging her."

Don concentrated very hard on all those parts underneath the hood.

"Dad?"

"What does it matter to you who I charge or don't charge?"

"Mom says she can't see how you pay your bills if—"

This got Don out from under the hood. He stepped up to Jake, pointing the wrench in his face. "Your mother worries too much about me. I live simply, Jake. I don't need a lotta crap to be happy. Just a roof over my head, something to get my hands dirty, and an occasional home-cooked meal. So you tell your mother I'm doing just fine."

Don backed off, but he kept his eyes on Jake, daring him to argue.

Jake raised his hands in mock-surrender. If his dad's face hadn't been so serious, he would have laughed. Nothing got under Don's skin more than hearing how much his ex-wife worried about him.

But something in what Don had said about the way he lived stuck with Jake. "Dad, are you still going to Mom's for Sunday dinner?"

Don turned his attention back to the car, but he grunted in what Jake assumed was a "yes."

"So that's your home-cooked meal for the week? That and whatever leftovers they send you home with?"

Don fingered a wire in the engine.

"Or is someone else cooking for you?"

Don tightened a bolt.

"Oh, my—Dad, are you sleeping with Bertie Flanagan?"

That got Don out from under the hood and in Jake's face again.

"You watch your tone, son."

Jake did his best to wipe the smile off his face.

"Not that it's any of your business," Don said, "but Bertie and I have . . . an arrangement. She's been lonely since Frank died, and with Missy out of the house, she misses cooking for people, she said. I told her to get a job at a restaurant, but I guess she don't want anyone bossin' her around. So she cooks for me, I fix her car."

Jake had a million more teasing questions to ask his father, but Don was blushing so deeply that Jake didn't want to upset his blood pressure. So he left him alone. Mostly.

"Does Mom know?"

"No, and it's even less her business than it is yours. Nobody knows. This is just between me and Bertie, and I aim to keep it that way. So don't go flapping your jaw to anyone, Missy especially."

"Missy doesn't know?"

"No. Bertie thinks it'll upset her. Missy doesn't think Bertie should ever move on from Frank, even though it's been several years."

"But you didn't think your son would get upset?"

"Are you upset?" When Jake shook his head, Don continued. "Didn't think so. It's a different situation. Frank died; your mother just had enough of me."

And here we go, thought Jake. The part where Don started taking digs at Marilyn, then Jake blew up and stormed out and didn't see his father for a few weeks. Right on schedule.

"I know, I know," said Don, pre-empting the blow-up with raised hands. "I don't blame her. I was a real jerk to her."

"That's one word for it." Another word was cheater.

"I wasn't good enough for her, Jake. And I knew that when I married her, but I believed her when she said it wasn't true. Then she got that job at the college, made all those smart friends, and who'd she come home to but a guy like me who can't ever get his hands clean?"

"So, what, now you're saying all the drinking and the cheating, that was just self-sabotage? There were other ways to destroy your life, Dad, without dragging us down with you."

Jake could see that Don wanted to give in to the anger in his eyes, to give in to the urge to have the row that both of them seemed to need.

Instead, Don said, "Just be careful with that professor, that's all."

Don turned back to Mrs. Flanagan's engine. It wasn't exactly the door-slamming blow-up Jake was used to, but he knew he was dismissed all the same.

Jake shook his head. He wasn't going to fix his father, and he sure as hell wasn't going to try to fix the weird relationship between his parents. Besides, it seemed that Don was finally moving on. With Bertie Flanagan. She was good-looking, Jake supposed, although he had a hard time thinking of her as anything other than Missy's mother. Jake's fingers were itching to dial Missy's number, but he had promised his dad, and besides, that wasn't fair to Missy, to find out through the rumor mill. Although with Mrs. Wallace coming into the shop, she'd find out soon enough.

But Jake had to tell someone. He thought of Grace. She didn't know his dad or Mrs. Flanagan, and he was pretty sure he could count on her to keep it to herself around Missy. He'd have to explain the whole back story so she got why it was so strange, but he had a feeling Grace would understand.

He called Grace and left a message when her voice mail picked up. Then he swung by her house on the way home, but her bike wasn't on the porch and no one answered when he knocked, though Mr. Bingley meowed at him from the living room window. Jake was starting to get mad when he got back into his truck. He tried to shake it off. She's not ignoring you, he told himself. It's been, like, six hours since you saw her. Give it a rest. She'll call you when she gets home, then you can tell her your dumb story and maybe she'll invite you over again.

Jake grumbled as he backed out of her driveway. It was just the amazing sex, rattling his brain. She'd call when she got home.

* * *

Grace waited three days to call Jake back.

She didn't do it on purpose, not really. When she got his message on Sunday night, her immediate reaction was to call him back, see if he might like to come over. But that would be too much too soon, so she waited. She realized she might be playing games, but she justified the delay by telling herself that she was just setting boundaries, establishing that their relationship, such as it was, would not be a see-each-other-every-day kind of thing. It would be . . . casual.

Not that she didn't think about him those days that she didn't call. But she was busy. Genuinely busy, and Jake on the brain did not help. Reading student journal entries for her intro class took enough concentration, so it didn't help that every time someone split an infinitive, her mind would wander. To Jake. And his hands. And his shoulders. And his abs.

And his smile.

That was what did her in. It was Wednesday and she was working from her home office. (Which featured wallpaper hung by Jake . . . she tried not to think about that.) She loved working here in the afternoon. The sun filtered through the bamboo blinds—they didn't really go with the room, but they were leftover from the previous owner and Grace was kind of renovated-out—creating stripes and swirls on the wood floor. Mr. Bingley loved it too. He spent so much time in the sunny spot in the turret that she put a throw pillow in there for him. It was the best she could do, decoration-wise. And she couldn't blame Mr. Bingley for lounging there. Just last week, she was having trouble focusing on an abstract for an article she was finishing up, so she just lay down on the floor and let the sun soak into her bones. It was nice. And it worked, although she had a hard time getting out of the sun to go back to writing. She had wanted to lie there all day, basking and stretching and napping on her floor, with occasional interruptions from Mr. Bingley, who joined her in the sun.

She was glad Jake didn't have a key. She didn't need him walking in on that.

And there he was again. She looked at the pile of journals—almost halfway done. If she called Jake, she could get her fix and then concentrate. Or maybe they could schedule something for later that would act as an incentive to get things done.

And now she was the kind of woman who lay on the floor with her cat and scheduled her love life.

Not love. Her like life.

Her sex life.

Before she could talk herself out of it—and she was trying—she had dialed Jake's number. He picked up with a distracted "Hello?"

"Jake? Are you driving?"

She heard him curse under his breath. Well, not quite under his breath. She could tell she was on speakerphone. "Hey, Grace."

"Sorry, do you want to call me later?"

"No, it's fine."

She paused, trying to puzzle out his tone. "Jake, are you mad at me?"

He sighed. "No. I'm annoyed with myself."

"Why?" It was nice to hear Jake got on his own nerves sometimes, too.

"I promised myself I wouldn't pick up when you called."

"Oh." She nervously tapped her pen on the pile of unread journals. She had waited too long. Ugh, this *was* a game. "Do you want me to hang up?"

"No."

"Do you want to hang up on me?"

He laughed. Grace let out a breath. "What's up?"

"Nothing," she said, tapping away at the infinitive-splitting undergraduate homework. "Just grading papers."

"Already? Isn't it, like, the second week of school?"

Grace shrugged, which, of course, Jake did not see. "Not big papers, just reading journals. Mostly to make sure they do the reading."

"Do they?"

"Most of them. I can usually tell if they just read the plot summary. Or if they're really in tune with the themes, especially early in the book. That's usually a sign that they got their ideas somewhere else."

"Grace Williams, Literature Detective."

She laughed. "Kind of. Actually, that's pretty good motivation to keep working."

"Is that why you called? For motivation?"

"No, I just . . ." Why was she suddenly shy? The man had seen her naked, for heaven's sake. And not just *seen* her naked. They, like, did stuff.

"Grace?"

"Just wanted to see if you wanted to hang out. Maybe come over and watch a movie. I'm making frozen pizza for dinner."

"Sounds tempting," he said, sarcastically. "The pizza, I mean. I mean the pizza doesn't sound tempting, but the hanging out does." He made a short, dismissive sound. Was he shy, too?

"Great, I have some more grading to finish up—"

"Well, I don't know if I can. I'm on my way back from a job."

Oh, a job. That was good. She knew he did something in construction, but Grace hadn't heard of him working since she'd met him. It was good for him to have a job.

"Okay, well . . ."

"I have to see what time it is when I get back."

"Okay."

"I just don't know right now."

"Okay, Jake. It's fine. Just, you know, if you can. No big deal."

"Okay. See you later. You know, if I don't see you tonight."

"Which is also later," she reminded him.

"Yeah. So see you later no matter what."

She laughed softly and said good-bye. She didn't really want to hang out with him. She had work to do, and she didn't want to start something with Jake. She had a feeling he'd be trouble, and not just in the stuff-falls-apart-when-he's-around way. Because stuff fell apart when he wasn't around. More in a he'll-break-your-heart kind of way. But that was fine, because she wasn't about to give her heart. Not to Jake, not to anyone.

Chapter 16

Jake knocked on her door just after sunset. He'd gotten home, taken a shower, and was going to see if there was a game on. Then Mary Beth came up and told him Todd was making eggplant parm if he wanted some, which he did, but sitting down to dinner with his sister and her husband when he'd told Grace that he might come over didn't seem very nice. Of course, she'd waited three days to call him, which also wasn't very nice. But as his mother often reminded him, two wrongs didn't make a right. So he skipped dinner, forgoing the to-go box offer from Todd because he didn't want them to ask questions when he asked for two helpings, and because he was annoyed that Grace had waited so long to call, so she didn't deserve Todd's eggplant parm. Which meant he wouldn't get any either, but Jake was pretty sure there'd be enough left over for breakfast tomorrow.

Logic firmly in place and pizza box in hand, he knocked on Grace's door. She pulled the curtain aside, then opened the door with a surprised look on her face.

"Jake! And pizza!"

She was wearing the little pink dress that she'd worn to the Fourth of July barbecue, the one that was just a bit too short. Her feet were bare and her face looked freshly scrubbed. She had her hair pulled back in that messy ponytail of hers. It was barely dark and she looked like she was ready for bed.

Jake congratulated himself on his timing.

"Better than frozen," he said, and let her take the box from him as he stepped inside.

"Have a seat," she said, indicating the couch. She put the pizza on the coffee table and went into the kitchen. Jake followed her.

She was reaching up in the cabinet to get plates as he swung through the door. Stretched up like that, he could see the muscles in her calves and her dress was inching up even higher and he had never had less of a taste for Todd's eggplant parm.

"Let me," he said, coming up behind her. And if he crowded her a little so that when she came down off her toes her back ended up flush against his front, well, he was just trying to be a gentleman. And if he leaned in to nuzzle her neck, it was just to let her know that he wasn't mad at her anymore for not calling.

"You smell good," he said, because she did. Like vanilla. Like dessert.

"I just took a bath," she said, tilting her head to the side so he could find out whether she tasted as good as she smelled. The thought of her in that big claw-foot tub, wearing nothing but bubble bath, made him forgive her even more for not calling.

"Jake," she whispered as his lips trailed over her neck. He didn't know if that meant to stop or to keep going, but she moved easily when he turned her around so they were front-to-front, and she opened her mouth for him when he kissed her, and she let out a *whoosh* of breath when he wrapped his arms tight around her waist. Then she pulled back, just a fraction, just enough that their lips were separated, and looked into his eyes.

"Hi," he said, because he had no idea what that look meant.

"Hi," she said with a smile. He leaned in to kiss her again, and this time she kissed him back, hard, wrapping her arms around his neck and snaking her hands through his hair. He was about ready to lift her up and see how sturdy that kitchen counter was, when he heard a low growling sound.

She pulled back abruptly and immediately started that full-body blush he liked so well.

"Sorry," she said, backing up enough to put a hand on her stomach. "I haven't eaten since breakfast. Got sort of carried away with grading."

"Engaging stuff?"

"Hardly. But after we talked, I got into Grace Williams, Literature Detective mode, and the time kind of flew by."

He liked that he made her work easier. He didn't like that she was too hungry to make out, but there would be time for that after pizza.

He stepped back and picked up the plates while she turned the oven off and threw her unthawed pizza back into the freezer. She grabbed a roll of paper towels and followed him into the living room. He liked that she was no-nonsense about her pizza. He was, too. Although he probably wouldn't have even bothered with plates.

She shooed Mr. Bingley off the couch and sat down next to him, their thighs touching. He wanted to run his hand over her leg, lift up that little pink dress and see if she was wearing more cute underwear, but she tucked her legs up underneath her, away from him, so he turned his attention to the pizza.

"I hope pepperoni's okay."

She inhaled deeply as he opened the box, her eyes closed in pleasure. Pepperoni seemed okay.

"What are you watching?" he asked. There were a bunch of white people in long dresses talking quietly on the TV screen.

She looked up nervously from her first bite of pizza. "We can change it."

"Why? Is it porn or something?"

"No!"

"Too bad."

"It's *Pride and Prejudice*."

"Ah. Smart people porn."

"There's a TV marathon on. I couldn't resist."

"Haven't you seen it before?" He was pretty sure he'd seen it before. Mary Beth was more than a little obsessed.

"Yes, about a million times. So we can watch something else if you want to."

"No, this is good." Jake figured if they watched something that she'd already seen, she wouldn't mind if they stopped watching it. For sex.

It was a long movie. Grace had enough time to eat four pieces of pizza, which turned Jake on. Then she stretched and leaned into him, which turned him on more. He toed off his shoes and stretched out, pulling her over him.

"This is everybody's favorite part," she said, wrinkling her nose. The main guy, Mr. Darcy, had a squinty, tortured look on his face. Then he squinted some more and dove into a pretty murky-looking pond.

Grace scoffed, but she kept her eyes glued to the screen. "I can always tell that a student hasn't read the book when they talk about how Darcy dove into the lake. That absolutely did not come from Jane Austen's mind."

He rubbed a lazy circle on her lower back. "Why are we watching this movie if you hate it so much?"

She jerked her head up, practically beaning him on the chin. "I don't hate it! I think it's a wonderful adaptation of the book. It's a little too focused on the romance, but I don't know how you would translate her subtlety of narration onto film, so that's fine."

"What's your deal with romance?" he asked.

She tried to sit up all the way, but he held on to her waist. "What do you mean?"

"I mean you read those trashy paperbacks—your words," he said when she looked as if she was going to protest. "But then you're obsessed with everyone else's obsession with romance."

"Just in Jane Austen! It's an important part of the work, but—"

"And in real life. You talk about not wanting to be a spinster, but then you don't want to date—"

"Is that what you want? To date?"

Jake shook his head. "No, but I'm not obsessed with it like you are."

She pursed her lips together in a mock pout—at least he thought it was mock—and laid her head on his chest. "I just don't want it, that's all."

He continued making circles on her lower back again. "Why?"

She shrugged. He should let it go, but he wanted to know. He didn't care, not for his own sake, but he was curious. Just curious.

"Did you get your heart broken?"

She sighed and lifted her head. "Of course I did. Hasn't everyone?" Jake had, probably. He wasn't sure. Which might mean he hadn't. But he was having enough trouble fighting down a bubble of rage that was rising in his chest.

He tucked a finger under her chin and made her look at him. "Somebody hurt you?"

She shrugged him off and put her head back on his chest. "It's not the end of the world." He continued rubbing her back, hoping she would start talking.

"It was another professor. He was sort of my mentor in the English Department, but he studied the later Romantics, Keats and Shelley and all that, you know."

Jake didn't know, although he vaguely remembered reading long, painful poetry in high school.

"We used to play this game, poetry versus prose, and for every point lost, the loser had to take off an article of clothing."

"Wow," said Jake. That was so nerdy he could barely get turned on by it, even with the promise of a naked Grace at the end.

He managed to get a little turned on.

"Anyway, I really admired his work. That's how we first connected. He was older, but he was still kind of a fox. He was divorced and had teenagers, so I wasn't thrilled about the idea of an insta-family, but by then I was so turned on by his mind, I figured the rest would work itself out."

"But it didn't?"

Grace snorted. "No. He was always a little flaky with details when it came to anything but the Romantics. He forgot to enter final grades all the time, he was always misplacing his cell phone. Oh, and he wasn't divorced at all."

"What?"

"He brought his wife to the departmental holiday party. I was supposed to be in Ohio with Jane and her family, but I had to finish up a grant application, so I postponed my trip. And I figured, hey, why not surprise him at the party. Boy, was he surprised!"

"You had no idea he was still married?"

"No, because he told me they were divorced. He still talked to her all the time, but I figured it was just an amicable split. They seemed to mostly talk about the kids. He tried to convince me that they were just trying to put up a united front for the holidays. You know, for the kids."

"But you didn't buy it?"

"Oh, I bought it. I'd already forgiven him and was mentally planning our New Year's Eve together. But our department secretary had a little too much eggnog, and she pulled me aside and told me the truth."

"And you believed her?"

"She had never led me wrong before. She was the one who told me about the grant I was working on. Which I didn't get, by the way. Anyway, once I confronted Lou about it, he confessed all. So I started applying for jobs, and here I am."

"Broken-hearted?"

She lifted her head so their eyes met. "No. I was. And my pride was hurt, probably worse than my heart. But I'm over it now. I swear."

"Good," said Jake. Lying there on the couch, feeling the warmth of Grace's skin through the thin fabric of her dress, Jake felt a niggle of worry. She'd been attracted to the Married Professor's brain, that was what made her love him. Jake knew he had a lot of good qualities, but professor-level smarts wasn't one of them. Was that why she was with him? Was she slumming until her broken heart healed? Until something better came along?

But then she leaned up to kiss him, and her lips against his made him forget to consider his dad's warning, and the evidence in front of him, and when he ran his hands all the way up her back he felt that she wasn't wearing a bra and he forgot everything else and just felt Grace.

Chapter 17

Grace jerked awake at the sound of a crash. She looked around, disoriented, for what could possibly be broken this time. The first thing she noticed was Jake's warm body, face down on the bed next to her. She forgot all about her house falling down as he shifted in his sleep and the sheet slipped past his waist. Good Lord, that was a perfect back. Wide, strong shoulders, smooth muscle tapering down to a narrow waist. And that butt. His butt made her wish for poetry.

Even that stupid tattoo between his shoulder blades was sexy. She first saw it at the swimming hole, but hadn't gotten a close look at it until last night. An angry-eyed falcon was wrestling an overly muscled tiger. She hadn't known what to make of it when she first saw it. Then he told her he'd gotten it on a dare, and she knew even less what to make of it.

But it would take a lot more than an ill-advised tattoo to mar the perfection of that back.

He stirred and rolled over, which gave her the opportunity to admire the perfection of his front. But then he squinted up at her and she thought it might be impolite to stare.

"Are you staring at me?"

"No!" she lied.

He gave her that crooked grin, even sexier when it was tinged with sleepiness. "Are you ogling my naked body?"

"Don't be ridiculous."

"I'll show you ridiculous," he said, and he ripped off the sheet. She shrieked as he threw himself at her, but, well, if she had to get mauled, might as well be by a hot, naked man.

"Do you have class this morning?" he asked once she was pinned underneath him.

She shook her head.

"What are you doing awake, then?"

"Oh!" Stupid reality, she thought. "Something fell."

"What?"

"I have no idea. The noise woke me up, and then . . ."

"Then you got distracted by my physical perfection?"

She hit him on the shoulder, but only because he was right. He sat up, taking the sheet with him.

"Hmm," he said. "Now I'm feeling distracted."

"Jake!" She pushed him off her, then reached over the side of the bed for her nightgown.

"I can't believe you wore that to the Fourth of July party."

Somewhere between the couch and the bedroom last night, the truth had come out. "I told you, it was an accident!"

Jake just shook his head. "Absent-minded professor." He turned in the bed to look for his boxers. "Uh, I think I see what broke."

He turned Grace's chin toward the closet, where the bar and the clothes it had previously been holding were all in a mess on the floor.

"Oh my God! How did that even—" She didn't finish her sentence. Just stared at the pile of clothes.

"You probably hung too much on there."

"I didn't! It wasn't shaky at all!" Jake heard a muffled meow from the back of the closet, and, after a while, Mr. Bingley jumped gracefully out.

"Mr. Bingley! Are you hurt?" Grace said, lurching toward her cat.

After determining that Mr. Bingley wasn't hurt, just a little angry, and that he'd probably climbed on the bar and caused it to fall, Jake got to looking at the problem. It looked like one of the pieces holding the bar in place had come off. Easy fix.

"Do you have a hammer?" he asked Grace.

Grace nudged him aside with her hip and dug through the clothes at the bottom of her closet. Her butt squirmed adorably as she pulled open a box from underneath a pile of everything. "It's in here somewhere," came her disembodied voice from the back of the closet.

"You might want to keep your tools more handy. You know, in case you need them."

"I know you can't see my face, so you'll just have to trust that I'm giving you a withering look. Ah, here it is." She came out of the closet, triumphantly holding the smallest tool kit he'd ever seen.

It was pink.

"I need a hammer, not a nail file," he said.

"Ha ha. There's a hammer in here. And one of those screwdrivers with the head you can switch out. Although I think I broke the screwdriver."

"Why is it pink?"

She opened the tool kit and handed him a hammer that looked like it wouldn't even crack a teacup. "My sister gave it to me."

"She must know as much about tools as you do."

"It was a gag gift. My condo fees in California included a twenty-four hour maintenance man."

Of course. Why do it yourself when you can pay someone else to do it for you? But he bit his tongue, because she looked so cute and proud of that ridiculous hammer.

"Grace, this hammer isn't going to do anything."

"Why not? It's a hammer."

He took the hammer from her hand and swung down hard, just once, on the wall of the closet. The head of the hammer neatly detached from the handle.

"You broke my hammer!"

"This is not a hammer, Grace. This would barely be good for opening a piñata. And now it's not good for anything."

"Hold on. I think I have some superglue in here."

He put his hand on her hip to stop her from going back into the mess of the closet. "Glue is not going to help. I have some tools in my truck. You need a man hammer for this job."

"This hammer is perfectly fine! At least it was until you went all caveman on it."

"This is a girl hammer. It's not even a woman hammer. This is, like, a kid's hammer. I'm telling you, you need a man hammer."

"Can you stop saying 'man hammer' please?"

"Why?"

"It's weird. And it's degrading to women. Tools don't have to be gendered."

He shook his head.

"I know it's dumb that my hammer is pink," she said, "but when you say it's a crappy hammer and then associate it with a woman, that implies that women are bad at fixing things."

"You can't fix things, you said so yourself."

"Yes, but that's not because I'm a woman. My incompetence is completely gender-neutral."

"Fine. I'm going out to the truck to get my gender-neutral hammer, and then I'm going to fix this bar, not because I'm a man, but because I am just a generally superior human being."

"Thank you," she said with a curtsy. So he smacked her on the rear, threw on his clothes and went out to his truck to get his tools. Then he came in, fixed her closet, and taught her all about the gender dichotomy.

The house liked where this was going. Banter was definitely a good thing. And Grace was starting to learn that she liked Jake, and that she needed him. Shouldn't take too much more.

Chapter 18

Grace's first semester at Pembroke passed much more quickly than she ever would have imagined. She only had to fail one freshman who didn't show up for class and did not respond to offers of extra credit assignments. The angry phone call from his parents had been brief, and the follow-up with her dean was just a formality. Her evaluations from her students were pretty good, and she got a few peppers on a website that rated how hot your professors were. That last honor was dubious, at best. Jake had laughed his head off when he heard.

She couldn't believe how easy things were with Jake. They saw each other a few times a week, whenever they were free. There was no set plan, no hurt feelings if one of them wasn't available, and lots and lots of great sex when they were. He had to go out of town for a job for most of October, but he was back in time to persuade her to dress up as a sexy professor for Missy and Kyle's Halloween party. She agreed on the condition that he dress up as a sexy construction worker. He ended up looking like one of the Village People—seventies moustache and all—but they had a great time at the party.

That was the only time they really went out as a "couple." Because they weren't a couple. Marilyn invited Grace to spend Thanksgiving with them, but she ended up going up to Jane's instead. Priya was delighted to see her Auntie Grace, which made up for the curry tofurkey Jane's mother-in-law made for dinner. She was preparing to go back again for Christmas. She had taken the bus up for Thanksgiving, but this time she had too many presents (mostly for Priya), so Jane agreed to drive down and get her. As long as Grace could guarantee her some time with Handsome Jake.

Grace didn't like the idea—having her sister hang out with Jake felt too much like he was a boyfriend. But Jane insisted, and Jake didn't mind.

They both wanted her to get a Christmas tree, which she thought was ridiculous since she wouldn't be home on Christmas Day, but Jake insisted and Jane didn't mind, so she went along with it. Of course they had to chop their own, so they headed to a tree farm on the outskirts of Willow Springs.

"The way that man swings an ax, it's just not right," Jane said as Jake made the first few strokes to the trunk of their chosen tree.

"I hadn't noticed," Grace said. "God, I forgot how cold winter is." She shivered under her down coat, sweater, and long johns.

"California girl," Jane teased. "Another few winters, you'll toughen up."

"I don't know. Are my lips blue?"

"Why don't you ask Jake?"

"Grow up," said Grace, but she was smiling when she said it.

"Grace, come on," Jake called. "Take the last swing."

"Go on, Gracie. Knock that sucker down!" Jane chimed in.

Grace shook her head and stomped her feet to get feeling back into them, then she took the ax from Jake. "What do I do? Just hit it?"

"Yeah. With the sharp edge."

She stuck her tongue out at him, moved a step back and took a swing.

"Try to hit the part that's already been cut," Jake suggested mildly.

"I tried! This is stupid, you do it." She shoved the ax at him and he jumped back.

"Okay, as much as I want to take sharp objects out of your possession, I really think you should do it. Come on." He pulled her toward him—ax pointing downward—and turned her so their arms lined up. Then he wrapped his hands around hers and, together, they raised the ax.

"Ready?" he whispered in her ear. She nodded, and he swung even higher and then *whap* right into the tree. It didn't move, so

Jake gave the trunk a gentle push. It fell into the frozen ground with a *thump*.

They tied the tree into the bed of his truck (well, Jake tied it while Grace and Jane stomped their frozen feet) and when they got to Grace's house, she watched Jake maneuver the tree into the stand in the living room.

"He just moved that whole tree by himself," Jane whispered to Grace from the kitchen doorway.

Grace looked at her sister. "You're drooling. And you're married."

"I know, I know. But our tree is only as tall as Priya, so it's not as much fun to watch Dev with it."

"Hot chocolate?" Jake asked, brushing tree dirt all over her living room floor.

He had done a lot of work, so she kept her mouth shut about the mess. She nodded and turned the kettle on.

"Be right back," he said, then ran out the front door.

"Gah," said Jane. "I don't know how you do it."

"Do what?" Grace asked.

"Keep your hands off that guy for more than three seconds."

"You realize you sound like an old perv?"

"I don't care, look at him!"

Grace laughed and pulled mugs down from the cabinet. She rubbed her hands up and down her arms. She was still freezing.

"Seriously, Grace. How are you not falling in love with him? He's strong, he's hot, he just chopped down a Christmas tree for you and he built a fire. I can't believe that even you are immune to those charms."

Grace chook her head. "I'm not immune. I just don't do that."

"That's not how it works, Grace. You can't just *not* fall in love with someone you so clearly love."

"I don't love him, Jane. I like him. A lot. He's one of my best friends here. And, yes, I have a different relationship with him than I do with my other friends."

"A sex relationship," snorted Jane.

"Great, very mature. Yes, a sex relationship. But that's it. We're friends, and we have great sex. Amazing sex. But I don't love him, Jane."

Jane smacked her on the arm and Grace was just about to give her an older sister what-was-that-for look, but when she turned around, she saw Jake standing there. He was holding an old shoebox with a red bow stuck to it. She couldn't read the look on his face. He was smiling, but it wasn't that sexy, sideways smile that made her nuts. He just looked sort of blank. Blank and smiling.

"Jake—" She started to apologize, but what for? They both knew what their arrangement was.

"Here," he said, handing her the shoebox.

"What is it?" she asked.

"Open it and find out, dummy," said Jane, trying to cut some of the tension by throwing Grace under the bus.

Grace opened the box and pulled back the tissue. Inside was a set of vintage glass ornaments. She picked one up. It was a scene of a church surrounded by trees. The roof and the trees were painted bright red and green, and the stars were dotted with gold glitter. There were about half a dozen hand-painted bucolic scenes in the box.

"Wow," she whispered.

Jake looked like he was blushing. "I just thought, since you didn't have a tree before, that you probably didn't have any ornaments. And I thought you would like these. They're kind of old and falling apart."

Grace laughed. "That's my style. Thank you, Jake. These are amazing. I feel terrible, I don't have anything for you."

Jake waved his hand. "This isn't really a Christmas present. It's just—I just saw them and I thought you would like them, that's all."

"I do. They're gorgeous." She stepped over and kissed him on the cheek. She really wanted to kiss him on the mouth, but she was still holding the box of ornaments and she didn't want to drop them. His kisses had a tendency to make her lose essential motor skills.

He smiled at her. "I'm glad. Now make me a hot chocolate, woman." He smacked her on the rear and stalked out to the living room.

Jane didn't say anything to Grace, just raised her eyebrows and poured boiling water into the hot chocolate. Grace told her to shut up anyway.

Jake could have done without walking in on Grace telling her sister that she didn't love him. He knew she didn't. He didn't want her to. He didn't love her. That was why their relationship worked so well. Strictly casual.

But he still didn't like to hear it.

At least she liked the ornaments. He'd worried they might be stupid. They were nice, but they were cheap, just a few bucks at the mission charity store. But Grace liked vintage stuff, and the box said "Made in England," so he figured, why not? And all night he caught her sneaking glances at the ornaments where they hung on the tree. Either that or she hated them and couldn't stop looking at them because they grossed her out. But every time she looked away, she had kind of a wistful look in her eye.

She liked them all right.

So after Jane went to bed, making a point of telling them that she would be asleep as soon as her head hit the pillow at the other end of the house, Jake took Grace's freezing hands in his and led her upstairs. He unwrapped her and, quietly, warmed her up.

Things felt different. The house had thought this was a done deal, but tonight things had changed. It felt . . . sad. Like things weren't going to work out as planned. Maybe it was just a misunderstanding. Grace and Jake argued all the time. But this wasn't a normal fight. This was Grace willfully ignoring what was in front of her face. This was Grace picking and choosing among the parts of Jake that he offered, instead of enthusiastically embracing all of him.

This was not the road to happily ever after.

Chapter 19

Grace didn't come back to Willow Springs until just before classes were ready to start. She had planned to return home right after the holidays, but Priya's adorableness made it difficult for her to leave. And then she found out her conference paper had been accepted, so she spent time refining her talk and doing more research at the state university library, which was much larger than Pembroke's. She hoped to turn this paper into another book, and this time she was aiming at the university presses.

And she read *Pride and Prejudice* about sixteen more times. Her new work was focusing on *P&P* in particular, and the way family relationships were presented. She knew Austen revealed subtle personality traits by the way her characters addressed each other and referred to each other; she just had to identify them all, and then categorize them. She was toying with clever titles, but all she could come up with was "Miss Jane If You're Nasty" and that had absolutely nothing to do with anything.

She was getting a lot of work done in Ohio with Jane, so she asked Helen to continue feeding Mr. Bingley, and stayed until the middle of January.

She knew she was being a coward. She had talked to Jake on the phone, a little, and he had a knack for sending her texts at the most inappropriate times. (Because it was obviously his fault that she forgot to turn off the phone when she went into the university library reading room.)

When she got back into town, she ran into Mary Beth at the public library, where Grace was shamefully returning some very overdue books. Mary Beth told her that Jake had taken a job in Florida for a month. Grace figured that was that—she and Jake had fizzled out. She was a little bummed, but it wasn't the end of the world. Which was just how she wanted it.

Meanwhile, Henry had decided to go forward with his paper on the Spinster House. He checked with her first, which she appreciated, but she didn't really feel it would be right to stop his scholarly endeavors. He promised not to include any current pictures of the house, except for close-ups of the Tulley glass in the turret. She wanted to ask him to be kind to Ree Summers, but that didn't seem fair either.

He had been over a few times, consulting with Grace on details, sharing new discoveries with her, and taking lots of pictures of the windows. Most of his discoveries didn't mean much to her—someone was really someone else's aunt, but that person had been dead for a hundred years, so it had little bearing on her current situation. They did discover that he was not as allergic to Mr. Bingley as he seemed after that first visit. The second time he came over, he asked her to put the cat upstairs. Grace didn't like the idea, but she did it anyway, closing Mr. Bingley in her bedroom with a promise of a fresh can of tuna once Henry was gone. But Mr. Bingley got out and joined them in the living room. Grace really thought Henry overreacted—was it necessary to scream and hide behind the couch?—but it worked out okay in the end. No sneezing, no red eyes, no asthma attacks. Well, Mr. Bingley seemed permanently prejudiced against Henry—she'd never heard the cat hiss before—but other than that, things were working out.

Henry even asked her out to dinner a few times, but Grace always turned him down politely. She just didn't feel like dating. Henry was nice enough. He was handsome, and they had a lot in common. Helen said she was being an idiot, and that if she was going to let someone like Jake Burdette fizzle through her fingers, why not go out with Henry?

"On second thought, if you're going to let someone like Jake

Burdette fizzle through your fingers, maybe you don't deserve Henry. You can't have all of them, Grace."

But she didn't want Henry. She didn't want Jake either, she was pretty sure. She just wanted to keep her head down and do her work. She didn't need a relationship, and she didn't need everyone in town telling her she did.

At least her house was leaving her alone. Helen didn't mention anything breaking over the holidays, and when Grace came back, there were no floods or missing walls or holes in the floor. So, even if he came back, she wouldn't have to see Jake.

Good, she thought. That was what she wanted.

One of the things the house had learned in all of its years was that people believed that absence made the heart grow fonder. The house couldn't get a good read on the level of Grace's heart's fondness, but Jake was definitely absent. Even when the house did try to create a disturbance, Jake did not come to fix it. The other one, Henry, was around quite a bit. The house was okay with that because more Henry might make Grace realize what she was missing with Jake, or might make Jake jealous enough to realize what he was missing. It wasn't working yet, but there was still time.

Chapter 20

Jake stayed out of Willow Springs until winter was good and done. Spending the winter in Florida was one of his smarter ideas. A buddy had bought a "handyman special" outside of Miami and hired Jake to take charge of the renovation. Jake didn't have his contractor's license in Florida, so he was more of a project manager, which was fine. It turned out to be a much bigger job than they had planned—black mold, asbestos in the basement. Nothing he hadn't seen before. Well, the alligator in the decrepit swimming pool was new, but now Jake had the name of a wildlife removal company in Florida, so that was good.

He could have stayed down in Florida forever, although urban living was not his style. Nor were alligators. But he had a few contacts down there, and everyone was satisfied when the job was done, even if they persisted in calling him "Hillbilly Jake."

It was Mary Beth who gave him a reason to come home. She was pregnant, she screamed at him over the phone in January. And even a pool-dwelling alligator wouldn't get him to admit it, but he cried when she told him. A baby. He talked to Todd, who told him part of him wanted this baby to be Daddy's Little Girl, but the other part didn't want boys looking at his little girl like he looked at her mama.

"You might want to wait until the baby's born to worry about that," teased Jake, knowing that they were waiting to find out the gender. As if having a baby wouldn't bring enough surprises.

"Yeah. You're right." Todd sounded so serious.

"Of course, the baby could be a boy." Jake couldn't resist taunting his brother-in-law.

"Sure. Yeah, of course. I've heard boys are easier, so that could be good."

"Really? Who did you hear that from?" Jake asked, thinking back on all the trouble he'd gotten into since he could walk.

"I don't know, somebody. Not Marilyn, obviously. Everyone's giving us advice and . . . it's a little overwhelming."

"How's Mary Beth?"

"She says she's fine, but I think she's freaking out."

Jake knew his sister well enough to know that the signs of stress were a lot more subtle in her than in other people. He was glad Todd knew that, too.

"She's kind of obsessed with the nursery," Todd continued. "I don't suppose—"

So Jake was headed back to Willow Springs to build a nursery for his niece or nephew. It wouldn't take long, although he had some ideas for a convertible space that could grow with the kid. If he had his way, this would be a super-nursery.

Mary Beth told him that Grace had hosted the baby shower at her house, which was nice of her, he guessed. He didn't like that MB was such good friends with Grace. It meant he would probably have to see her. Over the holidays, he'd started out texting Grace, but it took longer and longer for her to reply and he started feeling like an idiot, so he quit. But in a town as small as Willow Springs, it would be hard to avoid her. So he wouldn't. This was his town, dammit.

Grace was reveling in the weather. Seasons didn't change in California. It was pretty much the same all the time, which was nice if you liked sunshine and warmth. Grace did, but she liked this, too. She liked that every day could be something different, and that on the first warm day after a cold, gray spell, everyone poured outdoors. She even liked that she had to check the weather before she got dressed in the morning.

She was pretty bummed by the forecast for spring break. Thunderstorms were predicted all week, and although this morning it was sunny and unseasonably warm, said the local weather guy, expect heavy winds and rain before the sun goes down. She took the opportunity to ride her bike into town, checked out a few vacation books from the library, picked up some groceries, and had lunch with Helen and Mary Beth. Mary Beth was glowing, which was a vast improvement over the green shade she had been sporting at her baby shower. She told them that Jake was coming back to town to build her a nursery. Helen said that was sweet, and Grace felt both of the women watching her to gauge her reaction. That was sweet, she agreed, but it had nothing to do with her.

The rain started before lunch was finished. Helen offered to drive her home, but there was no way Grace's bike would fit into her car, so she rode as quickly as she could. By the time she got home, the sky was dark as midnight and rain was coming down in sheets and her egg carton was soaked through. As she unlocked the front door, a gust of wind blew across her porch and the door slammed into the house. She muscled it closed and locked it behind her. Almost as soon as she was inside, the sky turned an ominous black and the howling of the wind was only drowned out by the claps of thunder that shook her windows.

Grace saw Mr. Bingley dart under the couch, and as the rain battered her windows, she wanted to join him. But she had to be a responsible homeowner, so she ran around the house, making sure all the windows were closed and locked. Upstairs, she noticed her bike was still on her front walkway and thought about leaving it, but images of her one mode of transportation falling prey to rust had her rushing down the stairs. The door flew out of her hand as she opened it, and she could barely walk into the wind as she inched toward her bike. A bolt of lightning split the sky. This is dumb, she thought, but she was already out there so she went as quickly as she could. As she picked up the handlebars, a gust of wind lifted the bike practically out of her hands. She rushed back to the house—a little easier, with the wind at her back—and threw the bike into the foyer, then wrestled the door closed. She was just catching her breath, wishing she had a towel as she wiped water out of her eyes, when there was a small beep and everything went black.

Somehow the storm seemed worse with the power out. She felt her way to the kitchen and dug around for the emergency matches. She did a mental inventory of every room in the house that had a decorative, scented candle, and started gathering them up. She coaxed Mr. Bingley out from under the couch and under the blanket with her, and settled in. Then she decided she was too close to the window—California earthquake drills had taught her that windows were bad places in a storm—so she pulled the couch into the center of the living room, lit the candles, and settled in to read her way through the storm.

But she couldn't concentrate. The wind was lashing rain against the house—it felt as if she were at sea. And every time the thunder clapped, Mr. Bingley dug his claws into her leg. The lightning made her jump, and something crashed upstairs. She ran up to check and found the windows of the turret had blown in. She ran into her room for her sneakers and grabbed an armful of towels. She thought she could tack them to the wall and that would prevent more rain from coming in. Then she remembered that Jake had broken her hammer, and that dinky hammer probably wouldn't have held up to the job anyway. So she focused on damage control. She grabbed the papers that were blowing everywhere and ran them down the hall to her bedroom. She snatched her laptop and yanked the printer out of the wall and deposited those on her bed. And her books. Her office had shelves and shelves of books, and the wind was blowing rain and glass around the room, so she gave up prioritizing and started grabbing armfuls off the shelves. She stopped running all the way to her room with them and started just tossing them in the hallway. All the while, the thunder clapped and she saw the wind blow a tree down into the street. There was noise everywhere—thunder, rain, limbs breaking, pounding.

She stopped in the hallway with an armful of books and realized the pounding was coming from downstairs. Someone was pounding on her door. Her mind conjured up an opportunistic mass murderer, but quickly shifted to someone stranded out in this weather. She raced down the stairs, tripping on books and sending piles down the stairs with her. She fumbled with the lock and yanked open the front door, preparing to hustle the person inside, then get back to her waterlogged office.

But when she opened the door, it wasn't a stranded stranger.

Lightning lit up the sky momentarily, but it was enough for her to see who it was, and the fear and relief she felt crashed over her like a wave.

"Jake," she whispered.

Jake should have waited for Grace to invite him in—they were nothing to each other now, after all. But he was wet and cold and about to blow off the porch, and as soon as the door opened, Grace had broken down in tears.

Not exactly the greeting he was hoping for, but he chalked it up to the storm. He pushed the door shut and before he had even properly turned around, Grace was wrapped around him, squeezing him within an inch of his life. He clutched her back, taking a moment to revel in the familiar feeling of her body close to his. But he had come here to check up on her, so he pushed her back a step.

She was soaking wet, her hair drooping in stringy waves around her face. As he looked at her more closely, he saw that she had a small cut on her cheek. He held her at arm's length and saw her legs were scratched up, and there were more little cuts on her arm.

"Grace, are you okay?"

She gave him a watery nod, wiping her eyes on the hem of her shirt. She recoiled a little when she saw the blood her cheek left behind.

"Am I bleeding?" she asked.

"A little. What happened? You're all cut up."

"Some of that is Mr. Bingley. The rest must be from my office." He followed her gaze up the stairs and saw the mess of books. That was not like Grace, to treat books so badly. "The window broke. I was trying to get the books out."

"Grace, you could have been seriously hurt! What if the glass had gone into your eye!"

"I wasn't thinking, Jake. I was just trying to save my stuff."

He wanted to argue that her books wouldn't be much use to her if she was blind, but he saw that her hands were shaking and her lips were pursed so hard they were turning white. She was probably crashing from her adrenaline rush, but he knew Grace well enough to know that her books would come first. Or at least that she wouldn't be able to relax until they were taken care of. He tried to feel sympathetic—they were her livelihood, after all.

"I'll get them," he said and headed up the stairs. She followed him, and together they made a mini-fire line and got the bookshelves clear. He was about to close the door, but she ran in and grabbed a box from behind the overstuffed chair. When she was out, she nodded and he shut the door.

"I'm going to board up the windows." He had thrown plywood into his truck before heading to his mother's house. They had a big sunroom and he wanted to get their windows covered. But by the time he got there, his dad was already there, and he and Will were hammering the boards into place.

Grace shook her head. "I don't have—"

"I have the stuff in my truck."

Her eyes widened. "Don't go out in the storm!"

"We have to get that boarded up or the floor will be destroyed."

"What if you get struck by lightning!?"

He smiled. She did care.

"Don't give me that stupid smile. I just don't want you dying on my property!"

He wanted to laugh then, because if she was teasing him, she was fine. The color was coming back into her face and she wasn't shaking anymore, so he took her face in his hands and kissed her. Just quickly, but not so quickly that she didn't have time to grab onto his arms and hold him in place a little longer.

"I'll be right back," he assured her. He got out to the truck and was swinging the first sheet of plywood out from under the tarp that covered it, and he almost hit Grace with it.

"Get back inside!" he yelled over the wind.

"Shut up!" she said, and grabbed an end. He let her take it, then followed her with another one. They got the broken windows boarded up, Grace holding one end of the board and the flashlight, Jake hammering as fast as he could. With the windows covered and the power out, it was easy to believe that the storm had passed them over, that it was a normal, quiet night, just him and Grace, standing in a turret.

But Grace was shivering again, her shirt soaked through. Jake's jeans were heavy with water, and he thought his feet might be pruning inside his shoes.

"I think you left some stuff here if you want dry clothes," she said.

He nodded. "You should change, too. Try to clean out those cuts."

She led the way to her room, flashlight first. She pointed it at a pile of folded clothes on top of her dresser. Shorts, boxers, socks. No shirt, but she handed him an oversized Pembroke sweatshirt and he put that on. He felt his way into the bathroom and hung his clothes over the shower curtain, hoping they would dry by the time he had to leave. Kyle would never let him hear the end of it if he saw him wearing a Pembroke shirt.

When he got back to Grace's room, she was sitting on the bed, the flashlight in her lap pointing to a random spot on the wall. "Hey," he said gently, and she slowly lifted her head to him. "You okay?" He brushed a finger under her chin.

She nodded weakly. "Just tired."

"Let's get you dry." He pulled at the hem of her shirt and she lifted her arms and let him pull it over her head. He took the flashlight and found her least sparkly cat sweatshirt while she shimmied out of her wet jeans. She slipped on the sweatpants he handed her while he tossed her clothes over into the shower as well. When he got back to the room she was fumbling with a pair of thick, wool socks.

"Here," he said, and he slipped them on over her icy feet. He held her hands tight in his, trying to warm them. "Okay?" he asked. She nodded, but when he got up to go, she clutched at his sweatshirt, so he sank down on the bed next to her and wrapped his arms around her and together they rode out the storm.

The house was quiet. The storm outside was terrifying, but the house had endured worse. The beautiful stained glass was shattered, but Grace had barely noticed. What were a few broken windows when Jake was back?

Chapter 21

Jake woke up alone. It took him a moment to recognize Grace's room, even with the sunlight streaming through the window. Sunlight. Obviously it was morning, and obviously the storm was over. The alarm clock was dark, so the power must not be back on yet. He rolled out of bed and looked out the window. There were branches everywhere, and one of the old maples in Mrs. Wallace's yard had fallen, blocking his truck in the driveway and taking out part of Grace's fence. Maybe that was the worst of it: no power and some cosmetic damage.

He knew that would be a miracle, and he needed to get out to see what needed to be done. But first, he had to find Grace to make sure she was okay.

It didn't take long. She was sitting in the hallway surrounded by stacks of books—she had been busy. But she wasn't looking at the books. She was sitting cross-legged in front of the box he'd seen her pull from the office last night. She was thumbing through the contents. They looked like pictures from where Jake was standing, but he couldn't really tell. Her hair hung over her face, so he couldn't tell what she was thinking. From where he stood, she was as distant to him as those fallen trees outside. And he wanted in.

Grace had woken up to the sun on her back and her hands under Jake's sweatshirt. He was sleep-warm and breathing heavily on her hair where she lay cuddled into him. Then last night came back to her in a flash—the storm, the broken windows, and Jake coming in and saving the day. She eased away from him and watched him for a minute, his face relaxed in sleep. She ran her fingers lightly over his brow, this strong, hard-working man who always seemed to know when she needed him. When he stirred, though, she stopped. When she was sure he was still asleep, Grace crawled out of bed and went to survey the damage.

The view outside was pretty bad, but she would deal with that later. In the hallway, her books were still in the haphazard piles she and Jake had made last night in their rush to get the office cleared out. She was grateful that he hadn't asked any questions, just followed her lead and got her books out of danger. A lot of them had sentimental value, but they were also her work. Since she was a kid, books had been her calling, and the fact that Jake was willing to help her rescue them meant a lot to her.

He meant a lot to her. She didn't want to admit that, but it was true. Now that the storm had passed, he would probably want to talk, want some explanation about why communication had petered out, want to know if they'd pick up where they left off. She wanted to, but she wanted it like it was in the beginning: fun and a little distant.

She stacked books for a while, arranging things in neat-ish piles along the walls. When she came across the box, she stopped. Jane had given it to her at Christmas, even though Grace didn't want it. It was one of those small photo boxes from a craft store, and Grace had teased Jane that she was turning into one of those Pinterest moms. Then she opened it up and tried to give it back. Jane closed it for her, but made her take it home with her to Willow Springs.

The box was full of photographs. There were maybe fifty in there, stacked unevenly because of the different sizes and weights of paper. The one on top was a couple in a very early eighties wedding, complete with big hair and poufy shoulders. But Grace didn't laugh. She recognized it immediately.

It was her parents' wedding picture.

Jane had hers framed and hanging on the wall next to a picture of her and Dev at their beach wedding, mixed in with snapshots of Priya playing in leaves, next to a snowman, a sandcastle, face covered in ice cream. It was part of Jane's life. Grace was not so ignorant of symbolism to realize the significance of the fact that Jane had her picture on display, while Grace's copy was in a shoebox.

It wasn't the greatest picture of either of her parents. Their smiles were too wide and her dad, especially, looked like he had a double chin. The lighting was weird and made her mom look like her hair was thinning under her enormous veil. The whole thing would have been a family joke if it weren't for the eyes. Both of her parents were looking at the camera, and you could see in their eyes their happiness, their unadulterated joy, at the fact that they were finally married.

Grace remembered that when her dad came home from long business trips, he'd give each of his girls a kiss, then sit in his chair. Inevitably, Grace or Jane, or both, would climb on his lap and he would pick up the photo from the side table and tell the girls about the happiest day of his life, when he married their mother. Their mother would blush and try to shush him, but eventually he would shoo the girls off his lap and dance her around the living room. When Jane turned twelve, this kind of mushy behavior disgusted her to no end, but Grace liked it. It made her happy to see her parents so happy, and it made her feel safe that there was such a thing as love in this world and that two people could find it and create more people, and more love, and it would last forever.

"Who's that?"

Grace jerked her head up to find Jake standing before her, rubbing the sleep out of his eyes. She wanted to put the picture on the bottom of the pile, shove the box out of his view, but he'd already sat down next to her. Their knees touched and he reached for the photo.

"My parents," she said, and started shuffling through the rest of the pictures. Ballet recitals, soccer teams, father-daughter square dance. Ugh—Grace with braces. Just what she wanted to relive.

"They look really happy."

Grace snorted. That was an understatement. They looked psychotically happy. "They were."

"Where are they now?" It was the first time Jake had asked any questions about her family beyond Jane.

"Dead."

He sucked in a breath. "I'm sorry."

Grace shrugged.

"They must have been young."

Grace took the picture back, but didn't return it to the box. She nodded.

"What happened?"

She looked up at Jake. He was being nosy, and she was tempted to tell him as much, to tell him to mind his own business and leave her alone. But that wasn't what she really wanted. She wanted him here, in her life, her best friend, and it wasn't fair that she keep this from him. Maybe this would help him understand why they could never be more than friends.

"My dad died first. He was traveling for work. He worked for a software company so he was always on the road, setting up systems with different companies. I didn't really understand all that he did, but he was away a lot."

"Must have been hard for you."

She shrugged. "It just was. And when he was home, we had him all to ourselves. I don't even think he had any friends, outside of work."

"He was a good dad?"

"The best. Patient. And funny. And . . . I don't know, just the best. I never felt unsure around him, you know?"

"Not really, but it sounds nice."

"It was. And he loved my mom. They were nuts about each other, as you can see by the crazy wedding face." She held the picture between her fingers, almost lowering it into the box, but not quite ready to let it go yet.

"He died in a car accident. He was hit by a semi. The driver fell asleep. My dad was killed instantly, so I guess that was good."

Jake didn't say anything. She saw him lift his hand, as if to put it around her shoulder, but he stopped and rested both hands on his lap.

"My mom was devastated. We all were, of course. I was a junior in college, and Jane had just started her freshman year. We were at opposite ends of the country, my mom by herself in the middle. She was alone when she heard."

"And you went home to her?" Jake prompted.

"Of course. I flew in from California, and Jane drove from Virginia. She got there first. When she picked me up from the airport, she told me she was really worried about Mom, that she wasn't eating or sleeping. I tried to be the big sister, told her that was normal, and that we would take care of her."

Grace's voice broke and this time Jake did put his arm around her. She leaned into him for a second, but sat up straight again. She wanted to finish this story.

"When we pulled into the driveway, I remember telling Jane to put on a smile, let Mom know we were happy to be there with her, for her. I don't know why I thought it was important that we smile—our father had just died—but it seemed vital at the time."

Grace put the picture away and put the lid on the box. She closed her eyes and continued. "It didn't matter. When we got inside, Mom was taking a nap. Only she wasn't. She wasn't asleep. Jane lost it, and I remember going into some kind of super-mode. I called 911, I tried CPR. When the paramedics got there, they started asking us questions about pills and alcohol, but there was nothing in the room. We tore the place apart later, but there was nothing. She just . . . died."

"Oh, Grace." He rubbed her back while she wiped her eyes on her sleeves.

"Officially, it was a heart attack. I remember at the funeral—we buried both of them at once—I overheard a neighbor saying that it was romantic, that my mom couldn't live without my dad and she died of a broken heart." Grace let out a strangled laugh. "I had never heard such utter bull in my entire life. It wasn't romantic. To be so tied to someone that you literally cannot live without them? That's only romantic in books and movies. In real life, it . . ." For once, Grace couldn't come up with the word she wanted.

"Sucks?" offered Jake.

She smiled, keeping her eyes on her fingers entwined in her lap. "Yeah. It sucks."

This time, when he pulled her close, she let him hold her, let his murmurs soothe her. She felt better, telling him.

"So, now you know," Grace said, sitting up.

"Now I know," he said, softly, wiping an errant tear from her cheek.

"And now you know why I don't do love."

He didn't say anything, just nodded and kissed her last tear away.

The house felt heavy and lost. Grace and Jake were back together, but sitting in the hallway swapping sad stories was not what the house had in mind. The house had never been wrong about a couple in over one hundred years, and it wasn't going to start now.

Chapter 22

It had been no ordinary thunderstorm. It was a *derecho*, and there were snazzy news graphics to prove it. Most people in Willow Springs didn't really care what it was called, they just wanted electricity. A week after the storm, only about half of the town was back, which was pretty good, considering the number of trees that had been uprooted and thrown around like toothpicks.

The power on Grace's block came back the next day. Grace took the happiest shower of her life, then went to fetch Mrs. Wallace, whose power was back on, but who now had a tree where her kitchen sink used to be. Grace probably wouldn't have noticed had she and Jake not gone exploring the morning after the storm.

So Mrs. Wallace and Lucy were staying in Grace's room and Helen was staying in the office, boarded up windows and all. Grace was sleeping on the couch. Mr. Bingley was staying wherever Lucy wasn't. It was an awkward arrangement, and as it entered its second week, Grace was amazed that she wasn't pulling out her hair. But she never felt crowded, even when Mrs. Wallace dried her knee-highs on the dining room chairs. The house, somehow, made room.

Nobody thought of the arrangements as relief efforts; it was just neighbors doing what they did. The Red Cross came in and administered some much-needed first aid and distributed water and food, but the emergency shelter stayed largely empty. Grace was pleased to see a few of her students around town—apparently the Pembroke population had cut their spring break short to come help. She began to see them everywhere, wearing borrowed work gloves, dragging tree limbs, delivering meals, and generally doing what they were asked.

Everyone was pitching in. People kept coming up to Grace and telling her how great Jake was, using his connections to get construction equipment, and he was spotted all over town operating a tree-removing crane. Grace just smiled even though it had nothing to do with her. And she thought it was pretty short-sighted of people to thank the man who gave Kyle a chainsaw.

But in the end, it was Kyle who cut up the tree in Mrs. Wallace's kitchen, and he rallied the Pembroke rugby team into loading the pieces into the back of his truck.

The damage that upset people the most, though, was the destruction of the Library Window. Henry was particularly devastated, especially when he heard that Grace's turret windows hadn't survived either. But to his credit, he sprang into action. There was a glass artist in West Virginia, apparently, who studied the Tulley school of stained glass, and who would be able to travel to Willow Springs to restore the window. Henry sweet-talked her into cutting her rates and staying in a local home instead of an expensive hotel, but the estimate was still more than anyone in the town could imagine paying.

"Such a shame about that window," said Mrs. Wallace as she, Grace, and Helen sat around the dinner table. "It brought such joy to so many people."

"I learned to read under that window," said Helen. "And poor Henry."

"Yeah. Poor Henry." He had been coming over every day, devastated. At first Grace was glad to try to help, although she didn't think she was doing much aside from listening to him complain about the tight-fistedness of the library board. Knowing some of the library board as she did, Grace knew it wasn't a matter of not being willing to pay, but it was either the window or staff salaries. Five years of staff salaries. It was not a choice Grace envied.

But it was a beautiful window, and Grace felt the same frustrated impotence that there was, apparently, nothing to be done.

"Did you hear Miss Fairway's first grade class had a bake sale?" Helen asked.

"That's so sweet," said Grace.

"They raised a couple hundred dollars," said Mrs. Wallace.

"What?!" said Helen and Grace.

"That's a lot of cupcakes," said Helen.

"No, people just came out, paid ten bucks for a cookie, that kind of thing. The library board agreed to start a fundraising campaign. They're going to announce it tomorrow." Grace was always amazed at how Mrs. Wallace knew what was going to happen before it happened. She was either a psychic or incredibly, efficiently nosy.

"I wish we could do something to help," said Grace. She could make a donation. It wouldn't be much, but it would be something.

"Another bake sale?" suggested Helen.

"How about a bikini car wash?" suggested Mrs. Wallace, and Grace slapped Helen on the back so she didn't choke on her lasagna.

"Maybe we can throw a party. Serve a lot of booze and leave a tip jar out," suggested Helen, once she recovered.

"It would be nice if we could do something with a book theme," Mrs. Wallace said.

"A book sale?" Grace suggested, lamely.

"No, too many sales. I like your party idea, Helen. What about a tea party?"

"That will only appeal to half the town. You'll never get men to a tea party," said Helen. "Believe me, I know."

They all slumped in their seats, fresh out of ideas. Until Helen gasped and jumped out of her chair. "I've got it!"

"What?" asked Mrs. Wallace, clutching her chest.

"I like the party idea, Mrs. Wallace. And I like the book idea, Grace. So what kind of theme party can we have that will draw a lot of people? Something that combines an author who is appealing to members of the community and a topic that, say, we have a local expert on?"

"Um . . ." Grace wasn't sure where Helen was going, but it was making her nervous.

"Jane Austen! We can borrow costumes from the Pembroke theater department and have dance lessons and then have a big dance party at the end! We'll do some traditional English country dances!"

"Sounds boring," said Mrs. Wallace.

"Afterwards we can have a DJ," added Helen.

"Okay, I'm in," she said. Lucy barked.

"Grace?"

Grace thought about the fast-approaching end of the semester, the conference paper, her two unintended roommates. She had a lot on her plate. But then she thought about her roommates again, and Mary Beth and Marilyn, Missy and Kyle, Henry. She thought about how great it felt when she moved to Willow Springs and signed up for her library card, and how surprised she was by this great piece of art, just living with the public.

And her traitorous heart thought about Jake, and how Jake could be counted on to help out, especially if they got Mary Beth involved. And how she would have to spend time with him since she was the resident Jane Austen expert, consult with him on decorations and maybe even get him to dance. Would he dance? He liked to dance, he said, but this probably wasn't what he meant.

"Grace? Hello?"

She couldn't decide if the Jake thing was good or bad. Either way, she wanted to do something for Willow Springs.

She looked across the table at Helen and Mrs. Wallace, and nodded. "Okay. I'm in."

A string of little boys was following Jake.

The day after the storm, Jake paid almost all of what he'd made in Miami to rent a crane. He didn't know for sure that anyone would need it, but he'd been through enough storms in Willow Springs to know that, sometimes, you just needed some heavy machinery.

He started with his mom's house. Her tree was just blocking the driveway, so there was no major property damage, but it had been a while since Jake had operated a crane, so he wanted practice. He didn't tell Marilyn that. He hoped his certification was up to date, because he didn't have enough money to bribe Todd to keep his mouth shut.

Before the tree even hit the ground, there were kids gathering across the street. Parents, too, wanting to know if Jake was available to come down to their yard or if they could drive that thing (yes; no). But the kids were the ones who followed him. They stayed at a safe distance—he wouldn't run the machine unless they were all across the street—but as soon as the crane started lifting, he could hear squeals and "Awesome!" and it always made him smile. He re-

membered what it was like to be that little kid, completely fascinated by heavy machinery. And his dad had taught him everything
that was safe for him to learn. Well, mostly safe. Jake remembered
a few instances when his dad snatched his hand away from something, warning him not to tell his mother.

But he still had all his fingers, he could operate a crane, and he
was the daggun pied piper of Willow Springs. Which was a literary
allusion, he thought proudly. He wanted to tell Grace. Not about the
literary allusion, although he probably would because she'd appreciate it. But about the kids and crane. He hadn't seen her since the
day after the storm, not really. He'd seen her in passing, corralling
some Pembroke kids at a free lunch or riding her bike with supplies
under her arm. A few days ago he saw her standing up on the pedals
so she could see over the giant pack of toilet paper she had in the
basket. He should have stopped to offer her a ride, but by the time
he got finished admiring those strong legs of hers, she was gone.

He heard from his mother that Helen and Mrs. Wallace were
staying with her, and thought that was nice, although he wasn't
thrilled about the idea of spending an evening with Mrs. Wallace.
But he and Grace were friends. They cared about each other, even if
they didn't love each other. They had a connection, and it didn't feel
right with these long spaces between seeing each other. And she'd
opened up to him about her parents.

He'd spent a lot of time in Florida thinking about Grace, despite
his best efforts. She hurt his pride when she told Jane that she didn't
love him. But, really, that was what he wanted. He wasn't about to
make a life with a professor, and now more than ever, he understood
why she was not interested in any kind of forever with anyone. It
made sense. They were perfect for each other.

But heavy machinery made him feel like a man, and when he
felt like that, it was nice to have a woman around.

Chapter 23

Grace was carrying a mug of tea up to her office when someone knocked on the door. Startled, she spilled some hot tea on her hand. Then the hotness made her hand jerk, and she sloshed half the cup on her foot.

"Dammit!" She set the tea on the flat end of the banister. Mr. Bingley beat her to the door. He was meowing and pawing like he couldn't wait for her to get it open.

"Hey," said Jake when she pulled the door open. Before she could say anything, he smiled at her. Then he leaned down to pick up Mr. Bingley, who was practically crawling up his pants. "Hey, Mr. Bingley. Did you miss me?" He snuffled his face into Mr. Bingley's neck. Grace could practically feel the vibrations of his purring through the door. The cat's, too.

"Hi, Jake, come on in. Bring my cat with you." Grace closed the door behind Jake. "Who are all those kids?"

Jake shrugged. "I'm the local hero now. I have a big truck."

"I see."

"Technically, it's a crane, but it's big and yellow and loud, so I'm a hero."

"I heard about you and your crane. You're setting the hearts of Willow Springs's women all a-flutter."

"Is that right?" Jake let Mr. Bingley down on the floor and

stepped into Grace's space. "And you? Am I setting your heart a-flutter?"

"My heart doesn't flutter."

He pressed a soft kiss to her neck, then just lingered there, breathing her in. She shouldn't lean in. She shouldn't give in to the impulse to run her fingers through his hair and wrap her legs around his waist.

"So," he said, straightening abruptly and smacking Grace on the butt. He was in a good mood. Playful, even. Must be all that heavy machinery. She grabbed her tea and followed him into the living room, where he was already spread on the couch with his feet on the coffee table. "Where are your roommates?"

Grace tucked her hair behind her ear and sat on the arm of the couch. "Helen took Mrs. Wallace to the movies. I'm supposed to be getting work done."

"Oh. Do you need me to go?"

Grace didn't say anything, just shrugged in the general direction of her tea. She did need him to go. The house was quiet for the first time in a week and she had some tweaking to do on her presentation. But she could tweak later. Or tomorrow.

"Hmm. So they left you all alone?"

She shrugged again. Gosh, she really had a way with words tonight.

"Where's the dog?"

"Mrs. Wallace insisted on sneaking Lucy into the theater. And they've been gone for a while, so I guess it worked."

"Lucy likes the movies, huh?"

"She just goes for the popcorn. Besides, the previews are the best part."

"So . . ." Jake took the mug out of Grace's hand. He sniffed it, and raised an eyebrow at her.

"What? Spinsters can't drink tea?"

But he just shook his head and pulled her onto his lap. "You're no spinster." He kissed her nose. "Too cute to be a spinster."

"Cute, huh?"

Jake wrapped his hand around the back of Grace's neck and pulled her closer. "Very cute," he said against her mouth.

God, I missed him, she thought as their lips met, and danced.

She was not so stubborn that she couldn't admit that she liked the strong feel of him, the way his muscles were so hard but his lips were soft, even when they weren't being gentle. Like now, when he was kissing her as if his life depended on it.

He pulled back, gasping, and she blinked at him for a few seconds before she registered that he was not going to kiss her again. He was apparently just going to stare at her.

"When are your roommates coming back?" he asked her.

She shrugged. She didn't even remember what time Helen had told her the movie was.

"But they are coming back?"

She nodded. She wanted to say, yes, they're coming back, so quit wasting time, but she distracted herself by tracing Jake's lower lip with her fingertip. His lips were thin. She wondered if they felt swollen like hers did.

He bit her finger. She flinched. "Hey!"

"Do you want to go to my place?"

Grace had never been to Jake's apartment. She knew he lived above Mary Beth's garage, which sounded very quarter-life crisis to her. It didn't really suit him, although she supposed if he just worked sporadically, he would have to live frugally.

Then he kissed her quickly and sat back and she got distracted by those lips again. Really, the lips were nothing to write home about, but they were pretty talented. His whole face was talented. Heck, his whole Jake was talented.

"Grace?"

"Yes! Yes. Let's go."

Jake was nervous. He never got nervous, not about women at least. But he was nervous about what Grace would say about his apartment. It wasn't him; it was just a temporary, cheap place to live. Would she be more impressed that he usually slept in a sleeping bag in whichever house he was flipping?

He opened the truck door for Grace and smiled at her. Well, so what if it was silly. He wanted to open the door for her. He took her hand to help her out of the truck, as if she were wearing a ball gown and heels, not yoga pants and sneakers. As they walked up the driveway, he kept hold of her hand. Just in case she decided to bolt.

He could see Mary Beth puttering in the kitchen as they walked past. He usually honked or stuck his head in the door to let them know that he was home, and to see if there were any leftovers. But tonight, he just rapped gently on the window. Mary Beth jumped a foot, saw it was Jake, and threw the dish sponge at the window. She mouthed a word she probably didn't mean—probably—but stopped when she saw Grace. When she saw Grace, Mary Beth gave her a sheepish wave, and Grace sheepishly waved back at her. Jake thought the polite embarrassed wordless conversation could take all night, and he had other plans for all night, so he pulled Grace away from the house and up the stairs to his apartment.

Grace started looking around the second he let her in the door. It was a mess; he had kind of hit the ground running as soon as he got back from Florida. Not that he was a great housekeeper, and not that Grace was in any position to judge dirty clothes thrown all over the floor, but he didn't want her to see what a slob he could be. He wasn't sure why, but he didn't want Grace thinking anything bad about him.

Not that it mattered.

It did matter. That was the problem. But it was a problem quickly solved by pulling his sweatshirt over his head. Grace always seemed easily distracted by his body. It was a burden he was prepared to deal with.

She fell for it, and he was glad for many reasons when she walked straight into his arms.

"You in a hurry?" she asked.

"A hurry to get started."

She hummed a little at him, then stepped back and ripped her own sweatshirt over her head. Purple. She was wearing a purple bra that was lace all over and he could see right through it.

He growled.

"Did you just growl at me?" she said, laughing.

"Don't tease me, woman."

"Don't what?" she asked, running a finger down the center of his chest.

"I've been driving a damn crane all day and I'm tired."

"Too tired to—"

"Hell, no. But you should take pity on me."

"Because you've been working hard." She kissed his pectoral. "Helping out your neighbors." She kissed the other one.

"Yeah," he said, or he thought he said. His breath seemed to have run out on him.

"Poor man." She hooked her finger into the waistband of his jeans and led him over to the bed. His bed, dammit. He should be taking the lead. But she shoved him down and he sat, hard, and just stared up at her.

"Poor, tired Jake," she said, and shimmied out of her yoga pants. Good Lord, the panties matched. She pushed him back and he lifted his hips as she eased his jeans down to the floor. She ran her hands up his legs, then slid them over his hips to pull his boxers down. "Not too tired," she murmured as she tossed them over her shoulder. They went wide and landed in the bell of the floor lamp by the door. Jake watched, dazed, as the lamp wobbled then crashed across the doorway.

Grace turned to the lamp, then back to Jake. "Sorry," she said, and started to climb off him.

"Nope," he grunted, and grabbed her waist, crashing her into him and knocking them both back onto the bed. Even in the newly dim apartment, he could see her smile. "I could fall asleep at any time." He tilted his chin up and she kissed him. "I don't want to rob you of the opportunity to shower me with pity and praise."

"Hmm," she said, and traced a gentle finger across his brow. "Brave, selfless Jake." Her lips followed, forging a soft, wet trail down his cheek, across his neck. "Hero to the community." She gently nipped at the pulse in his neck, then shushed his gasp with a kiss. "He just gives and gives."

Grace's voice was getting softer and breathier, and as her lips touched every inch of his skin Jake lost track of what she was saying. He was great. He was a giver. He didn't care, though, not while her lips and tongue swirled down his torso, across his stomach, then lower, and he couldn't hear a thing because he was too busy feeling Grace and her magnificent, talented mouth.

He was close to losing control and although Grace hummed in pleasure, he didn't want her to have her way in this. He wanted to be closer to her, inside of her. He pulled her up and she scrambled onto his chest, tossed off-balance and then again when he shoved her panties down her legs. She was laughing, catching her breath and settling her knees on either side of his hips. She produced a foil packet—sweet, magic Grace—and tore it open with her teeth and then she was rolling it on him and rolling herself over him and all he could do was hold on. He watched her writhe and sway over him, watched his hands roam over her pale skin and the rough lace of her bra, and when he shifted, he watched her face go from smug to surprised, so he did it again, then again, and she tossed her head back and shouted, and so did he, and when she collapsed, breathless, on his chest, his arms flopped out to his sides and he lay there, covered in Grace, while their hearts slowed.

He wanted to say something about how *she* was a giver, or maybe a joke about driving his crane, but he was tired and she was soft. She shifted and placed a kiss on his chest, then his neck, and his arms came up and smoothed a gentle line down her back.

Chapter 24

Jake was spooning Grace, hard. She'd been awake for a while, trying to figure out how to get up without waking him. He'd been tired. Oh, he perked right up when she climbed on top of him, but no sooner had they shouted each other's names and collapsed in a tangle than he was asleep. Sometime in the night they'd shifted, and now her back was squished against his front, his arm in a tight band around her waist.

She wanted to lie there with him, have a lazy morning, but her brain wouldn't let her. She should have brought some work with her. Grading a few papers would probably put her right back to sleep. But she hadn't. They left her house in such a hurry—neither of them wanted to risk Helen and Mrs. Wallace coming home early from the movie—that she only grabbed her keys and phone. Besides, it wasn't very romantic to say, hey, I haven't seen you in a week and you're crazy to get into my pants, but let me grab a little homework first.

She'd dreaded seeing him again after her hallway breakdown, and had never told anyone about her parents, certainly not any romantic partners. That was a deep, secret part of her no one needed to see. He'd just happened upon her in a moment of weakness, and once she started talking, she wasn't able to stop. She was afraid that the next time she saw him, he'd be full of pity and treat her with kid gloves. She didn't want that. She wanted him to treat her like Jake always did.

And, oh, he had treated her like Jake.

He shifted in his sleep and his hold on her loosened. She took the opportunity to scoot out of bed and into the bathroom. His bathrobe was hanging on the door, so she slipped it on and went to retrieve her phone from where she'd dropped it last night. Six text messages, all from Helen. They went from amusement ("Operation Sneak Dog Into Theater: Success!") to concern ("We're home— where are you?") to all-out worry ("Srsly were you abducted??") to relief ("Talked to MB—have fun getting abducted by Jake!"). And then just a series of emoticons. Grace probably should have left a note, but the Willow Springs grapevine seemed to have taken care of it for her.

She pulled the curtain aside—it was barely light out. No wonder Jake was asleep, it was so early. That, and the giant yellow crane sitting in the driveway. She looked over at him and felt her heart go all warm and gooey. He was a good guy. A good friend, and a good guy. And muscles.

She put her phone down on the desk, preparing to dive back into bed with those muscles, when she noticed it wasn't a desk at all. It looked like a drafting table, one of those big white ones that slanted slightly downward. There was a light attached to the top and she flicked it on, glancing quickly at the bed to make sure Jake was still dead to the world, then took a look at what was on the desk. She wasn't snooping, she told herself. Just . . . okay, she was snooping. But she was curious. Jake rarely talked about himself, unless the topic was directly related to the person he was talking to. Like mentioning how he'd tried to read *Pride and Prejudice* for English class. He was so charming and focused on her that the fact that he had whole other facets surprised her. It shouldn't have, and it wasn't fair that she'd assumed the part of Jake she saw was all he was. So she'd rectify that by snooping.

These looked like architectural drawings, mostly for interiors, but a few outside drawings as well. The lines delineating rooms were marked with tiny, precise measurements, but the notes around the room were messier, as if the person writing them was just jotting ideas down. There were notes all around the margins as well, with words like "warm, light, neutral" and "modern, clean." And "yuppie."

That was how she knew they were Jake's notes.

"What are you doing over there?" the yuppie-hater mumbled from his bed. "Come back to bed."

She did, but she brought the drawings with her.

"What is this, Jake?" She was excited, and didn't know why.

He opened his eyes, just a sliver, then rolled over and shoved his face into the pillow. "I can't see. It's not even daylight."

Grace could wait. She scooted down so she was lying next to him, but she kept looking at the drawings. She thought they were all for one house, but there was a veranda on one drawing that didn't make any sense on one of the others.

"Grace."

He was muttering into the pillows.

"Go back to sleep," she whispered.

"I can't sleep if you're sitting there looking at my stuff!"

"Well, tell me what they are." She put the drawings aside and leaned in to kiss his shoulder.

He turned to look at her then. His face was bleary and pillow-marked, and his hair was sticking out and he was sort of scowling at her, but he looked so cute she knew he couldn't possibly mean it.

"They're my work."

"Are these the plans for your jobs?"

Jake paused and looked at her. "What exactly do you think I do for a living?"

"You're in construction," she answered.

He flipped onto his back and looked up at the ceiling. "It's a little more than that."

She propped her head up with her hand, facing him. And then, because she couldn't help it, she ran her fingers up and down the line of hair on his chest.

"I flip houses."

Grace stopped her trail in the center of his chest. That was not what she was expecting. "Like on those TV shows?" She loved those shows. When house hunting, she was particularly addicted to them.

"Yeah. I mean, the shows are not entirely realistic, but yeah."

"Are you telling me I shouldn't believe everything I see on television?"

"Not with the crap you watch."

She jabbed him in the chest and he retaliated by grabbing her arm and flipping her so she was underneath him. She leaned up and kissed his chin.

"So, what, you buy old houses and fix them up?" she asked.

"Basically."

"Around here?"

"Some. Willow Springs has a lot of great architecture, and a lot of it has been neglected. And you fancy college people just love a fixed-up old house."

She wanted to *hmph* in disgust, but he was right. She did love old houses.

"Sometimes I go to other parts of the state. Sometimes Ohio, although I'm not licensed there, so I have to hire a local contractor."

"And that's what you were doing in Florida?"

He nodded.

Her chest felt lighter, but she ignored it. Besides, Jake was still lying on top of her. She didn't feel that much lighter.

"Is that why you came to meet me when I moved in? To see if I would hire you to fix up my place?"

"No, I was there because my bossy older sister made me be there."

"Ah."

He rolled off her, but pulled her close to his side. "It's good money, and I can work more or less when I want to. As you can see, I live pretty simply."

She nodded, even though he couldn't see her. But he must have felt it, because he continued.

"So I buy two or three houses a year, fix them up, and put the money in the bank for the next house."

"And stay in your sister's garage until that comes up?"

He shrugged, and her head jostled along with it. He moved a hand up to her neck.

"I'll buy a house for myself one day. When I find the right one."

Grace wondered what the right house for him would be. He was such a guy, but now that she saw his apartment, she realized that it didn't suit him at all. The apartment was bland and bare, despite the mess. She tried to picture him in a modern house, all clean lines and bachelor-simple. That didn't fit either. He would probably be happy in a house like hers, one that had a lot of charm but needed some TLC to bring it out.

"So you had absolutely no designs on my house?"

"None," he assured her.

"My house isn't good enough for you?"

He laughed, and she felt it down to her toes. "No, it's too good. That house isn't in bad enough shape to gut and flip."

"But if you had to. If, say, Mary Beth made you, what would you do to my house?"

"If I was flipping it to sell? I'd probably gut the kitchen."

Grace gasped. "I love that kitchen!"

"Yes, but you're not normal. Most buyers want an updated kitchen. Something at least from this century."

"Hmph. Fine. What else?"

"I might take out that swinging door to the kitchen. Maybe knock that whole wall down and open up the space. And I'd try to find room for another bathroom downstairs."

"What about the turret?"

He rubbed his eyes. "Ugh, that turret is a nightmare. I'd probably just put some throw pillows in there and let the buyer deal with it."

Grace shook her head. "I tried that. It doesn't work. Do you think my house needs all that other stuff?"

"No. Maybe the kitchen wall. I hate that swinging door."

Grace started to protest that she loved it, that it enabled her to make a grand entrance. But the truth was, the door was a pain in the butt. Often, literally.

Jake stretched underneath her. "What time is it?"

She shrugged. "Early. What are you doing today?"

"Just driving my crane around."

"Manly."

"You want to come watch?"

She did. She bet Jake wielding heavy machinery was even sexier than Jake with hand tools. "I can't. Papers to grade. Ugh, and I have to go to a planning meeting." Mrs. Wallace, it turned out, was a force to be reckoned with when she had a mission. The library board loved their Jane Austen fundraiser idea. Now all they had to do was make it happen.

Jake turned so he was facing her. "Is it an early meeting?"

She shook her head. "This afternoon at the Daily Drip."

"Plenty of time." He slid his hands to her waist. "Why are you wearing my robe?"

She tried to think of something pithy about protecting her modesty, but she was too slow. Jake captured her puzzled mouth with his and she forgot all about grading and planning and Jane Austen.

Chapter 25

"The library meeting room is still out of commission." John, the library director, shook his head sadly into his mocha latte. "And I'm afraid it would be too small for what you have planned."

"Pembroke's out," Marilyn added, placing a definitive check on her notepad. "One of the trustee's daughters is getting married there that weekend."

"I don't suppose she'd want a Jane Austen-themed wedding?" Mary Beth asked.

"What's more romantic than Jane Austen?" asked Mrs. Wallace. "Just don't tell me that Will is catering the wedding. We have to have Will."

"Will is available," said Marilyn. "And he'll donate his services if he can claim the first two dances."

"I'm dying of the romance," Helen gushed, flopping dramatically in her seat.

"Speaking of dances, did you guys get the YouTube videos I sent out?" asked Giselle, one of the dance teachers at Pembroke.

Everyone nodded, even Henry, who thought the dancing was the worst part of the plan. Nobody believed him for a second. John admitted that he and his wife had been practicing, too. Mrs. Wallace updated them on the costumes—the theater department at Pembroke was donating suits and breeches for the men, and the Willow

Springs Community Players had a pile of empire waist dresses they were fixing up for the women.

It was all coming together. The Pembroke Chamber Music Group was going to play, the food was set, the costumes were in progress. The only thing left was to find a venue.

No problem.

"If only we knew someone with an old house," Mary Beth said with a sigh, dropping her chin into her palm.

"If only," agreed Mrs. Wallace. "Someone with a nice, old house with a big yard."

Grace felt the back of her neck prickle.

"Yes," said Helen. "Someone with a scholarly expertise, like, say, a PhD, who might be able to host and help with finishing touches."

"Where, oh, where," said Mrs. Wallace, "can we possibly find such a person?"

All sets of eyes at the big coffee shop table turned to look at Grace.

She thought about the floorboard sticking up in the front hallway, and the fact that things tended to fall without warning.

"I only have one bathroom." It was the most practical excuse she could come up with.

"So? Both of my bathrooms work," Mrs. Wallace offered. "People can pee at my house."

She could do it, probably. She wanted to do it. But she had a lot of students pulling extra credit and had a senior thesis to advise. Plus she was leaving for the conference in a few days, and wouldn't get back until right before the fundraiser.

But she really wanted to do it. She thought about Jake, and what he'd said about Pembroke people being different from Willow Springs people, and now here were half a dozen of each, crammed around a few pushed-together tables in the Daily Drip, working together to restore the Library Window.

The only person who was vehemently against it was Henry.

"It's too much for you, Grace," he said softly to her. He'd been stopping by her office more and more, and she found herself confiding some of her stress to him.

Not the stress about Jake.

Which wasn't really stress. Just . . . she didn't know what. It was stressful that she thought it *should* be stressful, but wasn't. It was easy. She was into him, he was into her, and that was it. The ease was what made her nervous. It had never been this easy. She kept telling herself what she always had in all of her pre-Lou relationships—that she could walk away any time. And she could. She would. At least, she would if she wasn't sure someone in town would find a way to get them back together.

There was no point in fighting the inevitable. And she did like him. So, for now, they were together.

Also inevitable: she was having a Jane Austen party at her house.

Jake nodded hello to the guys working at his dad's shop and headed for the office. Don wasn't there, though, so he wandered around until he found his father and his cousin, Keith, in the yard, leaning over the open hood of a diesel pickup.

"Hey, Dad. Hey, Keith."

"Hey, Crane Man," Keith said, shaking Jake's outstretched hand.

Don smiled at him. "How's it feel to be the town hero?"

"It would feel better if it would make people forget about the time I ran the football captain's helmet up the flagpole," Jake said.

"Small towns have a long memory," said Keith.

"It was the night before the state championship. Jake here nearly cost them the game."

"Hey, if he'd quit picking on my math tutor, I wouldn't have had to do it."

Don looked at Keith. "See what I mean? Town hero."

Jake knew his dad was joking, but liked the note of pride he heard in his voice all the same.

"What's this?" Jake asked, indicating the truck.

"Just bought it," said Keith.

"Yeah, I don't think I told you congratulations on getting back into the veterinary business." Jake gave his cousin a pat on the shoulder. "And congratulations on the baby."

"Thanks. Mal's due any minute now."

Jake remembered when Keith's first wife was killed by a drunk driver. It tore the whole family up, and he was glad as hell that

Keith had found happiness with Mal. He was a good guy; he deserved it.

"Shouldn't you be getting a station wagon or something?" Jake asked. "I don't think a baby seat will fit into this thing."

Keith flushed. Don piped up, "Fixed up a four-door and delivered it last week."

Jake just smiled. Keith was a quiet guy, and Jake didn't want to torture him with more attention. So the three men retreated into the engine, decided it was sound, and fiddled around with some more stuff just to make sure.

"So, how's your professor?" Don asked Jake.

Jake rolled his eyes. "She's not my professor, Dad. And she's fine."

"Jake here has been seeing a Pembroke gal," Don told Keith.

Jake shrugged. "Nothing major."

"But you like her?" Keith asked.

"Sure, I like her. You gonna give me love advice now that you're an expert?" Jake had always looked up to Keith like an older brother, but he didn't need to hear more of the same she's-too-good-for-you crap he got from his dad.

Keith raised his hands in defense, and kept his mouth shut. He checked his watch. "Hey, I gotta get back. If I'm gone much longer, Mal's gonna think I'm stranded by the side of the road."

"Say hi for me," said Jake. He gave Keith a one-handed man-hug, and they waved him off.

"She's a good girl," Don said.

"The truck?"

Don cuffed him lightly on the back of the head. "No, Mal."

"Yeah, she's great."

"I hear your professor's pretty great, too."

"Dad, don't start—"

"I'm serious! Marilyn loves her. Of course, Marilyn loves everyone. But I heard your professor's throwing a big Jane Austen party to raise money for that library window."

"Yeah, I heard."

"You going?" Don asked.

"Hadn't thought about it. I think we have to dance."

"I know." Don bowed and turned with an imaginary partner.

"I'm taking Bertie. She got me fitted for this fancy coat and everything."

Jake couldn't believe it. His dad didn't even wear a coat at his own wedding.

"Wow. That will be . . . interesting."

"You might as well resign yourself to fate, son. If Mary Beth isn't dragging you, your girlfriend will."

"She's not my girlfriend."

Don looked at him. "Why not?"

Jake shrugged. "It's complicated, Dad. Well, no, it's not complicated. That's the way we want it. Uncomplicated."

Don shook his head. "You're a fool."

"What?"

"You heard me. Anyone can see you got it bad for this girl. What's this 'uncomplicated' nonsense?"

"Weren't you just telling me that she's too good for me?" Jake asked.

"No, I told you that you were too different from each other."

"Great. First Keith, now you. You're getting laid, so you can give out love advice?"

"Watch your tone, son. I just mean I may have been misguided."

"So now she's not too good for me?"

"I'm sure she is, but that doesn't matter. I was married to your mother for almost twenty years, and I spent the whole time trying to convince her that I wasn't good enough for her."

"Dad—"

"No, listen. I've been thinking about this," Don said. "Because of your professor, and because of Bertie. Your mother's stubborn, and she's determined to see the good in people. I did my damnedest to get her to see that I was no good. I did things I'm not proud of, son, but she got the message. It took pert near twenty years, but she got it."

Don wiped his hands on the rag he pulled from his back pocket. He did it carefully, focusing on his fingernails. "I got what I wanted. I got her to see that I was no good for her. Stupidest thing I ever done."

Jake just stood there, watching his father rub his hands with a dirty rag. He knew Don was a miserable, lonely man, and Jake never understood why he'd treated his mom so badly. Learning that it was a self-fulfilling prophecy wasn't exactly comforting, but he got it. Didn't like it, but he got it.

"I'll never forgive myself for the way I treated your mother when we were married. And not just 'cause it made me lose the love of my life. She didn't deserve it. I didn't deserve it. At least she never thought so. Instead of being the man she knew I could be, I took the coward's way out. I didn't trust her, that the version of me she saw was the real me, dirty fingernails and all."

"Geez, Dad." Jake didn't know what to say. He'd never expected such . . . emotional clarity from his father. Bertie must be doing him good.

"The reason I bring this up, son," Don said, "is because I don't want you to make the same fool mistake with your professor."

"Dad, she's not—"

"I know, I know, she's not your professor. But I know you, son, and I can see that you want her to be. And I don't know what's holding you back, but if it's because you think she's too good for you, well, I advise you to leave that up to her to decide."

"That's not it, Dad. We're just . . . different."

"Because she works with her brain and you work with your hands?"

Jake shrugged. "Yeah, that's part of it." The other part, that neither of them did love, seemed like the kind of argument his father was ready to poke holes into.

"Jake, I've seen what goes into planning one of those houses of yours. It takes as much brains as it does muscle to get that done."

Jake blinked. Was that a compliment?

"Dad, it's just different, okay? Her whole life is . . ." He waved his hands around his head, unable to explain exactly how Grace's world worked.

"How do you know that? Does she talk to you about it?"

"Yeah, sometimes." Jake loved to hear her talk about her work. She had great stories about her students, and when she got on to Jane Austen, her eyes lit up and her hands started waving and even though he didn't always know what she was talking about, he loved to watch her.

"Do you talk to her about your work?"

"Sure." Since she found out about his business, Grace was bombarding him with questions—probably knew enough to open up her own house-flipping business now. He wasn't worried about the competition though; she still didn't have a hammer.

"So you both love what you do, and you share it. Probably talk about a lotta other stuff, too, right?"

Jake saw where his father was going. He wasn't wrong. He and Grace had never had a shortage of things to talk about. But that was because they were both talkers, not because they had anything in common.

As soon as Jake thought about it, he realized how wrong that sounded. He'd never talked to any woman the way he did with Grace. They stayed up for hours, just talking. Well, not always just talking, but there was an ease to their conversation that he found himself missing when they were apart. He just liked being with her.

"And you have some," Don waved his hands vaguely, "chemistry. Right?"

"Yeah, Dad, we've got chemistry." Chemistry and electricity and fire. They had it in spades.

"And when you don't see her, you miss her, right?"

Jake didn't say anything.

"Sounds like love, son."

Jake shook his head. "Dad, it's more complicated than that." Even if he did love Grace, which . . . well, he was pretty sure he did. But it didn't matter. Love was off-limits for Grace. He couldn't betray her like that.

But damn his father for bringing it up. Because saying it out loud gave him hope, and that was one thing he'd promised Grace he wouldn't do.

"Love is complicated, son. That's always true. But I bet this Grace of yours is stubborn like you are. And I bet, brainy as she is, she's convinced herself that you're all wrong for each other."

Jake had no idea how Grace felt. Well, she didn't love him, he remembered overhearing that loud and clear over the holidays. But that was a long time ago. And the look in her eyes, the intensity between them when they had sex . . . they were making love, that was what it was.

"I'm just saying, don't let some dumb pride get in your way like

I did. And don't let some stupid preconceived notions of Pembroke people prevent you from being happy."

"When did you become such a love guru, Dad?"

"Eh, don't listen to me. You're probably right. She probably is too good for you." Don clapped him on the back as they walked back to the shop.

She probably was. But it still got Jake thinking.

Chapter 26

Grace was running around like a chicken with its head cut off. She'd overslept and couldn't find anything, and now the cab was outside, waiting to take her to the airport.

It was Jake's fault, of course. Helen and Mrs. Wallace had moved back home, so Jake had come over last night and they celebrated her roommate-free status on every available surface of the house. He was acting strange, kind of intense, and she was a little relieved that her early flight gave her an excuse to send him home so she could get a good night's sleep. Which hadn't worked because she spent the whole night tossing and turning, unable to stop thinking about the look in his eyes as he hovered over her, or the way he held her close and she melted into him. And then, when she finally did get to sleep, she slept so hard that she slept through her alarm.

And now she was tearing up the house, trying to find her cell phone. Fortunately, she'd packed the night before, conference clothes neatly folded in her suitcase to minimize wrinkles, and conference notes and a backup flash drive in her shoulder bag. Everything was by the door, ready to go. Everything except her phone. She threw the door open and gave the cabbie a signal that she was almost ready.

Then she heard a faint twinkling sound. Her phone. She froze, trying to find the source of the sound. She followed it into the living room, then to the couch, where Mr. Bingley was dozing in a sunny spot. A sunny spot on top of her phone.

She shooed him off and then, without looking, picked up the phone.

"You're going to miss your flight," Jake drawled in her ear.

"I know! I know. I couldn't find my phone."

"Did you find it?"

"Ha ha. Yes, Mr. Bingley was hiding it."

"He must not want you to go. Smart cat."

"It's just for a few days. And then when I get back there's the Jane Austen dance and then . . ."

"Grace, Grace," Jake said soothingly. "Deep breaths. Focus on one thing at a time."

"Right, yes. Focus on the conference."

"I was going to suggest focus on getting to the airport."

"Crap, yes."

"Listen, before you go—"

"Jake, I'm going to be late!"

"Just quickly, I promise. I left some tools over there."

"What? Where? I didn't see any."

"I'm sure I did."

"Which ones?"

"Grace."

"I know, I know, I wouldn't know them if they hit me in the head. Fine. Well, I'm leaving. Do you really need them?"

"I really do. I'm sorry. Can you leave a key under the pot or something?"

"Grr. Yes, fine." Grace pulled the door closed behind her and locked it. Then she took her front door key off the key ring and placed it under the pot of herbs on the edge of the porch.

"It's under the basil," she told him.

"Thanks, babe. Have a good conference."

"I think I'm going to throw up."

"Don't throw up. Knock 'em dead. You're a genius, remember?"

Grace smiled. Jake was too charming for his own good.

"Grace?"

"Yeah?"

"Get to the airport."

"Right! Yes. I'll, uh—"

"Call me when you get there?"

"Yeah, sure."

"Talk to you later."

"Okay."

"Grace."

"Yes?"

"Airport."

"Yes! I'm going! 'Bye!" Then, before she could say anything stupid, she hung up the phone and got into the cab.

Chapter 27

Three days later, too much wine and not enough sleep later, Grace returned from her conference. She lowered her sunglasses as the cab pulled away. Was Willow Springs always this bright? She started to dig through her purse for the keys, but then remembered Jake and his tools. He'd better have put that key back, she thought.

Nope. No key under the basil. So she started to dig through her purse for her cell phone, preparing to lay into Jake and then make him come over and let her into her own house, and then maybe invite him to stay.

The man himself opened the front door.

"You're back," he said. That solved two of her problems, but she was still annoyed. Then Jake smiled and the residual annoyance melted away. He looked good, in a well-worn gray T-shirt and loose, faded jeans.

"You're in my house," she responded.

"I was just, ah, finishing something up. Come on in." He held out his hand for her suitcase, and she gladly passed it over.

"Yes, thank you. I will come into my own house," she said.

"So, how are you? Are you tired? How was your talk?"

"Jake." She dropped her purse and looked around. Her house looked the same. Mr. Bingley meowed at her, then ignored her. Jake seemed more excited to see her than her cat was, and she had to admit, it was nice coming home to him. Even though this wasn't his home. But he was there anyway.

She shrugged out of her coat and he took it from her, hung it in the hall closet. He did know that this was her house, right?

She'd been thinking about Jake more than she should have while she was gone. How she wanted to talk to him before she went to bed. How, after she finished presenting her paper, she wanted to share with him the way that opening with a joke had been a really bad idea, but eventually, people warmed to the topic. How she ran into one of her old colleagues from UC who told her that Lou was divorced now and on probation for shacking up with one of his undergrads.

That was natural. They were friends. She should want to share with him. But this wasn't just sharing. This was the kind of intimate, inside-joke stuff that she normally just shared with Jane because Jane knew the back story and would appreciate the nuances and absurdity. Now she had that feeling of intimacy with Jake. She felt a momentary pang of guilt that she'd replaced her sister, but that wasn't it either. She still had Jane, but she also had Jake.

Grace had been working very hard at keeping her friendship with Jake separate from her sexual attraction to him. But she realized that was impossible, because they weren't separate. She was attracted to him *because* of their friendship. And his body. And maybe his body had come first, but now it was the whole Jake she liked, and the way the whole Jake fit with the whole Grace.

She was in deep doo-doo, as Priya would say.

She wanted to run away, but this was her house. She should kick Jake out, but didn't want to do that either. She needed space and time to sort it out, to tuck these feelings away until they subsided. But she'd had that time, and all she did with it was think about Jake.

She was so lost in her own thoughts that she barely noticed when Jake took her hand and led her upstairs. Okay, she thought. He missed me, too. But he didn't lead her to the bedroom.

"Close your eyes," he said, stopping in front of the door to her office.

She raised her eyebrows, but then he raised his back at her, and the end result of the eyebrow standoff was her standing in front of him, his hand over her closed eyes, as he opened the door.

"Okay," he said, moving his hand away.

Grace gasped and took a step back, right into Jake. But then she took a step into the office, not understanding what she was seeing. When she'd left, the turret windows were still boarded up, and her books were boxed so Helen could use her bookshelves as a dresser. But now, the space was transformed. There was no other word for it.

The walls had been freshly painted, and even her accent wall had been repaired where the water had damaged the wallpaper. The books were lined up neatly on the shelves, not at all how she would've done it, but they were unpacked. Her desk was back, and there was a new cushion on the chair.

But it wasn't the parts that had been refreshed and repaired that had her heart beating in her throat.

Her turret, her favorite and most troublesome part of the house, was transformed. The boards were gone, and the sun shone through sheer curtains hung over new windows. The random easy chair she had stuck in there in an attempt to make it cozy was out in the larger part of the room. Instead, there was a bench that wrapped the curved edges of the wall, painted to match the trim and overflowing with colorful throw pillows. There was a soft ottoman in the center of the "C" of the bench that left just enough room for legs. Even the narrow spaces between the windows were not neglected—small bud vases were attached to the wall, with wildflowers she recognized from her yard.

It was perfect. It was cozy and light and the ideal spot to curl up with a book or a cat or a friend.

"Jake," she whispered. She turned to find him waiting in the doorway, his face eager although she could tell he was trying to hide it. She knew his face so well. "You did this?"

"Do you like it?" He took a step toward her.

"It's perfect. But how? Why? When?"

He laughed and held her face and kissed her lightly on the lips. "I've been thinking about it for a while. I know you were having trouble figuring out how to use the space, and that's kind of my deal, you know?"

She nodded and put her hands on his wrists. She couldn't tear her gaze away from his eyes.

"And I was going to suggest it as a project we could tackle together, but then I thought I'd just surprise you. I couldn't save the stained glass, but I tried to inject some color anyway. Do you really like it?"

She threw her arms around his neck. "I love it. It's more than I could have imagined." She turned to look at her cozy turret nook, but she kept an arm around his neck. She couldn't let go of him yet. "It's so clever. And so comfortable. And the flowers. Oh, Jake, I love it." She turned into him, and this time she grabbed his face and kissed him.

She let him up for air, and then let him talk. He was animated, excited to explain how he planned the surprise, how he had Missy convince Kyle to help him. He talked about measuring and installing and testing the softness of the pillows, and Grace was listening, but also panicking. This was the most romantic thing anyone had ever done for her. It showed her how much Jake cared and how well he knew her. And part of her craved that, wanted to devour Jake and his generous heart, but the other part of her, the familiar part, told her to *run*.

"Grace?"

Grace let go of Jake's hand. He shook it out, confirming that she'd been squeezing way too hard. And he had wonderful hands. Beautiful, talented hands. Hands that were gentle and firm and hard and soft, all at the same time. Perfect hands.

She tried to be rational. She wasn't going to die because of Jake. Her parents' story was not her story, she knew that. But she couldn't get the message through to her heart, or her sweaty palms, or her shaking knees.

"I wanted to do something for you," Jake said, taking her face in his hands again. "I love you, Grace."

That shouldn't make her want to vomit, should it? But suddenly all of the crappy food she'd eaten at the conference waged warfare on her entire digestive tract and she thought if she didn't get out of there, she was going to throw up all over this gorgeous turret that he made just for her because he loved her and she was really, really ill.

"Grace? Grace, honey, are you okay?"

She nodded, her lips pursed tightly together.

"Sit down. You look like you're going to pass out."

Oh, passing out. That would be better than throwing up. Her body liked that idea better.

"Grace? Come on, now. You're making me really nervous."

Nope. It wasn't pass out or throw up that her body wanted to do. Apparently, it was burst into big ugly tears and run from the room. She ran down the hall, looking for some privacy, for somewhere to slam the door and get away from Jake and his love.

She chose the bathroom just in case.

The tile floor was cool under her knees and it felt good to lean her forehead on her arms against the bathtub and let the deep, shuddering breaths work themselves out.

There was a knock on the door, then the handle rattled as the door opened. She thought she'd locked it.

Jake stood in the doorway, arms crossed over his chest—one of her favorite parts of him that now she'd never see again. He looked down at her and then up at the crown molding.

"Those aren't happy tears, are they?" he asked quietly.

She could feel the hurt coming off him in waves and was ashamed. She was ashamed for acting like a child and ashamed that she couldn't love him back, this wonderful man who meant so much to her. But she couldn't. She wouldn't. She tried. Sitting there on the bathroom floor, she tried to say the words he needed to hear, but every time she started to speak them, her throat closed up and she thought she'd be sick.

"Can you at least look at me?"

She didn't want to. She wanted to stay on the bathroom floor forever, maybe crawl into the bathtub later, just to mix it up. But she looked up anyway.

He crouched down so he was at her level.

"I love you."

Was he trying to torture her? She clutched at her shirt. She thought she might be having a heart attack. But she kept her eyes on him, as he asked. She couldn't love him, but she could do as he asked.

"Jesus Christ," he muttered, then stood up. He ran his hands through his hair, then over his eyes. He looked tired. He looked excited before; now he looked tired.

"This was not the reaction I was hoping for." He rubbed absently at his chest. "I don't know why I thought it would be different. You told me, didn't you?" He looked down at her again and she nodded. Yes. This wasn't her fault. She'd warned him.

"Grace, I'm not like your parents—" Whatever he wanted to say, he stopped mid-sentence. But Grace got the point. She'd heard it before. We're not like your parents. She hated when people said that, because underneath, there was always a "get over it already." She was grateful when she heard it, though, because it made it easy for her to walk away.

But this. She took a shuddering breath. This was killing her.

"You know what? You know that. I know you know that here," he said, tapping his head. "So I'm just going to pick up what's left of my pride and go."

"Jake," she croaked as he turned away.

"What? Do you want more? You're everything to me, Grace. Everything. And I thought . . . well, I was wrong. That's fine. That's your right. But I have to go, okay?"

It wouldn't be fair to make him stay. To, essentially, tell him she didn't love him, but then tell him she needed him. That was not right, and Jake deserved to be treated right.

So she didn't say anything, and in a moment, he was gone.

Jake tore down the stairs, then tore back up them to grab his tool belt from the office. He was tempted to throw something through those damn turret windows, but he'd worked too hard to destroy them just for spite.

He felt used. He felt like a fool. Of course she didn't love him. She'd told him she couldn't, that she didn't do love. He hadn't believed her, so shame on him. Or maybe Don was right the first time. Pembroke people did not mix with townies. They were just too different. But Jake thought he had a chance, he thought he felt something between them. So how did he show it? By building something. By working with his hands, the only thing he knew how to do, to prove himself to a woman who worked with her head. He should have listened to Don. He should have listened to himself, back when he first met her.

He just wasn't good enough for her.

Jake squeezed his eyes shut. That wasn't true. He knew that wasn't how Grace felt, but he couldn't stop himself from going there. Besides, he thought for sure she loved him back, and he was obviously wrong about that.

He needed to get out of there. He needed to get as far away from this house as possible. He took the stairs two at a time. He reached for the front door, but then he was face-down on the floor. He looked back. A floorboard had come up. He remembered Grace mentioning that to him, and him promising to bring a cinder block over to show her how to use water and weight to flatten it out.

So much for that, he thought. He got up and slammed the door behind him.

The house shook, indignant and hurt. That was certainly un-called for. Jake, who'd always treated the house with such care, was gone. And Grace was hiding out. The house could feel her, her emotions like water pouring out of her, and Grace trying to scoop them back in with her hands. But she couldn't hold them, and the house thought maybe soon she'd give up trying and call Jake back. But it didn't happen. She stayed in, he stayed out, and the house settled down and admitted defeat.

Chapter 28

Grace's breath stopped when she heard the front door open. He's come back, she thought, and her heart raced at the thought.

But the happy chatter she heard downstairs told her it was not Jake.

"Grace?" Jane called. "Grace? Your front door was unlocked, you doofus. I hope you're home!"

She heard footsteps on the stairs, and smaller footsteps running downstairs. Priya was probably after Mr. Bingley.

There was a light knock on her door. Before she had a chance to tell her sister to go away, Jane came in and turned the light on.

Grace squealed and threw the covers over her head.

"Grace, what are you doing? Don't you have a party to throw or something?"

Grace mumbled from her cocoon. She knew she should get out of bed; she should've gotten out of bed hours ago. The library's Jane Austen Fundraiser Extravaganza was this evening. But it was hours away, and she needed to sulk.

Her covers were thrown back and Jane stood over her. Grace watched her face segue from sisterly indignation to sisterly concern. "Grace, what's happened?"

"Nothing," she insisted, sitting up, looking at the alarm clock. She really needed to get up. "Just being lazy."

"Is that why your eyes are red and swollen?"

"Yes. They were too lazy to make themselves presentable."

"Grace."

The problem with having a sister who was a confidante was that she always wanted to help, even if Grace didn't want her help. Grace wanted to be sad and alone and puffy in her bed for the rest of her life.

She shifted to make room as her sister sat on the bed. Then Jane toed her shoes off and got under the covers.

"Tell me."

Grace found the edging on her duvet cover infinitely fascinating. But Jane poked her and she knew there was no getting out of it.

"Jake loves me."

Jane blinked in surprise. "Handsome Jake?"

Grace nodded.

"Just Friends Jake?"

"Don't crow, Jane. You were right, okay? It was never going to work."

"Is that why you're crying? Because you want to be friends with benefits and he wants more?"

Grace shook her head. She could feel the lump in her throat coming back, and she was pretty sure her tear ducts couldn't take another crying fit.

"So he told you he loved you, and then . . ."

Grace sighed. "I locked myself in the bathroom and he went away."

"Mature."

Grace threw her head into her hands. "I know! And he re-did my turret and it was perfect—it is *perfect*—and I said thank you and he said he did it because he loved me."

"I'm assuming 're-did my turret' is not a euphemism."

Grace gave her sister a look. "No. Go look."

Jane got out of bed and Grace waited. Not hearing anything, she got impatient, climbed out of bed and shuffled into her office.

"Grace . . ." Jane was breathless. "This is so you."

"I know."

"And he did this for you?"

Grace nodded. "When I was at the conference. It was a surprise."

"Geez. I'll take him if you won't."

"You know, one day Dev is going to overhear you."

Jane shrugged. "Oh, he has. But he knows my sick sense of humor. And he knows I love him more than any man in the world. That helps." She linked her arm through Grace's. "So that's it?"

Grace rested her head on Jane's shoulder. "I guess."

"I would ask you how you feel about all this, but I think finding you oversleeping in a dark room is my answer."

"I can't do it, Jane. He knows I can't. I told him about Mom and Dad."

"You did?" Jane nudged her up, surprised. "You never tell anyone about that."

"Well, I told Jake. I thought we understood each other. I thought he got it, that I don't do love. Friends, yes; sex, yes; love, no."

"You sound crazy, you know that? Love is not something you 'do.' It's something that happens between people, whether you want it to or not. Look at me and Dev. Do you think I wanted to fall in love with a guy who lived in a van while he tried to get his prog rock band off the ground? Or whose family didn't approve of me because I didn't look like them? Trust me, there was a lot of heartache I could have done without."

"But you did it anyway."

"Yes, because I'm stubborn, and so are you. And you know what? It worked. Dev lives in a house now, and his family loves me. And I wake up every morning feeling grateful for him and our beautiful daughter. Both of whom are downstairs, by the way. I hope Mr. Bingley is up for some toddler torture."

"But what if something happens? What if—" It was too horrible to say out loud. And, possibly, too ridiculous.

Jane turned to face her sister. "That's possible. Of course it is. Dev could die, or I could, or he could run off with a groupie, although most of his fans are hipster guys in their twenties, so that's unlikely. What happened with Mom and Dad was terrible, but it's not normal. People deal with things and they move on. You and I did it when they died. Well, I dealt with it. I'm seriously questioning your coping mechanisms."

"Well, why can't I deal with this and move on?"

Jane threw up her hands. "Fine. Do what you want. But look at this." She pointed to the turret. "This was built by a man who knows you. And if a man like that said he loved me, I would grab him and never look back."

"You can quit the smug married business," Grace said, sullenly. "Not everyone needs to be in a relationship to be happy."

"Do you know how badly I want to hit you on the head right now?" Jane asked. Grace took a step back. "I'm not suggesting you stay with Jake because he's a great guy, although he is. But, Grace, I know you better than anyone. I've seen how you are with him. I've heard how your voice changes when you talk about him. And if you want to pretend you're not in love with him, that's fine. You'll get over it, probably, but you'll be an idiot. And then I'll be the smart one and the entire balance of the universe will be thrown off, but I can't tell you what to do."

"Even though you want to."

"Even though I want to."

"Even though you sort of just did."

Grace could see that Jane was getting pissed off, and part of her wanted to needle her more. She was itching for a fight, or for anything that would keep her mind off Jake.

Then Jane sighed sadly and turned to leave.

"I'm scared," Grace whispered. Jane whirled around and enveloped Grace in a crushing hug. She could barely breathe, but she held onto Jane like a life raft.

"I know," Jane said softly. "I was, too. But it's worth it."

Grace hadn't thought about it that way. Her relationships were always good, and when they stopped being good, they were over. She never thought that the intensity of feeling, the forgiveness and compromise, the danger of heartache, would be worth it. But the good parts with Jake far outweighed the bad.

He was worth it, definitely. But was he worth it to her? Could she give him her heart, knowing she could lose everything? And, after what she'd put him through yesterday, would he even want it?

There were forty million people in Grace's house by the time she showered and came down to help set up. She stood at the bottom of the stairs for a minute, trying to take it all in. Her furniture had been pushed back against the walls, and Missy and Helen were setting up folding tables. As soon as they had the legs down, Mrs. Wallace would waft a tablecloth into place. People—she didn't recognize some of them—were tracking through the front door, making a beeline for the kitchen.

"Grace! You're up! Are you feeling better?" Mary Beth came through with a plastic container full of cupcakes. She stopped in front of Grace. "Have you seen Jake? I haven't been able to get hold of him. He's not upstairs, is he?"

Grace shook her head.

"Well, he'll turn up. He promised me he would. Listen, would you mind helping out back? I sent Todd to set up the tables and I'm not sure he understood my diagram."

Grace nodded, but it didn't matter, Mary Beth was already gone. Grace followed her through the kitchen, where the counters were piled high with Tupperware, and Will was shouting that he didn't have any place to work. She went out the back door, and froze.

Her back yard had been completely transformed. The lawn was neat, hedges trimmed, and someone had put up small arbors covered in fairy lights. There were paper lanterns strung between the trees, and the soft sounds of the band tuning up wafted on the breeze.

"Looks great, doesn't it?" Henry stood at the bottom of her porch steps and offered his hand. She took it and let him lead her through the yard. "Just think how it will look once the sun goes down."

"Magical," Grace said softly.

"Once I got Todd to stick to the diagram, it all fell into place. The tables are from the Lutherans, the arbors came from a Pembroke storage shed. I'm not sure where the lights came from."

"And the yard. It looks so . . . neat." Her yard never looked neat. She'd meant to get up and do some clean-up, but, well, she'd forgotten all about it.

"You did a great job with it," Henry said. "Even Kyle was impressed."

"But I didn't—" But she wasn't allowed to finish. Henry was leading her over to the dancing area, where Kyle was setting up a row of chairs.

"Hey, Professor," he said with a wink.

Henry rolled his eyes. "He's been like that all day. I think he thinks he's charming."

Grace shrugged. Kyle was charming in his own goofy way.

"I wanted to talk to you about something," Henry said, turning her away from Kyle and the dance floor. He took her hands and, to Grace's surprise, held on to them. "I meant what I said at the planning meeting."

Grace had no idea what he was talking about.

"I said I wouldn't dance unless I had the pleasure of the first two dances with you. I know it's bold, but . . ." he hesitated and looked down at their joined hands. "But I think it's right. I know you've been seeing Jake, but I think . . . I think we are well suited, don't you?"

Henry was a suitable man for her. He was calm and focused and they had professional and personal interests in common. He was handsome, and when she looked into his eyes, she saw he was sincere. But that's all. She didn't feel anything when she looked at him, except that his hands were getting sweaty and she wished he would let go.

"That would be nice," she said, tugging her hands free. "To dance with you," she clarified.

"But that's all?" he asked.

"I'm sorry, Henry. I just . . ."

"We'll just dance, then," he said, his face brightening.

Grace wanted to make sure he understood that she wasn't being coy or leading him on. She really did mean just to dance. But he turned and walked away, and then Todd thrust Mary Beth's diagram in her face and she spent the rest of the afternoon configuring tables and not thinking about Jake.

Jake would go to the party. He promised his sister, and he'd never broken a promise to her yet, no matter what it cost him. He would go, do the little dance she taught him, and leave. There would be a crowd—his mom had been downright gleeful as she took the RSVPs—so he could go, dance, and not see Grace at all. Or if he did see her, he could just say hi, thanks for the party, and leave and never see her again.

What he really wanted to do was dance with her, or maybe kiss some sense into her, but he knew that was a fool's dream. Grace had been absolutely clear with him. She didn't do love. And if he didn't get it the first time she told him, he sure got it now.

He would go to the party. He would dance.

But he wasn't wearing a damn costume.

When Mary Beth had first showed him the bright blue jacket he was supposed to wear, and the breeches and poufy shirt that went under it, he smiled tightly and took them. It was important to Grace, so he'd figured he could dress like a clown for one night. He was no longer feeling so generous.

So he was surprised to feel out of place as he filed into Grace's house with the other guests, all of whom were wearing jackets and breeches and dresses and feathers.

"Dude!" Kyle called, then squeezed through the crowd to get to him. "Where's your costume?"

Kyle was wearing a red coat with black lapels and gold trim. He had on the breeches, bright white and stuffed into a pair of tall black boots. And he was wearing a hat. A pointed black hat with a tremendous white feather on it.

"You look ridiculous," Jake muttered.

"I know. Missy wouldn't let me carry the sword. I mean, what kind of military man goes out without a weapon?"

Jake shook his head. His friend had lost his mind. Jake tried to feel grateful that he didn't have a woman to make a fool of himself over. It didn't quite work.

"Jake!" Mary Beth pushed through the crowd to him. "What are you wearing?"

Jake looked down. He had his nice jeans on, at least. And his shirt had a collar. He hadn't ironed it, but at least it was the kind of shirt that could be ironed.

"The pants didn't fit," he lied. "And I spilled coffee on the jacket."

Mary Beth gasped. "That's borrowed! We have to get that out before it stains—"

Todd grabbed his wife around the waist before she could run out the door to attend to Jake's fake-stained jacket. "We'll worry about it later. Come on, the dancing is starting."

Jake rolled his eyes and started to make a snarky comment to Kyle, but his friend was pushing his way through the crowd, shouting to Missy to save him a spot in the line.

The whole damn town had lost its mind.

He took his time getting outside, pretending not to see the disapproving looks people threw his way when they saw his clothes. He stopped in the doorway and got elbowed out of the way by a little girl in a bright purple dress. Then he was nearly bowled over by a woman chasing after her.

"Sorry! Oh, hey Jake." Jane straightened and squeezed his arm. She looked nice. Her dress was a similar cut to the little girl's, but Jane's was light purple and her hair was pulled back off her face. Which gave Jake the perfect view of her look of pity, even through her very modern glasses. "Nice outfit," she said, then continued her chase after the little girl.

Jake took the opportunity to follow her down into the crowd. He caught sight of the bright purple girl again, dancing gleefully in the arms of an Indian man wearing a purple jacket. The man met Jane in the middle of the line of dancers, bowed, and backed away while the girl clapped and squealed. Using his brilliant skills of deduction, Jake figured the family dancing together in matching outfits must be Jane's husband and daughter.

He was just congratulating himself on not being a total idiot when he saw her. She was wearing a moss-green gown that was cinched below her breasts and flowed down to the floor. Her hair, that unruly mess she never could seem to control, was pinned up elaborately, with flowers woven through. As he got closer, he noticed that they were the wildflowers that grew in her yard. And he noticed the snug fit of her dress, and how the green color made her eyes pop.

And he was way too close to her for a man who never wanted to talk to her again. At least not tonight. He ducked back into the crowd, but not before receiving a scowl from Henry, who was dancing with her. Jake wanted to tell him not to worry, he wasn't going to stand in his way. Instead he just stalked off to see whether someone had spiked the punch yet.

"Jake!" Jake was getting really tired of people shouting his name. And if one more person made a comment about his clothes . . .

"Whoa, what's the face for?" Helen asked. She pushed at his chest and he stepped back. "You're standing on my dress." She pulled the long blue and white fabric from under his boot.

"Sorry."

She smiled at him. He couldn't help but smile back. Helen's enthusiasm was always infectious. Jake regretted that if he and Grace were done, he probably wouldn't be seeing much of Helen, either. That was too bad. He liked her.

"I forgive you, but you can make it up to me by dancing."

"Oh, no," Jake said. Dancing meant being far too close to Grace. "I'm not wearing the right clothes."

Helen shrugged. "I'm wearing a corset. If I have to suffer, you have to suffer. Besides, Mary Beth told me you learned the steps."

He started to object again—he'd look like an idiot out there in his modern clothes, and he had just about enough of looking like an idiot lately—but Helen just took his hand and pulled him toward the dancing. The music stopped and the partners bowed and curt-sied, and Jake thought he was off the hook. But the band immedi-ately picked up another song and there was more bowing and curtsying and jostling new partners and new couples into the line.

"Look who I found!" Helen shouted over the music, squeezing into the space next to Grace. He nodded to Henry, who smirked in response. Jake turned to give a polite nod to Grace, but she was staring at him, her bright eyes clinging to his face. He wanted to pull her aside, ask her what that meant, ask her why she was danc-ing with Henry, but the music started and they all began to dance.

Grace couldn't stop staring at Jake. She tried to focus on Henry or on the steps that she was badly messing up, but she couldn't shake the awareness of Jake, inches from her. If only she could talk to him, explain how she felt, but every time she passed him, Henry was there, grasping her elbow and bringing her back to the dance.

She needed to talk to Jake, and she wanted to do it while they danced. That way he couldn't get away. She turned to Helen, who gave her a questioning look, but didn't say anything when Grace pulled her in and switched places with her. Henry started to protest, but Helen just shrugged and circled her new partner.

"Jake," Grace said in a low voice.

But Jake just shook his head and kept dancing.

Grace didn't know why he was here after she had been so horri-ble to him. He wasn't acting like he wanted her back, but he didn't run away, either. They passed each other on a turn, their hands con-necting briefly, and Grace felt electricity shoot through her gloves.

She was so dumb. She thought she'd explain to him that she still wanted his friendship, and nothing more. But then he touched her and she knew, without a doubt, that she could not settle for that. She loved him. She loved him, and he loved her, and if he would take her back, they could love each other. It was so simple. She was so frustrated with herself and so overwhelmed by her feelings, she couldn't help the quiet tears that streaked down her cheeks. When she passed Jake next, his eyes widened, but his steps didn't falter.

"I love you," she whispered, as their hands connected and they crossed partners. It didn't hurt nearly as badly as she thought it would. Her hands were sweating and she thought she was having a panic attack, but it wasn't too bad.

This time he did trip, just a little, but kept dancing.

"Jake, did you hear me?"

Henry, who was moving past just then, shushed her and gave her a look that said, "Focus on the dance."

Grace tried. Really, she did. But Jake kept passing her and they would touch, just for a moment, and she couldn't wait.

"I love you for so many reasons," she started as they passed again. "You're generous, and thoughtful." She turned and faced him, then took a step forward. "I love the way your mind works and"—step back and forward—"that you can look at something that's broken"—step back and forward—"and figure out immediately how to fix it." She stepped back, but held his gaze. As they circled each other, she continued, "You're patient. And you teach me things. And you're handsome. No, you're hot. That's not why I love you, that's just icing, you know?"

Grace had a whole list of Jake's admirable attributes. But, as always, she was getting lost in his muscles. That wasn't the important part, though. She took a breath, then took another step toward Jake. She was out of time with the music, but this was important. Jane Austen would forgive her.

"I'm scared. I'm afraid to take this risk, knowing I could lose everything, but you're worth it. You're—"

She fumbled for her words, but couldn't finish. Partly because she couldn't breathe, he was holding her so tightly, and partly because even Grace couldn't talk when Jake was kissing her. In front of all these people. Mrs. Wallace was probably having a heart attack, she thought. Then she didn't care and stopped thinking and just held on to the man she loved as he lifted her off her feet and spun her around.

The sound of thunder had Grace pulling back. But it wasn't thunder, it was applause. This wasn't the polite applause she expected at the end of the dance. This was thunderous, boot-stomping, cat-calling, Kentucky applause. And she and Jake were in the middle of it.

He smiled at her, that crooked smile that she had to remember to add to the list of things she loved about him. He pressed his forehead against hers and cupped her face in his hands. "Say it again," he whispered.

"I love you, Jake. I've been such a fool—"

"I don't care. I forgive you. It doesn't matter. Oh, Grace." He kissed her again. And again. And again.

The party lasted well into the night. Marilyn stood on a chair and announced that they had raised the funds to repair the library window, and the whole crowd, Willow Springs townies and Pembroke people alike, let out a cheer and kept dancing. Well, most of the crowd. The owner of the Spinster House was upstairs, showing Jake how much she loved him.

The house tried to settle around them, to give them some peace and quiet, but there were so many people in the yard. These two were impossible. First they hated each other, then they loved each other, then they refused to admit it. The house was exhausted. Maybe one hundred years was enough of matchmaking. Maybe it was time to take its talents in a new direction.

Epilogue

Grace groaned at the persistent nudge at her shoulder.

"Come on, Professor. Rise and shine."

Then she really groaned. She'd promised Jake that once spring break started, she'd help him tear down the wall between the kitchen and the living room. He was right, it was a good idea and it would open up the space and let some much-needed light into the kitchen. But did they have to do it so early in the morning?

She learned pretty quickly that Jake was an early riser. No matter how late he kept her up—and it was often indecently late—he was up at dawn, ready to tackle the day. And if the day didn't have enough in it to tackle, he made more. Now that he'd been officially living with her for six months, he was ready to put his mark on the house. And Grace was more than ready to help him with that. Or she would be. Later.

"Can't we start at noon?" she asked in a voice that she hoped was both plaintive and seductive.

Jake kissed her behind her ear and she squirmed into him. "Nice try," he breathed into her ear. She shivered.

"Can't you do that door thing?" she asked, turning into him without opening her eyes. He had taken the kitchen door down yesterday and they rejoiced by running back and forth through the doorway like kids. Then he took the door out to the garage, where he was planning on turning it into a table. She had no idea how he was going to do that; it seemed like a lot of work. Work he could be doing now instead of making her get out of bed to tear down a wall.

"That's a weekend project," he scolded. "This is a whole-week project."

She shimmied further underneath him. "I'll give you a whole-week project," she said, and nipped his nose. He kissed her, like she hoped he would, and she pulled him closer and felt his arms wrap around her and his legs tangle with hers.

A crash from downstairs had them pulling apart.

"What was that?" she asked Jake, who had been with her the entire time and could not possibly know what the crash was.

"Mr. Bingley?" he asked, but when they turned, Mr. Bingley was at the foot of the bed, cleaning his ears.

Jake rolled off Grace and out of bed. She groaned and followed him. It had been a suspiciously loud crash, and since the house had been devoid of suspicious destruction since the night of the Jane Austen party, this was probably worth investigating. Jake stepped into a pair of boxers, she grabbed her robe, and he led her out of the room.

When they got to the bottom of the stairs, Grace walked into Jake's back where he had stopped on the landing.

"Holy—" he said, and Grace followed his eyes to the living room. And the kitchen. Which they could now see from the living room because the wall had fallen down.

Grace coughed as a plume of plaster dust made its way to the stairs. "How did that happen?" she asked her expert contractor boyfriend.

"I have no idea," he said. "I'm just glad that wasn't a load-bearing wall."

Because, really, the whole wall was down. It was a mess, plaster chunks everywhere, pieces of the frame wobbling dangerously.

"I guess our demo work is done," Jake said.

"Does that mean we can go back to bed?" Grace asked, then bolted up the stairs as Jake chased her. She dove onto the bed, and Jake landed next to her. Mr. Bingley fled into the hallway and padded down the stairs, far from the giggles and squeals in the bedroom.

* * *

The light from the windows at the front of the house stretched back to reflect off the glass on the kitchen cabinets, sending the plaster dust dancing like fairies. The light would get brighter and stronger as the morning sun rose higher, and then the afternoon sun would reach through the kitchen. The house would be warm and bright and beautiful, the kind of place a person would want to stay in, to build a life in. The kind of place a person wants to stay in forever.

Sarah Title has worked as a barista, a secretary, a furniture painter, and once managed a team of giant walking beans. She currently leads a much more normal life as a librarian in West Virginia. Her first book, *Kentucky Home*, was published in 2012, and a follow-up novella, *Kentucky Christmas*, came out in 2013. Her novella *Full Moon Pie* appeared in the anthology *Delicious,* written with Lori Foster and Lucy Monroe. Visit her online at www.sarahtitle.com, where she talks about books and dogs and reality television. It's a very classy website.

More eKensington books from Sarah Title!

The best gifts are always a surprise...

KENTUCKY CHRISTMAS

SARAH TITLE

 A Southern Comfort Novella

KENTUCKY HOME

  A Southern Comfort Novel

Let your heart lead the way...

SARAH TITLE